THE WOMAN BEHIND HER

A gripping psychological suspense thriller

ANNA WILLETT

THE
BOOK
FOLKS

Paperback edition published by

The Book Folks

London, 2019

ISBN 978-1-6873-3782-5

www.thebookfolks.com

For my brother, John.
We've come a long way from Somerset Street.

Chapter One

Helen's last breath was unremarkable. A short intake over dry lips. Then nothing. Jackie didn't know what she'd been expecting. A dying declaration? A gasp of revelation? All she knew was when her Aunt Helen finally gave up and shuffled off her mortal coil she did so very much as she'd lived the last twenty years: quietly and without fuss.

Jackie set her aunt's hand down on the blue cotton sheet. Her skin felt warm, alive and at odds with her body's lack of sound or movement. The moment, although sad, was anticlimactic. Helen deserved more.

The nurse spoke from the end of the bed. Not her aunt's queen-size bed but a rented one brought in specifically for palliative nursing.

"She's gone." A pronouncement that didn't need to be made was delivered in a soft knowing tone. "I'll step outside and give you some time," the nurse said.

Jackie wanted to respond, to tell the nurse to make whatever calls needed making at such moments. She mostly wanted to tell the woman to take her end-of-life voice and get the hell out of her aunt's house. What she did was nothing, unable to take her eyes off Helen's pale

1

hand. Paper-thin skin over greyish blue veins. Veins no longer coursing with blood.

The door behind her whispered closed, telling Jackie she was alone. She continued to stare at her aunt's hand. The blood would be settling now. Jackie wondered if her aunt's mind might still be working. How long did it take for the neurons to stop firing?

"Aunt Helen?" Jackie forced herself to look up. The woman's lids were partially open, her mouth slightly agape. If not for the misty glaze on her eyeballs, Jackie would have said she appeared to be sleeping. Or at least drifting off to sleep.

"Wherever you're going, I hope it's nice." Tears blurred her vision. "You didn't find much love here, did you?"

Helen never married or had children. She'd lived a solitary life, as far as Jackie knew. A career woman. Jackie's mum used this term when describing her sister-in-law with admiration. She wondered if that's what her mother said about her, too. A kind way of calling someone a childless spinster. Only Helen had been more than a single woman. She'd been a journalist who travelled the world, possibly moving between a string of lovers. Not like Jackie, a thirty-six-year-old schoolteacher. An only child. When her time came, there wouldn't even be a frumpy niece to hold her hand.

Jackie brushed away her tears with the back of her hand. "I'll miss you." When said aloud it sounded too cheery, like something called out at the airport to departing friends. The final words captured by a remarkable brain as it dimmed into oblivion should have been profound – meaningful.

"I..." She tried again, but words escaped her.

She stood and kissed Aunt Helen's soft warm cheek and let her fingers touch Helen's hair. Once a mass of copper curls, it was now thinned and mostly white with a few strands of red: embers in the snow.

Jackie caught a scent, lemony and clean, as if her aunt had just bathed. A familiar smell, one which she would probably never know again. Somehow the loss of that fresh scent seemed heartbreaking. The depth of emotion was more than Jackie expected. Afraid she'd break down completely and begin wailing, she pushed herself up from the chair and left her aunt's room.

In the kitchen, the nurse, Susan or Sally, was on the phone. Jackie caught a snatch of the conversation as the woman notified Helen's GP. Not wanting to seem as if she were sneaking into her own aunt's kitchen, Jackie pushed one of the kitchen chairs aside, letting the legs scrape across the highly polished floorboards.

The nurse turned and gave Jackie a sad smile, which she didn't bother to return. Now that Helen was gone, there'd be no further need for the procession of palliative care nurses and the house could fall back into silence. Jackie shuddered and grabbed the kettle. She'd make tea and retreat to the spare room until the inevitable comings and goings ended.

"I've made the calls." Susan or Sally was speaking to her. "The undertaker will be here in about half an hour."

Jackie busied herself with the tea bag, unfurling the string and dropping it into a mug. "Thank you." She spoke without turning around. "I think I'll make a cup of tea and have a lie down in the spare room." *Hide until it's all over.*

"Good idea. I'll give you a call when I'm ready to leave." The nurse moved closer. For one horrifying moment Jackie thought the woman meant to embrace her. "It's better that she went during the day – that way things can move along quickly." She leaned against the kitchen bench, angling her head to look into Jackie's face.

She knew the woman meant no harm, but something in her tone worked on Jackie's nerves like teeth on tin foil. "Yes, very convenient."

"Oh. Sorry, I didn't mean it like that."

She'd hurt the nurse's feelings; she could hear it in the woman's voice.

"No. I'm sure you didn't," Jackie said, picking up her cup and hurrying out of the kitchen, desperate to put the awkward interaction behind her.

As she closed the door on the spare room, she heard the front doorbell. Ignoring the clanging and rattling of doors being opened, she set the cup down next to the bed. Over the last few weeks her aunt's spare room had become Jackie's haven. When Helen had her fall, she suffered a stroke and then a few hours later another. It became clear she wouldn't recover, so Jackie opted to bring her home from the dimly lit corridors of the palliative care unit. With the help of nurses from Golden Line, Helen had been able to die in her own house. Jackie didn't know why she felt such resentment towards the nurse when all she'd done was try to help. Maybe it was the woman's professional veneer and her ability to remain cheerful while another human being's life ebbed that irritated Jackie.

She sat on the springy double bed and took a sip of tea. Maybe she'd lived alone too long. Having someone else in the house, even a house that wasn't hers, felt stifling. *Maybe I'm just terrified because I can see myself in Helen. See my future.* She put the cup down and rubbed her eyes. What she really wanted was sleep. Deep uninterrupted sleep – the blackness blocking out the shock of watching her aunt die so unceremoniously.

Lying back, she pulled the patchwork quilt off one side of the bed and wrapped it around her like a cocoon. Warm and golden light dropped in from a crack in the curtains. She could hear voices, a murmuring of conversation. Most likely the undertaker. Something rattled, the sound similar to a stack of plates being plonked on a table. Jackie closed her eyes.

A crack woke her with a start. The light had faded, sinking the room into a murky hue that didn't quite chase away the gloom.

"I'm leaving now." The nurse's voice on the other side of the bedroom door brought Jackie back to full wakefulness.

Remembering her curtness with the woman, Jackie forced herself out of bed. Clothes rumpled from sleep, she opened the bedroom door.

"I just wanted to make sure you were all right before I go." The look of genuine concern on the woman's face made Jackie flush with shame at her callous treatment of the nurse.

"I'm sorry about earlier," Jackie said. The awkward apology tumbled through lips that felt thick with sleep. "I really do appreciate everything you've done for my aunt." The last word almost stuck in her throat. She clamped her mouth closed, willing herself not to dissolve into tears.

"It's never easy," the nurse replied.

Sandy. The nurse's name popped into Jackie's mind. Sandy reached out a sturdy arm and patted her on the shoulder. For an awful second it seemed like Sandy meant to pull her into the embrace she'd almost given earlier, but something in Jackie's posture must have made Sandy think better of the idea. She gave Jackie's arm a final tap. "Everything's been taken care of. Do you have anyone who could come over and stay with you tonight?"

Jackie ran through the short list of people she counted as friends. Hetty, a fellow teacher. A friendly colleague – someone to have an occasional coffee with, but nothing more. Lisa was the only real friend Jackie had, but not someone she wanted to call on in such circumstances.

"No." Jackie rubbed her eyes. "I mean, I'm fine... I'd rather be alone." She managed a smile, but it felt taut. "I'll walk you out." She hoped the offer indicated the discussion was over, but Sandy wouldn't be put off.

"What about a neighbour? I spoke to an elderly woman this morning. She mentioned knowing your aunt for years. I could pop over and—"

"No." Sandy flinched, but Jackie didn't care. Enough was enough. She was grateful to the woman, but her concern felt suffocating. Sandy was beginning to remind Jackie of the countless overly anxious parents of students she'd dealt with over the last fourteen years. If a few sharp words were what it took to get the nurse out of the house, then so be it. "I really do want to be alone." Jackie folded her arms over her chest and leaned against the doorframe.

Sandy took a step back and nodded. "Yes. Yes, of course. I'll let you get some rest."

"All right. Take care," she said, turning to leave.

The nurse wore a white zip front smock over navy pants that strained against her broad hips. As she moved, Jackie could hear the nylon material whooshing together as Sandy's thighs tested the constraints of the fabric. It wasn't until the front door clanged behind the nurse that Jackie felt able to unfold her tightly clenched arms. She opened her mouth and let out a deep breath into the silence. *When did I turn into such a bitch?*

Chapter Two

Jackie shuffled along the hall and into the kitchen. She hadn't eaten since grabbing a few biscuits mid-morning. The thought of food made her stomach growl. It occurred to her that grief should have sapped her appetite, yet even in the face of death the body craved food – food that her thickening waistline didn't need.

Appetite sated by a mostly uneaten ham sandwich and a handful of crackers, Jackie washed her plate and returned it to the cupboard above the sink. The stillness of the house made her twitchy. Not because she was used to noise and people: solitude was her way of life. But in the few weeks she had lived with her dying aunt, she had become used to the feel of another life. Even a fading spirit had a presence and now that presence was no more.

Restlessness drove her from the kitchen. Without thinking, she found her way into Aunt Helen's study. *My study now.* As Helen's only niece and closest living relative, Jackie would most likely inherit the house and any savings in her aunt's account. She'd have to make a decision on what to do with the place, but the idea of contacting Helen's solicitor and pushing probate into motion made her feel hollow; drained.

Instead, she sat at Helen's large oak desk, running her fingers over the smooth wood. This had been the spot where her aunt had most likely typed articles and pieces that focused attention on social issues and had won awards. The idea of Helen bent over her typewriter, maybe wearing shoulder pads and high heels, made Jackie smile. It was a nice image, one she wanted to hang on to.

This room, more than any other area of the house, reflected her aunt's personality – robust and filled with knowledge. Shelves lined two of the four walls, each packed with books, some fiction, others random volumes from various encyclopaedias. Old photographs and certificates crowded the walls.

Her aunt had quit smoking almost fifteen years ago, but the faint scent of tobacco still clung to the walls, reminding Jackie of the long thin cigarettes Aunt Helen had smoked and the way she lit each of them with a gold lighter. If she closed her eyes, she could almost hear the flick of the lighter and Helen's sharp intake of breath. Wanting to prolong the feeling of being connected to her aunt, Jackie opened the desk drawer and began picking through the assortment of pens and old stationery supplies.

She ran her hand over the wood in the drawer. The desk seemed like a relic from another age, dry and smelling faintly of wax. How long had it been since Helen had even used the writing table? On impulse Jackie pulled the drawer out and set it on the desk. The house would have to be cleared at some point and starting now seemed preferable to going through the filing cabinet and searching out her aunt's insurance, banking, and legal documents.

She pulled a yellowing notepad from the drawer. If she was going to make a start, a list would be a good idea. Having something to focus on, even if it wasn't where she should be starting, gave her a jolt of energy. She jotted down a short list of supplies, including boxes and packing tape. The contents of the drawer were of no use, so she left the study and returned with a black rubbish bag.

After one last check to make sure there was nothing of value, Jackie tipped the drawer into the bag. *What am I doing?* For a moment she stood over the desk, the drawer dangling into the rubbish bag. Being in the study was supposed to be a way of feeling close to Helen and here she was, tossing her aunt's possessions into the rubbish before her body was cold. The burst of energy and purpose left her as suddenly as it had come. Jackie sank back into the leather chair, holding the drawer to her chest.

It was only as her hands brushed the back of the drawer that she noticed the protrusion. An unevenness of tape and metal. With tears drying on her lower lids, she spun the drawer around. A key was taped to the back board. Jackie stared at the object understanding what she was looking at but still confused by its existence. Why would her aunt hide something in her own house? A house that only she had occupied?

Still sitting, Jackie let the drawer balance on her thighs. The tape looked old and yellowed by time. The key, blurry beneath the adhesive strip, was small. Too small to open a door. At least not a front or bedroom door. If her aunt had secrets, was it right for Jackie to dig them out? If Helen had gone to such lengths to conceal something, maybe whatever that something was should be left untouched.

No matter how she reasoned, Jackie knew she would push on even before she tugged the tape from the back of the drawer and held the key between her thumb and forefinger. Holding the object up to the overhead light, the key looked even smaller than it first appeared. Silvery, but rusted along the teeth and head.

Tapping her fingers on the edge of the desk and drumming out a *tick tack* rhythm, she tried to picture the lock that the key might fit. Something small and old, but not antique. Still tapping, Jackie scanned the room. In the corner sat a grey metal filing cabinet with a key protruding from the lock. Important papers and documents were worth saving and filing, but not important enough for Helen to hide *that* key.

The only other possibility was the small doors at the bottom of one of the bookshelves. Jackie crossed the room, but even before she put the key to the lock it was clear the mechanism was too small. And, when she jerked the ornate handle, the cupboard doors swung open. The little nook contained nothing more exciting than the smell of aged paper, a photo album, and a stack of magazines.

Sitting on the floor, Jackie again surveyed the study while rubbing the key between her fingers. Maybe the key was left over from the desk's previous owner. For all Jackie knew, her aunt had bought the large piece of furniture second-hand. From her position on the rug, Jackie considered the desk. It did look like an antique. Whatever lock the small scrap of metal opened could be miles away or even buried under mounds of landfill.

"I don't think so." As she spoke, Jackie tossed the key up and then caught it in mid-air. She had a feeling the key belonged to Helen and whatever her aunt had hidden was somewhere in the house.

The next most obvious place was her aunt's bedroom. Jackie swiped at a strand of frizzy hair that had come loose from the tight braid at the base of her neck. Had the hospital bed been removed while she'd been sleeping? Had the sterile-looking cot been left as it was when Helen still inhabited it?

With the house empty, did she have the courage to enter her aunt's room — a room where a woman she'd loved as much as her mother, if not more in adulthood, had died?

"Not without a drink." Jackie stuffed the key in the pocket of her baggy fleece pants and scrambled to her feet. A glass of wine was long overdue.

Later, in the sitting room, Jackie set her glass on the coffee table and took the key out of her pocket. She'd already half-decided that the key probably opened a jewellery box containing old love letters. Helen was quite a modern woman despite being a child of the late 1940s. If she went to such lengths to hide the letters, Jackie could only assume they were pretty raunchy.

She balanced the key on her thigh, watching it catch the light. Did she want to read her aunt's secret letters? Jackie had always idolised Helen and her stellar career. Over the last ten years, Jackie found herself fantasising about what it must have been like to be so well-travelled and courageous. Reading some long-dead man's lustful thoughts about her aunt seemed seedy and disrespectful.

Throat constricting as a fresh wave of tears filled her eyes, Jackie snatched up her wine glass. It was more than the cringeworthy thought of reading about her aunt's sex life. By seeing Helen's letters, Jackie risked reducing her aunt to a mere woman. No, worse. An old woman clinging on to something as pedestrian as a long-lost affair.

"Jesus, Aunt Helen. We can't both be tragic." Jackie sniffed and took a sip of wine.

Emboldened by a second glass of wine, she stood outside her aunt's bedroom. The door remained ajar. Beyond the narrow gap the room sat in darkness. She'd been in this room countless times, both before and after Helen's fall, although before it was unusual for Jackie to enter her aunt's bedroom. She'd only done so when asked to retrieve something. Jackie fingered a loose curl at the base of her neck, trying to work up the courage to move. There was nothing that could hurt her inside this room, yet as she snaked her hand around the door and flicked the light switch, she felt a shiver of apprehension.

Under a blaze of light, Helen sat up, her hair wild and her arms outstretched as the blue sheet fell into her lap. Jackie gasped and blinked. The hospital bed was gone, as was the imagined appearance of her aunt returning to life.

Jackie had a vague memory of something rattling over the floorboards as she fell into sleep. The nurse, Sandy, had been true to her word and had taken care of everything. The absence of the bed made entering less daunting.

"Okay." She pushed herself off the doorframe. "It's all okay."

For a second, she couldn't quite remember what she was doing and then her thoughts returned to the key. Standing in the room where someone so dear had breathed their last made her quest seem petty and childish. Or worse – selfish. Heat burned her cheeks. She was prying. She was going through her aunt's things not as one would in such circumstances to make arrangements, but to satisfy her own curiosity.

The right thing to do would have been turning off the light and going to bed. There would be plenty of time to go through Helen's things in an appropriate way, but she'd done things in an appropriate way her entire life. Work hard at school and stay away from parties. Secure a place at university and gain a degree. Find a job – a respectable job, but not one that would be too taxing. Jackie had done all those things and where had it gotten her?

Bitterness like sour wine filled her mouth as her lips puckered in and out. At thirty-six she was alone, working at a job she despised, and living in a two-bedroom unit. *Is this it? Is this my life?* Tears were flowing again. Not for Helen this time but for herself, for the lonely miserable life she'd carved out with such care.

She stumbled into Helen's room, her feet slightly unsteady. If this was her life, no wonder she wanted to read her dead aunt's racy letters. She dragged her sleeve across her cheeks, soaking her tears up on the fabric. What did it matter? Helen was gone. She was past caring about her secrets. If the letters gave Jackie some comfort or even a few hours of excitement, didn't she deserve it?

She began by going through Helen's wardrobe, then under the bed, and in the sturdy-looking nightstand. By the time she reached the trunk at the end of Helen's bed, Jackie's eyelids were drooping and the room seemed to tilt as though the house had been swept out to sea.

* * *

Hours later, ringing, distant but clear, dragged her from sleep. She had no memory of crawling into bed but was relieved to find herself inside the spare room fully clothed and not quite under the covers. As the phone continued to shrill, Jackie sat up and winced at the stab of pain in her head.

Not bothering to respond to the phone, she let her head droop into her hands. The events of the night before were murky, a slideshow of crying, drinking, and ransacking the house. With the memories crowding her mind and the phone bombarding her ears, she slid to the edge of the bed. It was only then she noticed the suitcase.

Chapter Three

She had no memory of finding the case or carrying it to the spare room. Memory or not, the valise was real and sitting on the rug under the window. Aged leather once blonde but now blotched and scarred with time; an anachronism with buckled straps on either side of the handle and a locking mechanism in the centre.

Without trying the key, Jackie had no doubt this was the lock she'd been seeking. The key. Her heart jumped with panic as she reached for her pocket and found it empty. Still bleary-eyed, she cast her eyes around the room, but aside from a few of her belongings and the wine glass on the nightstand, there was no trace of the key. Sure she was missing something; she scrubbed a hand over her face, trying to wipe away the confusion. Mercifully, the phone stopped ringing.

Silence allowed her to think more clearly, but with dark yawning trenches in her memory, retracing her steps became impossible. She licked her lips and grimaced at the taste of wine. What she needed was a cup of tea and a shower.

With the kettle boiling, she poured herself a glass of orange juice, which she drank in three gulps while standing over the sink. Before she had time to plop a teabag in her cup, the phone rang again. Cursing under her breath, she picked up her mobile. The number was unfamiliar. She considered dismissing the call, an idea she disregarded only because whoever had called twice in the last ten minutes would likely keep trying.

"Hello, am I speaking to Jacqueline Winter?" The man's voice was deep, almost old-fashioned in its formality. When she hesitated before answering, he pushed on. "I'm sorry to disturb you at such a difficult time, but we need authorisation before proceeding."

"What?" Jackie squeezed her eyes closed. Had she missed something? "I don't understand... What do you want?" The question came out brusque and demanding, not the way she'd intended.

The man on the end of the line chuckled. "Sorry. I should have identified myself. I'm Fredrick Marclowe from Marclowe Funerals." He paused, allowing the information to sink in.

Jackie opened her eyes. "Oh, yes. Yes, yes, the funeral." She hadn't thought about her aunt's funeral. "I'm still sorting things out." It was something to say, a way of playing for time.

The last thing she wanted was to deal with funeral arrangements. Arrangements that would involve meetings with people and end with her standing over an open grave. The idea of watching Helen's coffin disappear into the ground sent a ripple of dread across her belly.

"I'm just not sure..." She let the words trail off, not knowing how to disentangle herself from the conversation.

"It's all right, Miss Winter." His voice was calm, comforting. "Your aunt had funeral insurance. She filled out a plan. Everything's organised. All you have to do is sign the forms."

Jackie almost smiled. Trust her aunt to be proactive even about her own death. It should have been reassuring knowing that the responsibility was lifted from her shoulders, but instead she felt herself being pulled along. If the funeral was planned then she'd have no choice but to let the inevitable happen.

She walked around the kitchen, phone clamped to her ear. The undertaker, she couldn't remember his name, was waiting. Her eyes landed on the counter against the far wall and the empty wine bottle. Had she truly drunk all of it in a few hours the night before?

Reaching for the bottle, she noticed the spill and inside of the sticky puddle sat the key. "I don't feel well. I have to go," she said and ended the call, putting the phone down near the bottle while avoiding the acidic smelling liquid.

All thoughts of tea were forgotten. Jackie flopped onto the rug in the spare room. Before opening the case, she ran a finger along its leather, noting the rich grainy feel. She had no idea where she'd found the case. *I blacked out.* The realisation should have been upsetting or a cause for concern, but her need to find out what the case contained eclipsed anything close to worry.

The key slid into the lock and turned with a rusty groan. A puff of vanilla scented air escaped as the lid flipped open. She'd been expecting letters. In her mind's eyes she could almost see them, two thick bundles, each tied with ribbon. Instead, the case contained notebooks, at least twelve identical volumes. Inexpensive-looking books with stiff cardboard covers.

Not the sort of thing she'd have expected her aunt to use when keeping a journal. That was what the books had to be: diaries. Not an old lover's lusty ramblings, but something from her aunt – her aunt's innermost feelings. The notion of Helen keeping secret journals was infinitely more appealing than love letters.

Not yet ready to touch the volumes, she focused on the two pouches inside the lid. Elasticated fabric, floral-patterned, and faded; one housed a stack of photographs and the other a child's shoe, small and made of soft leather. The sight of the little sandal sent a shiver down her spine. It made no sense. Helen had no children. *Not that I know of.*

She'd been on her knees, but now she leaned back and to the left so her butt was on the rug. It was obvious now, all this secrecy and then the child's shoe. Maybe Helen had a child and gave him or her up for adoption. A shocking secret thirty or forty years ago now seemed tame. Disappointingly tame.

She reached inside the pouch and picked up the sandal. "Jesus, Aunt Helen. Why couldn't you confide in me?" She felt annoyed and bemused at the same time.

Helen was her idol, the epitome of independence and feminism, yet she'd hidden a secret for God knows how many years. Maybe she wasn't all that different from her aunt. She had never had a baby and kept it hidden, but hadn't she been hiding her unhappiness, concealing her misery under dowdy clothes and a layer of apathy? Her loneliness and disappointments were like the small shoe: a secret she'd kept locked away from the rest of the world.

All the moroseness and the drinking weren't just about her aunt's death. Losing Helen had been the tipping point because watching her die reminded Jackie of her own life slipping away, the years speeding up until soon it would be her in a take-home hospital bed.

She bent forward clutching the shoe to her forehead. She screwed her eyes closed willing herself not to dissolve into tears again. *No.* She took a breath and uncurled herself. This was about Helen. There would be time enough for self-loathing later.

The first journal wasn't really a journal but a novel of sorts – a story. The idea that Helen had written a work of fiction made Jackie's heart speed up with excitement. She'd always known Helen was an exceptional woman, but touching the pages in the notebook was like discovering a new layer to a person she'd thought she'd known. A creative layer that in many ways could reveal more about Helen than anything she'd said or done during her life.

17

The story was entitled, *Kiss the Wall.* The pages were filled with Helen's small neat, slightly sloping handwriting.

I kiss the wall, not with love, but with bitter lips. A mouth once filled with wine and laughter now only ashes.

For a moment, Jackie marvelled at her aunt's words, but as the story carried her along her aunt was soon forgotten.

It took Jackie a few seconds to realise the phone was ringing again. Pulling her attention away from the story, she scrambled to her feet and winced at the sound of her knees popping. A quick glance at her watch told her she'd been sitting cross-legged for two hours. No wonder her legs and back ached. It took her longer to reach the kitchen this time and once again she'd missed the call.

There was a moment of relief. She'd tried to get to the phone. It wasn't her fault she'd missed another call, but now she was free to return to the story. The characters, Elise and Dale, were swimming around in her head, calling out to her. She wanted to go to the spare room and lose herself in the saga of the people her aunt had created – people that seemed so real, yet so far removed from the real world.

She almost gave in to the idea, but then the phone shrilled and she decided it was better to get the call out of the way.

"Hi, Miss Winter. It's Fredrick Marclowe. Are you feeling any better?"

The question took her by surprise.

"I…" She had no idea what he was talking about, but it seemed easier just to go along. "Yes," she said. "I'm better."

"Good to hear." He sounded genuinely pleased. "If you're feeling up to it, I wonder if you can come in and sign the forms. Once that's out of the way—"

"I'm really busy." She tugged at a curl that had come loose on the back of her neck, realising she hadn't combed her hair or cleaned her teeth and it was now past lunch time. "I don't mean to be rude, but it's not convenient." She *did* sound rude. Rude and disinterested.

"Yes, I understand." He seemed unaffected by her curt manner. Jackie couldn't help wondering if dealing with grief made him immune to rudeness. Emotional people were often rude. She knew from first-hand experience that irate parents were offensive beings when they were upset.

She felt a stab of remorse; she was behaving no better than the parents she despised. The undertaker, like her, was just trying to do a difficult job and here she was making his life harder.

"No." The word sounded harsh so she softened her tone. "I mean, I'm sorry." She turned and headed back to the spare room with the phone pressed to her ear. "I'm being rude... It's just..." How could she explain it? *I don't want to deal with my aunt's death. I just want to hide in my bedroom reading about a love that I'll never experience.* "I suppose I'm frightened." She stared at the suitcase sitting on the colourful rug. "Dealing with my aunt's death is..."

"I would say difficult," he finished for her. "But *difficult* doesn't really describe what you're going through."

His words, the kindness in his voice, threw her off balance. "Yes." She sank down onto the bed. "It is difficult." She chuckled, not sure why that should be funny. "Difficult to say the least."

"If it makes it any easier, I can drop by after work with the forms," Marclowe offered.

The idea of a visitor, even if it was the undertaker, set off a spiral of panic. She wanted to say no and put him off somehow, but at the same time a part of her wanted to talk to someone who understood her pain. "All right."

Chapter Four

Dragging a comb through her unruly hair, Jackie noticed a few more strands of grey amongst the lacklustre brown. She had no idea why she was wasting her time smartening herself up for the undertaker. Maybe she was about to hit an all-time low and make a fool of herself in front of a guy trying to be kind while doing a difficult job.

The idea of her playing the seductress in jeans and an oversized T-shirt struck her as comical, and for the first time in maybe weeks she laughed. Not a scoffing laugh but a genuine giggle. Before turning away she gave herself a quick inspection in the bathroom mirror.

"You've been reading too many novels," she said aloud.

It was an off the cuff line, and as the words left her lips it dawned on her that what she'd found in the suitcase was in fact a novel. Judging by how many notebooks Helen had filled, maybe a few novels. So why was it that they'd never been published?

Back in the bedroom, she picked up the notebook she'd been reading when the phone rang. She was no expert, but it was good. No, more than good; it was brilliant. As a journalist, Helen would have had plenty of contacts. Why had she never had the novels published? Helen hadn't only avoided sharing her work; she'd gone to some lengths to hide the books.

Jackie flicked thorough the pages that were dry and beginning to yellow. If she hadn't opened the case, Helen's work might have been lost. Whatever modesty or lack of self-belief kept Helen from publishing, wasn't it only right that Jackie changed all that? She felt a calmness settling over her – a sense of purpose. For Helen's sake, the books should be published.

* * *

Fredrick Marclowe wasn't the sort of undertaker Jackie had imagined. A little older than he'd sounded on the phone, maybe early forties but lean with the slight tan of a jogger. Instead of a sombre black suit he wore dark pants and a pale green shirt with its sleeves rolled up and opened at the throat.

"Would you like a cup of tea or coffee, Mr Marclowe?" Jackie spoke over her shoulder as she led the man into the sitting room.

"Um… a glass of water and, please, call me Rick."

When Jackie stopped and turned, Rick was smiling. "All right, Rick," she said. "Call me Jackie."

Half an hour later, Rick had finished walking Jackie through the forms and the funeral her aunt had planned. To her immense relief, Helen had decided upon a private affair at the funeral home with strict instructions allowing for only a handful of mourners.

"Trust Aunt Helen to think of everything." Jackie held the list of approved funeral goers. "My mother won't be attending. She's on a one-hundred-and-forty-three-day cruise." She tried to keep her voice light, but felt a jolt of emotion.

Not quite resentment and more like longing and abandonment. A ridiculous feeling for a woman of thirty-six, but, nevertheless, it was there, always eating away at her, eroding her self-esteem, making her doubt her own worth. If her own mother was indifferent and almost bored by her, how could anyone else care for her?

If Rick noticed the quiver in her voice, he gave no indication. "Right. That leaves four of you." He picked up the glass of water from the coffee table. "As you can see, Miss Winter wanted the cremation to take place as quickly as possible." He nodded to the forms. "We can have everything ready by Friday, if that works for you."

There seemed to be no point putting it off any longer so Jackie bobbed her head in agreement. "Friday."

He took a sip of water and set the glass down. Jackie noticed his hands were tanned, strong-looking. When she looked up and met his brown eyes, he was watching her. She could feel the heat radiating up her neck. She felt like a child caught with her hand in someone else's school bag, so she dipped her head, pretending to re-read the forms.

"This is a big house. Are you here alone?" Rick asked.

The question seemed odd. He knew this was her aunt's house and surely he understood that she'd been looking after Helen in her final weeks. Jackie considered telling him to mind his own business, but with embarrassment still stinging her cheeks she couldn't quite muster the courage.

"I don't mean to be nosy." He spoke quickly making her wonder if he'd noticed her surprise. "I just wondered if you had anyone helping you through all this."

Jackie forced a smile. "Oh, yes. I have quite a few friends popping in on me." She didn't know why she was lying. What difference did it make what he thought of her? After Friday she'd never see him again, so why bother to lie? "I'm actually a bit overwhelmed by everyone's kindness." Why couldn't she stop the words dribbling out of her mouth?

He nodded and his eyes ran around the room. The lack of flowers or cards seemed painfully obvious. "Well, that's good," he said. She couldn't tell if he believed her or if he was just being polite.

"Anyway," he continued. "I'd better get going." He stood, so Jackie did the same.

At the front door, Rick paused. "If you need any help with all this, just give me a call." There was kindness in his voice, or maybe it was pity.

Suddenly, Jackie wanted to slam the door in his face and forget about the funeral and any other responsibilities. She wanted to shut the real world out and lose herself in Helen's books. Her hands curled into fists. "Yes, okay. Thanks." She managed a grin that probably looked crazed. "See you on Friday," she said, closing the door.

Chapter Five

Still feeling wrung out from the funeral, Jackie had no choice but to return to work on Monday morning. She arrived early, eliminating the chance of running into any of her colleagues in the parking lot and thus avoiding their well-meant condolences. The winter sky, soupy grey and flecked with purple, reminded her of the fabric-draped table where Helen's casket sat before being discretely removed for cremation.

Hurrying with a tote slung over her shoulder, Jackie's shoes *click clacked* out her presence to an empty school. When filled with children, primary schools were lively places, but once empty the walkways of the old structure had an abandoned feel that always made her nervous.

Not wanting to linger on the cement paths any longer than was necessary, she was careful to have her keys in hand. The locking mechanism on the classroom door, almost forty years old now, stuck. She'd requested maintenance on the lock before going on leave, but obviously her request had been overlooked. Shrugging deeper into her wool coat, she dropped the tote at her feet and used one hand to pull the lever towards her while jiggling the key with the other.

"Do you have a minute?"

Jackie jumped and dropped her keys. When she turned, the woman behind her smiled. Not a friendly grin, but a satisfied one. A smug look, knowing she'd startled Jackie and enjoying the moment.

"Margaret." Jackie tried to sound unperturbed, but the woman's sudden appearance had thrown her. "I haven't even unlocked the door yet. Maybe you could—"

"I won't keep you. I just want to have a quick chat about Felicity." Margaret Green had a way of rolling over people. A singular knack for boorishness that left Jackie feeling attacked and disarmed.

Jackie bent and scooped up her tote and keys. "I've been away for a few weeks, so I really need a bit of time to sort things out," she said, turning her back on the woman and pretending to examine the contents of her bag. "I'm happy to make an appointment and meet with you after school."

She could feel the woman behind her, moving closer and invading her space. "No, I can't do after school. As I said, it won't take long," Margaret insisted.

Jackie pressed her lips together and turned around. She kept the keys in her hand, refusing to be bullied into letting the parent into the classroom. If the woman wanted to corner her outside of school time, she'd have to have her *chat* standing on the walkway.

"What did you want to chat about?" Jackie asked.

It seemed impossible, but Margaret moved closer, so close their noses were almost touching. The parent's proximity made Jackie want to shove the woman away.

"As you know, Felicity has been having problems with some of the other girls in the class." Margaret's milky-blue eyes swam close as if expanding. "They're bullying her." The last three words came out too loud and with unnecessary indignation. "The woman they had here while you were off was hopeless. I want something done about

25

these girls." She raised her hand and for one awful second Jackie thought the woman meant to strike her.

Margaret didn't miss the way Jackie flinched. A smile lifted the corners of her frog-like mouth, making Jackie hate herself for being so weak and easily intimidated. In that instance, she thought about Elise, the heroine of her aunt's novel. The character was independent, strong and confident; a woman obviously based on Helen's own personality. How Jackie wished she could be more like Elise. More like Helen.

Meanwhile, Margaret was busily naming the group of four girls she believed to be picking on her daughter.

"Now…" She waved a finger in Jackie's face. "I want something done about this or I'm going to the principal." Margaret's wispy ginger hair floated around her face like tentacles. "We pay our fees. My daughter shouldn't have to put up with this, not in a Catholic school." Her voice was shrill and had reached a pitch of outrage that was sudden and overly emotional.

Jackie straightened her neck and swallowed. "I'll talk to the girls and see what's going on." Margaret's mouth drew down in disapproval, but Jackie pushed on. "If there *is* bullying—"

"I'm telling you there is." Margaret's cheeks turned an unattractive shade of pink.

"Yes, as I said, I'll talk to the girls involved. Now, I have a meeting so I must get on."

Over Margaret Green's shoulder, Jackie spotted Hetty, the year two teacher. When Jackie caught her eye, Hetty looked away and opened her classroom door. She wondered how long the other teacher had been standing there. Had she heard the way Margaret Green spoke to her? Had Hetty seen her flinching like a frightened child?

"I have to go," Jackie said. Dropping the keys back into her tote, she pushed past Margaret. "I have a meeting."

She hurried away, almost jogging, desperate to put space between her and the angry parent. Not wanting to look back, she prayed Margaret wasn't following her as she raced through the school.

The front office was locked, so instead of hiding in the toilets, Jackie loitered in the narrow walkway that led to the library. After five painfully long minutes feigning interest in various posters touting the advantages of reading, she thought it safe to venture back to her classroom. *I'm a coward.* The words repeated over and over in her mind as she raced past the first few early bird students.

* * *

Out of sorts and still flustered by her early morning encounter with Margaret Green, Jackie watched her students from her desk at the front of the room. Heads bent over the task at hand, the very air alive with whispers; it almost looked like the students were praying. A chorus of constant murmurs that reminded her of muttered chants. The weeks she'd spent with her aunt and the time after her aunt's death – time she'd been free to spend reading or taking long walks – seemed like a world away from the oppressive climate in the classroom. No matter how hard teachers tried, no matter how innovative the lessons, children didn't want to be shut up in a classroom all day.

In the early days of her career, Jackie tried outdoor lessons. While the students seemed excited at first, sitting under a tree writing out answers to the endless banal questions in their comprehension books soon became just another prison for the soul. It made no difference where the lessons took place, the inescapable truth was no one wanted to be there. *Least of all me.*

It had been easier when she had Helen. Having someone to share her feelings with and discuss the shortcomings of her career choice. Somehow Aunt Helen, with her endless capacity for joy and enthusiasm, made everything lighter – less solemn. But now Helen was gone and the world seemed bigger, making Jackie feel smaller.

"Maddie, Nora, Alisha and Lucy." When Jackie spoke, almost every head in the room bobbed up. "Could you come up here for a moment?"

Of the four girls in question, Lucy was the first to stand and approach the desk. The other three lagged behind, exchanging glances.

When the four students gathered in front of her, Jackie smiled to put the children at ease. "It's okay, girls. I just want to ask you what's been going on with Felicity." She kept her voice low so that the rest of the class wouldn't hear the discussion.

Nora scratched her head and Alisha pinned her eyes on the carpet. Something had happened, but Jackie doubted it was as Margaret Green had described.

"She keeps saying mean things." Lucy was the first to speak. She matched Jackie's whispered tone with tearless and unafraid eyes. Jackie liked the girl and admired her courage and strength of character. "She's always trying to tell us what to do." Lucy glanced at the other girls who were nodding. "She's so bossy."

"Yes," Alisha agreed in a lisping whisper. "She called me a baby and…" The girl's eyes filled with tears.

"It's all right, sweetie," Jackie said, and touched the child's shoulder. "You just tell me what happened. No one's in trouble."

"We didn't say she couldn't play with us." Nora's lower lip was trembling as she stumbled out the words.

Experience had taught Jackie that with young children tears were contagious, so she chose her next words carefully. "I know you're all trying very hard to be nice." She locked eyes with each girl in turn, giving them an encouraging smile. "I'd like you to give Felicity another chance. Ask her to join in your games." She nodded and the four girls nodded back. "If anything happens, tell me and I'll talk to her."

As the group of girls made their way back to their desks, Jackie's gaze landed on Felicity. The girl had her mother's ginger hair and froggy mouth. A mouth that was now puckered in anger at the boy next to her. With lightning speed, Felicity's hand shot out and grabbed the boy's pencil.

"Felicity!" The name came out louder than Jackie intended. The girl looked up, unimpressed with Jackie's admonishing tone. The way the child held her gaze made Jackie feel unreasonably angry. Uncurling her fists under the desk, she forced her voice into a more acceptable level. "Do not snatch things from other children."

All eyes were on Felicity now and, judging by the smirk on her face, she was enjoying the attention. Jackie waited for the girl to answer or give some indication that she'd heard Jackie's instruction, but Felicity remained silent, her pale eyes unwavering and defiant.

"Answer me, please," Jackie instructed.

She had the feeling the little girl was weighing her up, trying to decide how far to go. It was a ridiculous thought. Felicity was only nine years old. It was more likely that Jackie was letting her dislike for the girl's mother cloud her thinking. Whatever was going on behind the little girl's milky-blue eyes, Jackie couldn't help feeling relieved when the child finally nodded her acquiescence.

After lunch, Jackie watched the hands on the clock slowly tick towards 3:15 p.m. These endless afternoons were nothing new, yet for some reason the feeling of lassitude that came with the last hour of the school day seemed less acceptable. She'd watched her aunt die less than a week ago. Was it any surprise she resented losing time to a job that left her feeling used up and resentful?

When the buzzer sounded, she didn't bother to make the children wait while she ticked off a list of instructions for the next day. Instead, Jackie gestured to the door.

"See you tomorrow." It was an overly casual dismissal, but the kids didn't seem to notice.

As the last child shuffled out, Jackie let out a breath and sank back behind her desk. Two afternoons a week she had after-school duty shepherding children across a busy road. To her relief, today wasn't one of those days. Instead, she had time to drive home and change before dinner. While she'd put off seeing her best friend for over a month, now Jackie was looking forward to an evening with Lisa. An evening where she could relax and talk and maybe even laugh. Lisa was always able to see the funny side of life. The two of them were so different, sometimes Jackie wasn't quite sure how they had become friends. It would be nice to laugh again.

"Just a quick word." Margaret Green stood in the doorway, her raw-boned frame blocking the exit. "I've just spoken to Felicity and she told me you were angry with her today." She made the statement sound like an accusation.

"Margaret." The woman's name felt like lead on Jackie's tongue. "I wasn't angry with Felicity, I—"

Margaret moved into the classroom, her heels clonking on the vinyl flooring. "She's very upset. Did you sort out those girls?"

Not wanting to be cornered again, Jackie stood and began packing her tote. "I did offer an appointment after school, but you said you couldn't make it." She didn't want to have to look in the woman's milky eyes, so she kept her gaze on the desk, making a show of gathering up her keys. "So, I made a doctor's appointment," Jackie added and forced herself to look Margaret's way, afraid the lie was somehow apparent in her expression.

"I really must go, but I'd be happy to meet with you tomorrow after school," Jackie continued. "I have crosswalk duty, but I could see you at 3:30 p.m.?"

Meeting with Margaret again was the last thing Jackie wanted. But putting her off at least bought her some time to prepare. If the principal was available, she'd ask him to sit in. Dan Keegan wasn't much use running a school, but his presence might keep Margaret under control.

Margaret moved swiftly, crossing the room to stand beside Jackie's desk. "This is really important. I'm sure you can spare five minutes." There was something in the woman's stance, a shifting of weight and leaning forward that struck Jackie as menacing.

Jackie opened her mouth to protest but was cut off by a knock on the open classroom door. "Are you ready, Jackie?" Hetty asked, smiling and holding up her keys. "You said you'd help me load some equipment in my car." The year two teacher had a pretty face, small delicate features, and straight brown hair. Usually smiling and darting around the school like a happy rabbit, today Hetty looked composed, almost poised.

Was it Jackie's imagination or did Margaret take a step back? "Yes, on my way," Jackie said as she slung her tote over her shoulder and gestured to the door.

She meant to tell Margaret she was sorry she couldn't stop, but the woman spun on her heels and stomped out of the classroom without another word.

"You're a life saver," Jackie said as she turned off the lights and pulled the door closed.

Hetty shook her head. "When Felicity was in year two, Margaret Green tortured me." The young teacher flicked a strand of hair over her shoulder. "She's not an easy person to stand up to."

Jackie's usual reaction would have been to prickle and become defensive, but Hetty's dark eyes were solemn and kind. There was no judgement or condescension in her words. She'd witnessed Jackie's encounter with Margaret that morning and was trying to help.

Jackie's shoulders relaxed. "I know what you mean. I just wish I didn't have to deal with the woman. I wish she'd just vanish."

"Oh." Hetty frowned. "I'm sorry about your aunt," she continued, swiftly changing the subject. "This must be a difficult enough time without people like Margaret Green making it worse."

Here it was, the condolences Jackie had been dreading. As Hetty's words washed over her, she realised why she'd been so desperate to avoid her colleagues' sympathy: she was terrified their words of kindness would remind her of how alone she was. Well wishes would only rub her nose in the fact that she had no one to lean on.

But instead of reducing Jackie, Hetty's kindness soothed her jagged nerves. "Thanks," she said.

Hetty insisted on walking Jackie to her car, jestingly offering to be her backup if Margaret was somewhere lying in wait. Both women laughed at the idea of Margaret Green jumping out from behind a bush, but Jackie had the distinct impression that Hetty was only half-joking.

Chapter Six

For once, Lisa was early, rising out of her chair and beckoning Jackie over to a table near the bar. Crossing the busy restaurant, Jackie was painfully aware of how frumpy she looked while plodding her way through the fashionable crowd.

"Jackie." She winced as Lisa's voice rang out and all eyes turned their way.

Jackie smiled and tried to duck into her seat, but Lisa wasn't having any of it. Lunging forward, she wrapped her slim arms around Jackie's shoulders and pulled her into an embrace.

"I'm so sorry." To Jackie's relief, Lisa's voice was softer as she pressed her cheek to Jackie's shoulder. "Why didn't you call?"

Ignoring the stares from a group of young women in short sparkly dresses, Jackie patted Lisa's back while disengaging herself from the awkward hug.

"I know how busy you are at work and…" Jackie stuttered out the excuse, not sure how to explain her behaviour. Lisa was her oldest friend. She'd never been anything but kind and supportive, yet Jackie had deliberately kept her at arm's length.

"I would have made time." There was pain in Lisa's voice as she released her from the embrace and settled herself at the table. "You should have called me."

A string of reasons formed in Jackie's mind but died on her lips. Lisa had always been a good friend. Why hadn't she at least informed her about the funeral?

"I'm sorry," Jackie said and seated herself opposite her friend. "It was stupid of me to keep you away. I don't know why I do these things." Tears were building in her eyes, biting at the back of her throat. "I haven't been myself lately... I've been sort of..." Jackie closed her eyes and swallowed.

What could she say when she didn't really understand it herself? *I just watched my spinster aunt die and realised I was seeing my own future.*

"It's okay, babe." Lisa's hand closed over Jackie's. "We all go through stuff," she said, shrugging her tanned shoulders. "Everyone deals with things the best way they can."

Jackie opened her eyes and met Lisa's gaze. Her friend was watching her with a look of concern darkening her gentle blue eyes. How, she wondered, did she get things so wrong? She thought Lisa to be smug and self-involved. After years of friendship, she'd relegated Lisa to the role of fair-weather friend, not giving her the chance to offer real support.

"I wish I had called." As the words came out, Jackie recognised them as the truth.

Having Lisa with her at the funeral might have alleviated the cold dread that tore at her heart as she bid her Aunt Helen farewell then watched as the coffin was lowered into the unknown.

But her aunt's destination wasn't really unknown, at least not her earthly one. Cremation was a grim and final ending to a human life, one that chilled Jackie to the bone.

Without realising it, she wrapped her arms around herself, staving off the cold that came from within rather than the warm crowded restaurant. "I'm sorry." It was all she could think to say by way of an explanation.

To her relief, Lisa seemed satisfied. "That's okay, babe." She patted Jackie's hand, the warmth of her touch chasing away the cold. "I'm here now. Tell me what you need?"

Later, when their food had arrived and Jackie's wine glass was almost empty, she broached the subject that had, in part, been her reason for agreeing to the night out.

"There is something I wanted to ask." Jackie said, and picked up her glass, finishing off the last sip. "I... um..." She'd rehearsed this bit in her mind, but with Lisa watching her with glassy eyes from a second gin and tonic, Jackie couldn't quite recall how her little speech was supposed to go.

"I have a manuscript," she said noticing something creep across Lisa's features. It might have been amusement, but the look was gone too quickly for Jackie to be sure. Determined not to be put off, she plunged ahead. "I was wondering if you'd..." Realising she was holding an empty glass, Jackie set it down on the table and winced as the stem clanked against her plate. "I mean, I know you work for a magazine, so I wondered if you know anyone I could send it to." The words were out. Not quite as she'd prepared, but there was no going back now.

Lisa drained her glass before answering, and in the seconds it took her friend to tip the tumbler to her lips and swallow, Jackie wished she could rewind the last thirty seconds and forget she'd ever brought the subject up. *Kiss the Wall* was Aunt Helen's work. If she'd wanted it published, she would have done so. Helen knew plenty of people in the literary world; she'd have had no trouble securing a publisher.

"I had no idea you wrote." Lisa sounded genuinely pleased and Jackie felt a stab of guilt for assuming her friend would think it comical that she had a manuscript.

"Tell you what, send me the first fifty pages and I'll let you know if I think you're ready for publishing." Lisa tipped her head to the side as she continued, her dark pixie-cut shining like onyx under the artificial lights.

"All right," Jackie said. For the first time in months, maybe even years, she felt a buzz of excitement. "I'll get it to you tomorrow."

* * *

It was well past midnight when Jackie shut down her laptop and left Helen's study. *My study now.* She was almost startled by the thought, but not altogether unhappy. She'd always loved Helen's house and according to her aunt's solicitor, the place now belonged to Jackie.

Trailing her hand along the wall, she navigated the dark hallway that led to the spare room. It had taken her almost five hours to transcribe the first fifty pages of Helen's novel. Getting the entire first book typed up would probably take her a few days. The idea of spending days working in the study should have been daunting, but instead she felt energised – excited.

Still, in almost complete darkness, a sound caught her attention. A soft thud followed by a rustle. Jackie stopped moving and glanced back over her shoulder, taking in the length of the dim hallway. The noise had come from outside, somewhere near the study. No stranger to living alone, Jackie forced down the familiar prickle of fear that came with noises in the night. She'd learned years ago that almost always night-time disturbances could be easily explained: a cat on the prowl or a possum clamouring through the trees.

Yet, as she turned and made her way back to the study, images of her aunt lying in the austere hospital bed tripped across her mind. Flicking on the study light, she was relieved to see the room was as she'd left it.

"No ghosts here." She spoke to the empty study in a voice that even to her own ears sounded shaky.

Glancing at the window, she noticed the curtains were open. If there *was* someone outside, they would have been able to watch her working on her laptop. With the pane turned black by the lack of outside light, someone could be standing only inches away from the window and she'd never see them. He could still be watching.

Jackie's heart fluttered in an unpleasant pattern of jumps and drops as she crossed the room and jerked the curtains closed. In her mind's eye she could almost see him on the other side of the glass, face blank and eyes dark and soulless. *Where the hell did that come from?* She shook her head, trying to dislodge the terrifying image from her mind.

With the curtains closed, she fled the study and hurried to her bedroom where she checked the old-fashioned locking mechanism on her window and snatched the curtains closed. It was unlike her to let one little noise freak her out. Helen's death had hit her hard, maybe harder than she realised.

After a few minutes sitting on her bed rubbing her thumbs back and forth across her index fingers, she forced herself to go back to the study and check the window lock.

The mechanism was in place, but in the few seconds she had the curtains open, Jackie had the feeling someone *was* watching her. A sense so strong that it took all her will not to run screaming from the room. Instead, she tapped the catch, making sure to let her finger soak in the cold metallic feel of the lock. Once satisfied the room was secure, she let the curtain fall back in place.

Despite a feeling of weariness, it took her longer than usual to fall asleep. As she listened to a mild wind blowing around the outside of the old house, it occurred to her that she'd told Lisa she had a manuscript, but hadn't actually explained that her aunt was the author. In the few minutes before sleep finally took her, Jackie made the decision to clear up the oversight when she emailed her friend the fifty pages.

Chapter Seven

A rumbling similar to a giant bee swooping over the house in search of an equally large flower dragged Jackie from sleep. It was only when she pulled herself into a sitting position that she realised there had been no alarm to wake her and the giant bee was a garbage truck's grinding gears as it stopped and started along the street.

Snatching up her watch, she saw it was almost 7:20 a.m. "Damn." She flung back the covers, irritated by her own forgetfulness, and at the same time startled by the drop in temperature.

If she had any hope of making it to work before the first bell shrilled, she'd have to forgo a shower. Deciding a hot cup of tea would go further in kick-starting her foggy brain than a hot shower, Jackie padded towards the kitchen.

As she flicked the switch and set the kettle to boil, she noticed the almost overflowing bin sitting near the back door. "Oh, for God's sake." She'd forgotten to put the bins out last night. She could have tried running outside in her pyjamas and dumping the wheelie bin on the curb before the truck reached her house, but instead she poured the boiling water over her teabag and slumped down at the kitchen table.

Was this what grief and shock did? Did the feelings of loss and sadness steal away a person's ability to function and remember the simplest chores like setting the alarm on her phone or putting the bins out? Suddenly the idea of facing another day at school seemed like a torture she just couldn't bear. If she hadn't already taken weeks off to care for Aunt Helen, she'd have called the principal and feigned illness. But, as it was, she was already behind on her reports. Feeling resolute, she settled for a few sips of rapidly cooling tea before facing another day.

Dressed and ready to go in less than half an hour, Jackie remembered the fifty pages she'd typed the night before. She glanced at her watch: 8:05 a.m. Any further delay would make her late, but the idea of explaining to Dan why she was late for class seemed unimportant compared to getting the first part of the manuscript off to Lisa.

Early morning light dropped through the window, creeping across the desk like a carefully aimed stage light. Jackie crossed the room and flipped her laptop open. Dashing off a quick email and attaching the first part of *Kiss the Wall* took less than five minutes. It was done now. The pages were most likely arriving in Lisa's inbox at that very second and the idea of her friend reading the words Helen had so artfully put together made Jackie's stomach flip with relief. More than relief, anticipation mixed with joy, a feeling she hadn't experienced in a long time.

Just before shutting the computer down, it occurred to her that she'd forgotten to put Helen's name on the document. At dinner the night before, Lisa had assumed Jackie had written the manuscript. An assumption Jackie hadn't bothered to correct. *Why had she done that?* For a moment, Jackie couldn't quite remember what she'd been thinking while Lisa looked at her with a glint of admiration. Jackie had never been admired, not even by

Aunt Helen. Was it wrong to enjoy the experience, if only for a few days?

Her gaze drifted to the window where a hibiscus tree crowded the pane. Outside, unconcerned by the murky winter sky, birds sang their cheerful song. What would Helen think of her actions? Jackie didn't really believe in an afterlife, let alone the idea of someone watching from another plane of existence. Yet, the glimpse of sky and cheery birdsong didn't dispel the feeling that something was off.

Rubbing her thumbs along the sides of her index finger, she stood from her place at the desk. It was the notion of being watched that brought everything into focus. The curtains. Jackie's hands dropped to her sides and clutched the fabric of her loose-fitting pants. She'd closed the curtains before going to bed.

The memory was clear in her mind; the noise outside and then the feeling of being watched. She'd imagined someone staring in the window and drew the drapes together before going to bed. A sliver of uncertainty crept across her thoughts. At least that's what she thought she'd done.

Her eyes danced around the study as her fingers twisted the fabric of her pants. Could she have blacked out? Lost time? It had happened the night she found the key. One minute she was searching the house and the next she woke up to find the suitcase in the spare room. She'd been so excited to finally solve the puzzle of the hidden key that she hadn't given the hole in her memory much thought, but now the idea of moving around the house with no recollection of her actions chilled her.

Glancing at her watch, she was surprised by how much time had passed and how long she'd wasted fretting about the curtains. It was almost 8:15 a.m. With no option but to push the blackout to the back of her mind, Jackie raced out of the house.

* * *

Dan was sitting at the front of her class, a brightly coloured picture book resting on his knee. Despite the feeling of guilt at being caught coming in late, Jackie felt a prickle of irritation towards the principal. Her students were nine years old. Surely Dan knew they were past picture books.

"Miss Winter..." Dan's voice was overly loud as he snapped the book closed and stood while the children turned in their seats and twenty-eight childish eyes took in her harried appearance.

It took all her will not to cringe. "Sorry I'm late, everyone," she said. "But my car wouldn't start." It was the first thing that popped into her brain as she cursed herself for not coming up with something better during the fifteen-minute drive from Helen's house to school.

"Well..." Dan tossed the book onto her desk. "You're here now. That's the main thing." His skin was as grey as his receding hair. "Could you stop in my office after school?" There was joviality in his voice, but the tone didn't match the coolness in his stare.

Jackie watched the principal leave the room, her bag still clutched to her shoulder and her cheeks red from jogging from the parking lot. She wondered what he would do if she chased after him, grabbed his arm and told him she quit. Would he try and talk her out of leaving? After ten years at St Agnes, would anyone really give a damn if she walked out and never returned?

"Miss Winter." She recognised Felicity's voice without turning around. "We didn't have a teacher, so Mr Keegan had to read us a story." The child's voice was pitched high and dripping with recrimination.

"Yes." Jackie worked to keep the irritation out of her own voice. "I realise that." She moved across the room without looking at the children and dumped her bag on her desk. "Take out your handwriting books and start on letter 'H'."

"But we're up to letter 'J'." Felicity's tone had changed from accusing to smug.

"Do 'J' then," Jackie snapped and thumped the desk with her fist. "Or read a book… Just give me a damn minute."

"Sorry to interrupt." Hetty stood in the open doorway, her eyes wide and one pale hand clamped to her throat. "I just wondered if I could use your class' iPads, b… but I can come back later…" The young teacher was already backing out of the door.

Jackie realised her fist was still clenched and resting on the desk like a mallet. She tried to speak, to tell Hetty it wasn't what it looked like, but Jackie's mouth was devoid of moisture and her tongue felt stuck in place. And, if it wasn't what it looked like, what had just happened? In fourteen years of teaching she'd never spoken to a child with so much anger.

"It's okay, Miss Jackobe. I was just…" Jackie stumbled. When she was finally able to speak, the words sounded jumbled and half-formed, so she jumped to her feet meaning to follow the younger woman outside and explain what she'd just witnessed.

In her haste, Jackie's leg caught the edge of the desk and she stumbled. For one sickening second, she thought she might end up on the floor, but somehow managed to catch herself in an awkward side-step. When she turned back to the door, Hetty was gone and the room was abuzz with giggles and whispers.

Red-faced and with her lower lip trembling, Jackie turned back to the class. "Get on with your work."

* * *

The rest of the day passed with a slowness that seemed interminable. For once Jackie was glad she had lunch duty, preferring to spend half an hour walking the playground barely aware of the chaos around her than venture into the staff room. Her mind kept replaying the moment she looked up and saw Hetty watching her. Reliving the embarrassment and guilt over and over was like digging at a pus-filled scab; the pain kept coming, but she was unable to stop.

By mid-afternoon, the air in the classroom tasted sour and over-used like the recycled atmosphere on a long aeroplane journey. With the final bell still five minutes away, Jackie couldn't stand it any longer.

"All right." The children were waiting for a parting speech, reminders about homework and an exaggerated farewell. "You've been good today, so you may as well go early." There were murmurs of delight, a sound that would have usually brought a smile to her face. But in that moment, all she felt was panic. She had to get out of the room. Not just the room but the school where everything she did was watched by dozens of eyes.

It was only when she reached the parking lot that she remembered Dan had asked her to see him at the end of the day. The idea of walking back into the school and sitting in the self-important principal's office while he lectured her about getting to work on time made her muscles clench with anger. The man hadn't really taught a class in twenty years and had no idea of the pressures teachers were under. Her earlier fantasy of telling her boss to go to hell came back and this time she actually considered acting on it.

Warmed by the winter sun, the inside of her car was a welcome escape from the cold chill carried on the breeze. While the enclosed air was stale, she experienced a sense of safety, a feeling of separation from the rigours of her job.

"Maybe I should quit." Jackie spoke to the empty vehicle as she turned in her seat and dumped her bag on the floor.

When she twisted back to the wheel, she gasped and her knee bumped the keys dangling from the ignition. A shape washed in sunlight but clearly human stood in front of the bonnet. Squinting and using her palm to shade her eyes from the sun, the unmoving figure became clear.

Margaret Green remained motionless, her rust-coloured blouse flapping in the breeze and her fine hair whipping against her face. The only sounds in the car came from Jackie's breathing and the tinkle of metal as the keys swung near her leg. The moment seemed unnaturally long as she waited for the woman to move or speak. Instead, Margaret remained ahead of the car, frozen like a shop mannequin.

Jackie couldn't quite see the woman's eyes, but she felt them on her. Not sure what she was meant to do, Jackie turned the keys and started the car. *I could accelerate and drive over her. I could say the sun blinded me and I didn't see her.* The thought took her by surprise and for a second she was more freaked out by her own thinking than by Margaret's strange behaviour.

The sound of the engine must have broken the spell because, suddenly, the woman was in motion. She darted right and came alongside of the driver's door. Stooping, the woman's face filled the window. With Margaret out of the way, Jackie could have driven off and left the parent standing in the empty parking space, but instead she lowered the window.

"I know what you did." Margaret Green's voice was low, almost a growl. "You won't get away with this." Her eyes were glassy and for the first time Jackie felt not just uneasy but really afraid of the woman.

"I don't know what you're talking about, Margaret." Jackie's voice was thin, lacking strength or conviction. "I'm on my way home, so…" She trailed off, not wanting to aggravate the woman, but desperate to close the window and drive away.

"Yes, you do." Margaret had her hands on the door, fingers curled over the lip of the window. "Felicity told me how you screamed and cursed at her. You're not fit to be teaching and I'm going to make sure you lose your job over this." She was leaning in the window; her pink face so close Jackie could see the open pores on the woman's nose. "You'll be sorry you spoke to my child like that."

There was a look in the woman's watery blue eyes, a look that reminded Jackie of the way Dan had stared at her when she arrived late. A smug gaze filled with judgement.

Fear and unease vanished, swept away by a rush of anger.

"Get away from my car." Jackie leaned forward, not caring that their faces were so close she could smell the woman's breath; thick and reeking of coffee. "You'd better stop harassing me or you'll be the one that's sorry."

For the first time Margaret seemed uncertain. She drew back from the window, her frog-like mouth drooping downwards. With the woman clear of the car, Jackie slid the gearstick into drive, careful to keep her eyes firmly fixed on Margaret. As she pulled out of the parking space, she had the urge to say something else: a clever parting shot. But the anger she'd experienced only a moment ago was already dissipating, so Jackie settled for a final shake of her head.

By the time she was on the road, her hands were shaking. The encounter had left her rattled, but there was also a feeling of release. She'd stood up to the woman and by not showing up for her meeting with Dan she'd sort of stood up to her boss, too. Things were changing. She could feel the shift and welcomed it.

Chapter Eight

"Your aunt certainly left you well provided for." Andrew Drake flipped through the three-page document. "As well as the house in Regent Park, there's a modest shares portfolio, an account with a substantial amount of savings, and an investment property in the Swan Valley." The solicitor dropped the will onto his desk and rested his elbow on the arm of his chair. "It's not a complicated will, so probate shouldn't take too long."

Jackie suspected her aunt had been careful with her money, but had never imagined she'd accumulated so much. "I don't know what to say." She realised she was fiddling with a stray wisp of hair at the base of her neck and forced her hand back into her lap. "What happens now?"

As the solicitor talked through the probate process, Jackie's mind wandered. After a glass of wine the night before, she'd sent a text to St Agnes' assistant principal, Nick Chambers, and told him she was sick. Not bothering to actually call and speak to the man was something she'd have never ordinarily done. But not only had she sent a curt text, she'd followed it up a few minutes later with another message informing Nick she'd be taking the rest of the week off, only remembering to let him know who the text was from at the last minute.

In the light of day, Jackie had no regrets. Fuelled by the feeling that her life was set to change, she'd gone through Helen's filing cabinet and dug out the details of her aunt's solicitor. And now, sitting in Andrew Drake's office, her life had taken a dramatic turn.

"So, for now you can continue living in your aunt's house and I'll be in touch when probate is granted." He leaned forward. "If you have any questions, just give me a call."

Jackie's mind was buzzing with possibilities. At the same time there was a measure of sadness clouding her elation. She couldn't help but think of Aunt Helen, an independent and self-sufficient woman striving to support herself in a world where single women of a certain age are almost invisible. "Thank you, Mr Drake."

He smiled and although the man must have been close to his mid-fifties, there was something attractive in the way his dark blue eyes glimmered. "Please, call me Andrew. You know your aunt and I go way back," Drake said, sitting back in his chair. "I was just out of uni when I first met Helen. She was an amazing woman." When Andrew smiled, his face changed and he looked younger. "I was twenty-two, not much more than a kid, but I had a bit of crush on her." The smiled softened into a look of sadness. "I'm so sorry for your loss."

The words were familiar. Jackie had heard the same platitudes countless times since Helen died, but on Andrew Drake's lips there was genuine sorrow. Sorrow that made Jackie want to fold herself into the man's arms.

"Thank you, Andrew," she said. "That's very kind of you."

* * *

The Regent Park shopping precinct always made Jackie nervous. It was that same feeling she experienced in the restaurant, of being a frumpy woman out of place on the affluent streets of such a trendy area. Today, however, something was different. The shift in perspective that started when she stood up to Margaret Green seemed to be gathering momentum. As Jackie strolled the narrow streets, she could almost hear Helen's voice confident and calm in her ear. *You can't let the world decide where you belong, but to find your own way, you have to trust yourself.*

In the window of a small boutique, a dress caught Jackie's eye: a wine-coloured pattern that reminded her of exotic birds swooping and diving through a jungle paradise. It was the sort of thing she'd always wanted to wear but never had the confidence or the figure. On impulse, she entered the shop and asked the assistant if she could try the dress on.

Rather than looking down her nose at Jackie, the pretty young woman in the boutique was friendly and helpful. To Jackie's delight, the dress was too large and she had to ask for a smaller size, something she attributed to her lack of appetite since the funeral.

An hour later, she left the shop not only with the dress, but a green silk blouse, a pair of outrageously expensive black jeans and a dark blue puffer coat. It was the most she'd ever spent on clothing in one session, but instead of feeling guilty over her indulgences, her stomach flipped with pleasure.

Before driving home, she picked up a few supplies at the supermarket, including a packet of hair dye. *What am I doing?* She felt the weight of her worries lifting. *I'm trusting myself.* Maybe not completely but it was a place to start.

* * *

The late afternoon sky was clear of clouds, allowing the sun to take the chill off the air. Jackie tossed her purchases on the kitchen table and kicked off her shoes. Since moving into Helen's house, she had taken to walking down to the banks of the Swan River as often as possible. It was only a few streets away and the journey always helped clear her mind. Today, as she pulled on her battered trainers and stuffed her phone and keys in her pocket, she felt none of the murkiness that usually shadowed her thoughts.

With her hair secured in a tight ponytail, the breeze picked up the loose strands and danced them against her cheeks. Regent Park was an old, well-established suburb dotted with deep rooted wild fig trees and aged jacarandas. The streets were wide. Houses sat back on well-maintained lawns. It also possessed a leafy area where people liked to stroll. Her aunt's neighbour, a white-haired woman kneeling beside a catch of bare rosebushes, raised her head as Jackie strode past. The woman lifted a hand in greeting. Jackie responded with a cheerful wave. *I suppose she's my neighbour now.* It was only as the thought occurred to her that she realised she intended to remain living in Helen's house. The idea pleased her and added to her sense of beginning something fresh and new.

The walk to the riverbank usually took fifteen minutes, but today she slowed her pace. With work taken care of until next week she had time to just be. Time to meander.

The water looked as dark as a night sky and choppy as if a storm was churning beneath its surface. Jackie turned left and walked the path near the waterside, enjoying glimpses of surf skiers and small crafts as they cruised deeper waters.

Her destination was a little white bench under the shade of a wild fig tree. By the time she reached the rest point, her breath was coming in short bursts. *I need more exercise.* Flopping down onto the wooden seat, she draped her arms on her thighs and looked out over the river. She wondered what it would be like to be on a boat flying across the Swan while the setting sun scorched the sky.

Glancing right, she noticed a figure standing side-on about forty metres back on the path. It wasn't surprising to see others taking advantage of the dry afternoons and strolling the riverbanks, but something about the shape set

49

her nerves on edge. From this distance there was no telling if the shape was that of a man or woman. The person's dark coat and hood disguised everything but the lower legs, which were encased in dark pants.

Jackie snatched a look around, hoping to see someone else making their way along the track, but the area was deserted and the boats were so far out that the occupants would never hear if she called for help. Why was she thinking about calling for help? It was still light and the figure appeared to be doing nothing more than staring out over the water. Even as she rationalised and tried to still her uneasiness, her hand crept into her pocket and gripped her phone.

If he comes towards me, I'll get up and walk in the opposite direction. She snatched another glance to her left, but the path was still uninhabited. When she looked back, the figure had changed positions and was now facing Jackie. With his legs wide apart and the hood and coat moving in the breeze, he looked like a statue.

Shit. Things had gone from unsettling to downright creepy.

Not knowing what else to do, she stood and pulled out her phone. Maybe if he saw her calling someone he'd move on. She tapped at the screen then held the phone to her ear. When she looked back, he was still there, unmoving and obviously watching her. *Now what?*

Her hand was shaking as she held the phone against her ear. Should she call the police? If she did, what would she tell them? *There's a man staring at me.* It sounded ridiculous. There was nothing else for it but to walk in the other direction. The only problem was, she had no idea where the path ended. She'd never gone further than the white bench and for all she knew she could be walking to an even lonelier area, or worse a dead end. *Dead.* Her knees were trembling now. She'd have to risk following the path left; it was the only solution and the only way to put distance between her and the creep in the coat.

One more glance and she'd move. Maybe round the next curve and start running. Heart thumping, she turned her head, half expecting to see the man sprinting towards her. Instead, the path was empty. He was gone. She let out a puff of breath and swiped at her forehead with the back of her arm.

On the walk home she couldn't stop herself from grabbing furtive looks over her shoulder. Maybe she'd overreacted down at the river. Maybe the guy was just a creep that liked to stare at women *or* the whole thing could have been completely innocent. By the time she reached the house she was feeling steadier and more in control, and half-convinced that the whole incident had been a misunderstanding.

* * *

"I loved it." Lisa's voice was full of excitement. "If the rest of the manuscript is anything like the first fifty pages, you're onto a winner."

Jackie was sitting on the veranda at the rear of the house, sipping coffee and staring out over the wide expanse of the lawn. As night drew in, the incident at the river seemed miles away and almost silly now. Besides, she had more important things to think about. She'd known the story was good. Great in fact, but still hearing it from someone like Lisa sent a quiver of excitement down her spine.

"Thanks... I didn't—"

"I've already passed it on to a friend of mine at Thorn Publishing. He owes me a favour so I know he'll take good care of those pages." Lisa chuckled. "I hope the rest of the book is ready to go, because I've got a feeling you'll be receiving a full manuscript request."

Jackie hesitated before answering. She had been transcribing the notebooks and was pretty sure she had the first full novel ready. All that remained was to tell her friend the manuscript was Helen's work. It should have been the easiest thing in the world. All she had to do was say the words and clear up the misunderstanding. But it wasn't that easy, not really. Telling the truth now could throw a spanner in the works. Probate hadn't gone through, so legally she didn't really own the manuscripts, not yet anyway. And then there was Helen to think about. She'd obviously wanted the work to remain private. It might be better to keep her name out of it.

"Are you there, babe?" Lisa had stopped speaking and was waiting for an answer.

"I... Yes, I'm here. Sorry! I'm just so excited," Jackie answered, and heard her friend let out a relieved breath. "The rest of the manuscript is ready to go."

Lisa made a squealing noise that made Jackie laugh. "We should celebrate. Let's go out for drinks tomorrow night?"

Jackie thought of the dress with the exotic birds and smiled. "Sounds great."

After setting a time and a place to meet, Jackie hung up and hurried back inside. She only made it as far as the kitchen when her phone rang again. The number was unfamiliar but she recognised the voice immediately.

"Hi, Jackie." There was a whistling sound in the background, suggesting Rick was outside. "I just wanted to let you know your aunt's ashes are ready to be delivered."

The sense of pleasure she'd experienced only moments ago fizzled out, leaving her feeling exhausted and empty. Here she was making plans and being excited about the future while her aunt's remains were reduced to ash. Everything about her, her remarkable brain, fine features and wise eyes were gone.

"Oh." The word sounded weak. "I'm not sure what... what usually happens?" For some reason her mind threw up images of people dressed in black tossing handfuls of ash into the ocean. The picture made her shiver.

"Well..." Rick Marclowe stretched the word out. "Some people like to keep the ashes at home while others choose to have them interned with other family that have passed. If there is a family plot, you might want to have the ashes buried or scattered."

The burden of deciding what to do felt like a physical weight pushing down on her shoulders and neck. She dragged out a chair and sat at the kitchen table. "I think I'd like to bring her home."

"All right." His voice was gentle, soothing. He'd been so caring during the funeral and now the kindness in his voice reminded her of how much the man had done for her. She knew it was his job to support people through the trauma of a funeral, but that didn't take away from the gratitude she felt.

"I can come tomorrow, if that's convenient?" he asked.

"Yes, tomorrow… Thanks, Rick."

Chapter Nine

Rick arrived at twelve o'clock bearing a wooden box. Without opening the carton, Jackie knew it contained a black glossy urn that held what little remained of Helen Winter. She had expected the sight of the box to set off a rush of fresh grief, but instead she felt calm – relieved. Aunt Helen was home and because Jackie had decided to keep the house and sell her small unit in Balcatta, Helen would remain in the house she loved.

When Jackie showed Rick to the door, there was an awkward moment when the undertaker hesitated on the threshold. "Let me know if you need anything."

He seemed reluctant to leave. If she hadn't already made plans to see Lisa that night, she might have asked him to stay for dinner, which was something she wouldn't have dreamt of doing a week ago.

"Thanks for everything," she said. "I couldn't have gotten through it without you."

He nodded. "I don't think that's true. You're much stronger than you give yourself credit for." It was a surprisingly personal comment, one she wasn't expecting.

Jackie was still struggling with how to respond when Rick smiled and she noticed his eyes were hazel, flecked with dark brown. Eyes that made her think of honey and sunlight.

"I like your hair," he said.

Jackie touched her newly dyed copper-coloured hair. It was a big change, one she didn't know if she was ready for. "Thanks." She gave an uncomfortable chuckle.

A second later, Rick had wished her goodnight and was walking down the front path to where his car was parked near the curb.

* * *

"So, you had a moment with the undertaker." Lisa raised her perfectly arched eyebrows. "That new hair colour is really working for you."

Jackie couldn't help smiling. There was no one else in her life that made her laugh the way Lisa could. "I don't know if I'd call it a moment, but..." She picked up her glass. "He's nice."

They were in the city at a rooftop bar, a place with an overload of fairy lights and chunky industrial furnishings. It was the sort of place that usually made Jackie feel self-conscious, but tonight the trendy setting felt magical.

"Well, you look amazing." Lisa nodded to Jackie's new dress. "You've always been gorgeous, but it's like now you're finally realising what the rest of us could always see."

Jackie could feel her face colouring, but not with embarrassment. The warmth spreading through her body was in part alcohol induced, but also pleasure. She didn't feel gorgeous, but for the first time she thought she looked sort of attractive.

Looking down, she ran a finger around the rim of her glass. "I haven't told anyone this, not yet." A spark of excitement bloomed in her chest. "I've decided to quit my job." The last three words came out in a rush. It was the first time she'd vocalised the thought that had been playing around in her mind for weeks, and hearing it out loud made the whole idea seem real.

"Are you sure?" It wasn't like Lisa to be the cautious one and, when Jackie met her friend's gaze, she saw worry.

"I thought you'd be happy for me." It wasn't the reaction she'd been hoping for, but Jackie didn't intend to let anything dampen her excitement. "You know I haven't been happy for a long time and with…" She almost stopped, not wanting to think about her last few days at school. "It's been rough lately." Jackie rubbed her fingers across her brow. "It's always been rough, but there's this parent. She's been harassing me and—"

"Harassing you?" Lisa frowned. "What's the principal doing about it?"

Jackie laughed, but it wasn't a happy sound. "Nothing." She shrugged. "I haven't told him, but he knows. He knows what the woman's like because I'm not the first teacher she's gone after."

"I can't believe he's not supporting you, especially since you've just lost your aunt." Lisa shook her head. "What an asshole."

As her friend continued her diatribe, Jackie's thoughts returned to the moment she'd spotted Margaret standing in front of her car. She'd pushed the episode to the back of her thoughts, but now it was in the forefront of her mind so clearly, she could almost see the woman frozen while the wind had whipped her ginger hair into a wild halo.

"Jackie." Lisa touched her hand and Jackie jumped. "Wow, are you okay?"

"Yes." Jackie patted Lisa's hand. "Yes, I'm fine. I've made my decision." She took a breath before continuing. "I'm not going back. I'm supposed to give six weeks' notice, but all I stand to lose is a couple of weeks' holiday pay." She picked up her drink, a Long Island Iced Tea, a drink Lisa insisted they try. "It'll be worth the money just to never have to set foot in that place again." She could hear the bitterness in her own voice and tried to soften the impact of her words with a chuckle.

"Okay." Lisa picked up her drink. "Let's drink to it." She held the glass up to the light. "To the beginning of something big."

As they clinked glasses, Jackie felt a quiver of something that was in equal parts anticipation and fear.

* * *

After skipping her walk on Friday, Jackie was determined not to let the weird incident on her last visit to the river spoil her new dedication to exercise. She'd lost three kilos over the past two weeks, an achievement that was in part due to her daily walks. Besides, there was something free and wild about the Swan River. Staring out over the water helped quiet her mind. It helped her cast off the self-doubts and spend a portion of each day contemplating the future. A future that was looking brighter with each small change.

Seeing her neighbour at work in her front yard was almost as comforting as the wide, leafy streets of Regent Park. Jackie raised a hand in greeting and smiled when the woman did the same. *I should introduce myself.* She'd made the decision to stay and live in her aunt's house; she might as well make an effort to get to know her new neighbours. Something skirted around the edge of her memory. Something the nurse had mentioned on the day Helen passed away. Jackie tried but couldn't quite catch hold of the thought.

Shrugging deeper into her new puffer coat, she turned the corner to where the street sloped down and a glimpse of dark blue showed itself above the treeline. As her fitness level grew with each passing day, the walk became easier. Soon she'd have to find a different route: extend herself. *Maybe I'll try jogging when the weather's warmer.*

There were no houses on the small stretch of street abutting the stairs down to the river, just bushland and a disused nursing home set back behind an ageing cyclone fence. In the dusk's light, Jackie spotted a kookaburra sitting on the wire barrier and noticed something dangling from its long beak. Something scraggy and limp like a strip of fabric. She slowed her progress and turned to watch the bird.

Only as she drew closer did she realise it wasn't fabric in the bird's beak but a mouse. Grimacing as the kookaburra shook its head, tossing the tiny rodent's legs in a lifeless arc, Jackie stopped and covered her mouth. Turning away from the gruesome spectacle, she caught a glimpse of something out of the corner of her eye.

Before she could react, a hand clamped down on her shoulder and squeezed. "Don't think you got away with it because you're pretending to be sick." Margaret Green's fingers dug into Jackie's flesh, making her gasp and pull back in pain.

As she jerked back, Jackie stumbled, but managed to regain her footing. "Margaret?" The name came out as a cry of shock.

Jackie should have said more, but her brain was struggling to reconcile the woman's sudden appearance with the fact that she'd just grabbed Jackie's shoulder.

Margaret was wearing what looked like a dark running suit. Her hair was blowing wildly in the breeze and her eyes were wide, almost bulging out of her pale face. Still searching for words and telling herself Margaret hadn't meant to hurt her, Jackie was surprised when the woman took a step forward.

"You sicken me." The harshness of Margaret's words was as frightening as her closeness. "Just because you live in an expensive suburb, you think you can treat my daughter any way you want?" Spittle flew out of the woman's face and hit Jackie's cheek. "You don't get to do whatever you want." As she spoke, her voice rose and she jabbed a finger into Jackie's chest. "I won't let you do that."

Maybe it was the slippery cold feel of Margaret Green's saliva as it dribbled down her cheek, or it might have been the way the woman's finger stabbed between her breasts. Whatever the reason, something in Jackie snapped.

She shoved Margaret, driving the heel of her hand into the woman's shoulder. Margaret lurched back a few steps, her mouth open in a surprised circle.

"Keep your fucking hands off me." Anger stronger than she'd ever remembered feeling welled up and she couldn't stop the words that were coming out of her mouth. "You're crazy. No wonder your child is such an obnoxious little brat." She should have felt guilty for the things she was saying, but she didn't. Nor did she feel any sympathy for Margaret Green as her lips drew back and tears filled her eyes.

"I know you've been following me." Jackie was the one moving in now, crowding the woman with her body. "If you come near me again, I'm going to the police."

The slap came out of nowhere and rocked Jackie's head to the left. For a split second she saw lights dancing before her eyes. When she looked back, Margaret was grinning – a half-crazed smile that triggered something dark and violent in Jackie's soul.

She lunged forward and grabbed the front of Margaret's fleecy jacket, twisting the fabric so the woman was dragged forward. She could hear Margaret's breath coming out in puffs and the smell of her sour breath. Jackie wanted to hurt the woman and turn her grin into a grimace of pain.

Margaret shrieked and twisted out of Jackie's grasp. "You bitch." She spat out the words while rubbing her chest where her top was stretched out of shape by Jackie's grip. "You'll be sorry for this."

It should have been enough. Jackie should have walked away, but she couldn't. The rage was still boiling inside her as the slap still burned her cheek. Margaret's attack was no different from the way Dan had treated her, ignoring her need for help and allowing this parent to harass her. No different to the look of shock and disapproval on Hetty's face when she caught Jackie yelling at the children.

Jackie couldn't stop. She didn't want to stop. Without planning what she was about to do, her hand drew back and, suddenly, she was striking the woman, hitting her as hard as she could.

Chapter Ten

The house wasn't what she'd expected, at least not something as grand as the art deco structure. "What do you think a place like that's worth?" Veronika jerked her chin towards the building.

Jim shook his head. "More than I'll ever be able to afford. The cheapest places around here go for over a million."

"Mm." She hadn't really expected her partner to know about house prices, but if she had to guess, she'd put the value at closer to two million. "When we get back to the station, check out what older homes on large blocks are going for in this area."

"Okay, boss," Jim said, unclipping his seat belt.

They were still sitting in the car. She could tell Jim was eager, but for now she was content to watch the place. The lawn needed mowing and there was an upended hose reel on the west side of the garden. They were small things, but often small things had a story to tell. A car was parked in the wide driveway: modern but inexpensive. The vehicle didn't match the house or surroundings.

"You *can* call me Nika." Veronika Pope kept her eyes on the driveway as she spoke. "When she lets us in, wait a few minutes then ask to use the loo so you can have a look around."

"So, you think she's involved in this?" Jim asked.

Veronika grabbed her phone and stowed it in the inside pocket of her jacket. "We'll see."

* * *

A few minutes later, the two detectives were facing the large front door, listening to the bell sound its echoey clang somewhere deep in the house.

"Hi." Veronika held her ID up so the woman peering around the partially opened door could see. "I'm Detective Sergeant Pope." She gestured to Jim. "This is my partner, Detective Constable Drommel. We'd like to ask you a few questions about a woman you know, Margaret Green."

Veronika watched the woman's face, but shadowed by the door and only partially visible, it was difficult to get a read on her reaction. She noticed the woman's lids flutter a small tic that revealed nothing. People were always nervous when the police showed up on their doorstep, especially ones like Jacqueline Winter. A woman with no prior arrests was more likely to be flustered by their presence than one who'd spent much of their life dealing with cops.

"Can I have another look at your ID?" Jacqueline Winter's voice was hesitant but clear.

Veronika obliged Winter by holding her ID at shoulder height so the woman could get a better look. After a second, Winter nodded and pushed the door open.

"You'd better come in," she said, stepping aside.

They were shown to a sitting room on the left of the entrance. Veronika noticed the house smelled musty, suggesting it had been a while since Jacqueline Winter had opened a window.

"You have a lovely home," Veronika said, settling herself in a deep tobacco-coloured couch.

"It's not... Thank you," Winter said, and sat opposite Veronika and Jim.

Veronika watched the woman fold her hands and place them in her lap. She'd been about to say something about the house but changed her mind. It might be nothing, but like the neglected lawn, small things were telling.

"What's this about?" Winter licked her lips and leaned back in the armchair. "Only I'm having lunch with a friend and I was just in the middle of getting ready."

"It won't take long," Veronika said, side-stepping the question. "When was the last time you saw Margaret Green?" As she spoke, she reached inside her jacket and pulled out her notebook and pen.

"Why?" Winter shot back, her eyes moving between the pen and Veronika's face. "I mean why are you asking me about Margaret? I... I don't know her very well, only from school."

"So, was that the last time you saw her?" Veronika asked. "At school?"

Winter was clearly edgy. While Veronika waited for the woman to answer, her gaze flicked around the room. The curtains were open. Late morning light illuminated the spacious sitting room. The furnishings were expensive, if a little old-fashioned and worn. She noticed an open wine bottle on the floor next to the armchair where Jacqueline Winter was sitting with her knees firmly clamped together.

"Yes. Yes, it was at school." Winter reached up and touched the back of her neck. "It must be nearly two weeks ago now."

Winter's eyes were a dark shade of green and her hair a mass of copper curls. She was an attractive woman with angular features and pale skin. If not for the dark shadows under her eyes and her clavicle bones protruding from the neck of her blouse like salt-cellars, she would have been quite pretty. As it was, she looked tired and too thin.

"Can I use your bathroom?" Jim asked, rising from the sofa so suddenly that the shift in weight almost jettisoned Veronika off the seat beside him.

Despite the seriousness of the situation, Veronika had to stifle a smile as Winter gave the younger detective directions to the bathroom.

"Did you speak to her?" Veronika asked the question while Winter's attention was still on Jim.

"What?" Winter was on the edge of her seat now.

When Veronika spoke, she did so slowly. "Did you speak to Margaret Green when you saw her?" She paused and looked down at her notebook. Veronika knew exactly when Winter had seen Margaret Green but wanted to remind the woman in front of her that she was keeping note of her answers.

"When you saw her at school two weeks ago," Veronika continued. "Did you speak to her?"

"No." Winter was tugging at her hair now. "Maybe. I don't really remember. Why? What has she said?"

Winter's question threw Veronika off balance for a second. The woman was edgy. No. More than edgy. Jacqueline Winter was a bag of nerves. She was hiding something, but she genuinely seemed in the dark about their visit.

"Margaret Green is dead." Veronika delivered the news without trying to dress it up. "She was found in her car a few streets from here." She paused while Winter's already pale skin drained of colour. "It's been all over the news."

Winter shook her head. "I don't watch much television. I... I've been busy with... What happened to her? Was she..."

Veronika kept her expression bland. "I can't discuss the details of an ongoing investigation, but I can tell you we're interviewing everyone that had contact with Mrs Green in the weeks leading up to her death. So," she continued, "it would be helpful if you could tell us what she said to you the last time you spoke?"

Jim entered the sitting room. His reappearance made Winter jump. When she turned her eyes back to Veronika, they were watery, suggesting the woman was holding back tears. Veronika wasn't sure if the tears were about the news of Margaret's death or because Jacqueline Winter was a woman on the verge of an emotional outburst brought on by guilt.

"I can't really remember what she said." Winter closed her eyes for a second. "Just the usual, about her daughter, her progress at school and that sort of thing." When she refocused on Veronika, the tears were gone.

"What was Margaret like?" Veronika asked.

Winter glanced at Jim. "What do you mean?" she asked.

Changing gears in the middle of an interview was a tactic Veronika often used. It was a way of throwing the subject off course, keeping them jumping from one thing to the next and possibly forcing an admission. She hadn't made up her mind about Jacqueline Winter, but it was too early in the investigation to rule anything out.

"I mean..." Veronika held her pen poised over the notepad. "What sort of woman was she? Was she easy to talk to? Did she ever seem depressed or upset?"

Winter raised her shoulders. "I didn't know her very well. She only talked about her daughter, so... I wish I could help, but I do have an appointment." She looked at her watch and stood.

Jim slid forward but stopped moving when he noticed Veronika wasn't getting up from the sofa.

"You're a difficult woman to track down," Veronika said while flipping back through the pages of her notebook. "The school, St Agnes, has you listed as living in Balcatta." She looked up and locked eyes with Winter. "The Principal at St Agnes told me you resigned recently." She left the statement dangling in the air.

For a moment, no one spoke, but then Winter took the bait. "Yes, I quit." She held Veronika's gaze as she continued. "There seemed no point in letting the school know my new address."

"And your phone number?" Veronika asked. "The number the school has for you is no longer listed. Sounds like you didn't want to be found."

Winter held Veronika's gaze when she answered. "I changed my number a few years ago and you're right. I didn't want the school ringing me. The only time they do is when they want something."

The nervousness Veronika had noticed in the woman when the interview began seemed to have faded. As Jacqueline Winter showed the two detectives to the door, she seemed more composed.

"Just for my notes…" Veronika gave an apologetic smile and stepped out of the house onto the porch. "Can you tell me where you were on Saturday the 23rd of June?"

Winter was standing just inside the doorway, her arms hanging loosely at her sides. Veronika could see the question had taken the woman by surprise by the way her eyelids fluttered. But when she answered, Winter seemed calm.

"Here probably, but I can't be sure," Winter said, crossing her arms. "I'd have to check the date and get back to you."

"If you think of anything Margaret might have said to you during your last meeting, let me know," Veronika said, pulling a business card out of her pants pocket. "It's a bit crushed." She held the card out for Winter to take. "But my number's there, so you can reach me or just leave a message once you confirm where you were on the 23rd."

Winter stood in the doorway with her arms crossed over her chest. She hesitated and for a second Veronika thought the woman meant to refuse the card. When Winter finally reached out and took it, her fingers touched Veronika's. In the fraction of a second that their skin made contact, Veronika was shocked by heat coming off the other woman's hand.

As Veronika and Jim shuffled single file down the path towards their car, Winter called out to them. "You said I was difficult to track down. How did you find me?"

Veronika stopped walking so suddenly that Jim almost ploughed into her. As she turned back towards the house, she caught sight of an elderly woman in the neighbouring garden. The older woman saw she was being watched and turned her head, then bent over a patch of lawn.

Winter had stepped away from the front door and was standing on the path. Above her, clouds were gathering in the grey sky and a cold breeze lifted the woman's hair. Veronika wasn't one for flights of fancy, but there was something ominous in the way the coming storm seemed to surround the woman.

Veronika gave a tight smile. "The school gave me your mother's number. It took a few tries, but I finally got through to her."

It was a slight stretch of the truth. Veronika never actually got a hold of Winter's mother, but her mother *had* responded to a text giving her daughter's address.

* * *

"So, what do you think?" Jim asked as he drove them back to the station.

Veronika took a moment before answering. Jacqueline Winter wasn't an easy woman to read. Nor was she the usual type of suspect; not that there was ever a clear type. In Veronika's experience, there was no telling what could push someone over the edge and drive them to kill. Or, if a person had the capacity or inclination for violence. Often people cleverly hid those things, even from themselves.

"She's hiding something, but I don't know if that something is murder." Veronika leaned against the door watching the young detective as he drove. "How'd your look around go?"

"Interesting," Jim said glancing her way. "A few empty wine bottles on the table in the kitchen. Winter obviously likes a drink and is a creature of habit. There were at least ten bottles of the same type of wine in the pantry."

"Anything else?" she asked, already knowing by the pleased look on his face he'd found something.

"Yep." Jim nodded and slowed the car at a set of traffic lights. "There was a stack of unopened mail on the kitchen table, all addressed to a Helen Winter."

Veronika frowned, remembering the way Winter had been about to say something about the house and then stopped. Their victim Margaret Green wasn't a well-liked woman, which meant there were plenty of people they needed to interview. Her ex-husband Nigel was a standout, but he had an alibi for the night she went missing. While they hadn't actually found Margaret Green until at least twenty-four hours after her son called the father to tell him she hadn't returned home, the medical examiner's report put Green's time of death at somewhere between six and ten o'clock on Saturday, June 23rd, the same night Nigel Green was at dinner with his new wife and a group of friends.

"When we get back to the station, see what you can find on Helen Winter." Veronika paused and narrowed her eyes. "I want to know what her relationship is to Jacqueline Winter."

"Will do," Jim said. "So, you think Winter did have something to do with Green's murder?"

Veronika liked the young detective; he was eager to learn and had a sense of humour. Over the nineteen years she'd been on the force, she'd been paired with countless partners, mostly men. Apart from one horrific experience in her thirties and a few older men who thought they had to compete with her, Veronika enjoyed working in pairs. She liked volleying ideas back and forth and got a buzz off the sense of working towards a common goal.

"It's never that simple, Jim." She tucked a strand of blonde hair behind her ear. "There are things that put me on alert and one of them is—"

"Proximity," Jim finished for her with a sidelong grin.

"Yeah, yeah, yeah," Veronika said around a chuckle. "You can laugh, but proximity is rarely a coincidence. Margaret Green was found dead in her car only three streets away from where her daughter's teacher lives." She held up her hand and began counting on her fingers. "Jacqueline Winter has had several run-ins with Margaret. We know this from one of the teachers at Winter's former school. Then, two days after Green is murdered, Winter quits her job of twelve years and puts her house up for sale." She waved four fingers in front of her face. "I'm not saying she killed Margaret Green, but Winter definitely warrants a closer look."

Chapter Eleven

The police had found Margaret's body. Jackie thought back to the way the detective spoke, '*Margaret Green is dead.*' The words dropped out of the policewoman's mouth like stones, each one landing on Jackie's brain like a fresh blow. It had taken every ounce of willpower not to cry out and hold her head.

She looked at the business card still clamped in her hand. Detective Pope would be waiting for her to call and confirm where she was on the night Margaret died. *No*, Jackie corrected herself. She didn't die; she was killed. An image jumped into her mind: the half-crazed grin on Margaret's face after she had slapped her. It was that grin that had pushed her over the edge – pushed her to violence she'd never dreamed she was capable of.

Jackie dropped the card on the kitchen table, staring at the rectangle of thick paper as though it was something dirty and repulsive. What now? Would the detectives return? Her heart was jumping into her throat and then dropping like a hammer. She'd lied to the police. How long would it be before they found out?

Sliding down, grateful for the solidness of the kitchen chair, Jackie dropped her head into her hands. She had to think. Had to try and remember if anyone had seen her with Margaret that evening. They were down near the river. There were no houses in that area and only the derelict nursing home. It wasn't a thoroughfare, so that eliminated a passing car catching a glimpse of them.

Even as she tried to focus, images of Margaret's eyes wide and shocked kept overshadowing Jackie's thoughts. She had to get herself together and cling on to the knowledge that no one had seen her with Margaret. She'd told the police she hadn't spoken to the woman since the previous Tuesday at school. If she stuck to that, she'd be safe.

Glancing at her watch, she noticed she was late. Rick would be waiting, wondering where she was. The idea of cancelling their lunch date came to mind and was quickly dismissed. It was better to keep going as normal. Dropping out of sight would only make her look guilty. Besides, Rick was kind and gentle, and being with him made her feel...

She wasn't quite sure how she felt about the man. They'd only been on a few dates, nothing heavy or serious, but cancelling now could ruin everything.

She swiped at her face. When her fingers came away wet, she realised she was crying. Not for Margaret Green, but for her children who had been left without a mother. And, in part, for the new life Jackie was starting to build, a life that included the promise of success and maybe even love. She could let go and throw herself on Detective Sergeant Pope's mercy, or cling on and fight.

Sniffling, she wondered what her aunt would have done. *Not gotten herself into this mess in the first place.* If she were alive, what advice would Helen give? Probably not to sit snivelling but to take action.

Jackie pushed back the chair with a feeling of exhaustion. An old feeling that usually drove her to binge eat and drink herself to sleep, came and went. Not today. Today she would take control of the situation.

After sending Rick a text letting him know she was running late, she went through her phone and found Andrew Drake's number. Without hesitating, she called the solicitor's office and made an appointment for the following morning.

* * *

"Are you okay?" Rick asked after they'd ordered.

They were at a little café that overlooked the river. A place Jackie had chosen for their date because she thought it would be romantic. Instead, the view over the shifting water made her think of Margaret and the way her face looked when Jackie landed the first blow.

"Yes." Jackie wanted to be all right, so she forced a smile. "The view is amazing," she said, jerking her chin towards the water.

She thought of telling him about what happened that morning. Letting out all the details of the police visit, about the probing questions, and the way Detective Sergeant Pope's eyes bored into her as she asked where she'd been on the night Margaret was killed. Would he be sympathetic? Rick appeared to be caring. She didn't know him that well, but he seemed genuine in his affection for her. Perhaps it was time to trust someone. The very idea of putting some of the burden onto someone else was so enticing it almost took her breath away.

"There is something." Jackie tried to swallow, but her throat was dry.

Before she could continue, the waitress appeared with their food. In the minute it took for the woman to set their plates down, Jackie felt her courage failing. Laying something so extreme on a man she barely knew would most likely drive him away. Could she really trust him enough to tell him the truth?

"What were you going to tell me?" he asked, flipping his napkin open and draping it in his lap.

"I... I had an email from the publisher I told you about. He likes the pages I sent and wants to see a full manuscript."

"That's amazing." Rick leaned forward, his smile revealing teeth that looked impossibly white against his tanned skin.

His enthusiasm was catching. Jackie continued talking, telling him about the possibility of publishing three books in the series. All the while she watched his eyes, wondering what it would be like to trace the line of his brows with her fingers. For a while she was able to pretend that all the darkness crowding her life was someone else's problem and Margaret Green never existed.

After lunch, Rick took her hand and walked her to her car. The feel of his skin against hers made Jackie's heart beat faster. So fast that when they reached the car and he pulled her close, she was worried that he might feel the pounding through her chest.

"We should go back to your place and celebrate," he whispered. His warm breath against her ear made Jackie shiver.

When he pulled back, she could see herself reflected in his eyes. In that moment Jackie felt more alive than she'd been in a long time.

When she answered, her voice shook. "All right."

* * *

For a while in Rick's arms she was able to forget and lose herself in the heat of his lips and the pressure of his body against hers. Later, dressed in only an oversized T-shirt, she watched him scramble eggs and make toast.

"Breakfast at dinner time. Well, maybe late afternoon," he said, setting their plates on the table. "I'm glad you extended your leave. This way we get to spend more time together."

"Yes," Jackie said, shifting in her seat.

She wasn't sure why she'd lied about quitting her job, but there were so many lies, she had no idea how to start unravelling them. She picked up her fork as Rick dumped the pan in the sink and tossed a tea towel over his shoulder. As she ate, her skin still tingled from his touch.

"You look nice when you've just tumbled out of bed," he said with a playful smile before biting into a piece of toast.

For a second time she had the urge to blurt everything out. Maybe not everything but at least the part about the police visit. Instead, she pushed the eggs around the plate and searched for something to say.

"So, what did the solicitor say about Helen's will?" he asked, and then continued before she could answer. "Do you think you'll sell this place?" He used his fork to gesture up to the roof.

"No." Jackie was grateful he was making conversation, but was surprised by his chain of questions. "I've put my Balcatta place on the market and I've already had an offer."

"Huh. This is a big house for someone on their own."

Someone on their own. Jackie wasn't sure why, but the comment sparked a flicker of irritation. Maybe because it felt like he was reminding her that she was still alone even after he'd just crawled out of her bed.

"I'm aware of that." She didn't try to keep the curtness out of her voice. "My aunt lived alone here for years. Why should it be any more difficult for me?"

He looked startled by her response. "I didn't mean anything, it's just that this place is worth a fortune. I thought you might want to sell. You could travel… See the world."

"I don't want to sell and I don't need anyone making plans for me." She lowered her fork. She knew she was being unreasonable but couldn't stop herself. "It's been a big day and I'm really tired, so…" She let the words hang in the air, hating herself for ruining the amazing afternoon they'd shared, but at the same time wanting him to leave.

"Look, I'm sorry, Jackie," he said, getting up and coming around the table. "I didn't mean to upset you."

He was behind her now. She could feel the pressure of his hands on her shoulders and the smell of his scent, clean and with a hint of cologne. Moments ago his touch thrilled her. Now, she just wanted him gone.

"It's okay." She did her best to soften her tone as she reached up and patted his hand. "I'm just..." *Afraid the police are going to turn up and arrest me.* "Just trying to adjust to so many changes." She forced a laugh. "I'm a bit touchy."

"Okay." He kissed the top of her head. "I'll let you get some rest and call you tomorrow."

Ten minutes later Rick was gone. As the house returned to silence, Jackie ran her hands through her hair. The lies were piling up on her, making it hard to breathe.

Chapter Twelve

Dan Keegan put Veronika in mind of her high school math teacher, Mr Blomt. Like her old teacher, Keegan was caught in a time warp that started sometime in the late seventies where professional men wore nylon trousers with short-sleeved business shirts.

"Jackie had taken a few weeks off to care for her aunt," Keegan said, leaning back in his chair. "She'd only been back a few days when she texted my assistant principal to say she was sick." He pursed his lips. "It wasn't easy to get cover at short notice."

"Hm." Veronika held her pen over her notebook. "So, her aunt has been unwell?"

"Yes. Well, she *was* unwell." He frowned, his bushy brows pressing together like duelling mop heads. "She passed away just before Jackie returned to work."

So, the house must have belonged to Winter's aunt. Maybe that's what Winter had been about to tell them that morning. But solving the mystery of who owned the house didn't explain why Jacqueline Winter had been so edgy. Nor did it eliminate the fact that Margaret's body had been found in the area where Winter lived. Jim was at the station checking home ownership with the Regent Park shire. Veronika made a mental note to let Jim know what she'd found out.

"You didn't mention anything about Jacqueline Winter's aunt when I spoke to you the other day." She kept her tone casual, but couldn't help pitying Winter for twelve years spent working under someone like Dan Keegan.

"Why would I? You only asked for Jackie's address. There was no need to tell you her family history." Keegan gave a noncommittal shrug.

Veronika lifted her chin, surveying Keegan as he sat on the other side of the desk. His posture was relaxed, but his attitude was combative, making her wonder if he didn't like police or just any woman in authority. In a female dominated profession like teaching, Veronika wondered when, if ever, Keegan had faced an angry man. Probably never. Dan Keegan was obviously comfortable intimidating women.

"When I was here the other day, I spoke with Hetty Marsh. Is she at school today?" Veronika waited for Keegan to answer, but instead he simply stared at her while somewhere outside a child cried.

After what seemed like minutes, Keegan spoke. "Hetty is teaching and can't be disturbed." He shifted in his seat, moving forward so his elbows were on the desk. "I can give her your number and have her call you at a more convenient time, Miss Pope."

Veronika smiled and tipped her head to the side while slowly closing her notebook. "It's Detective Pope."

Keegan's brows arched in surprise, but Veronika continued before he could respond. "A woman is dead and her daughter happens to be one of your students. I would think that finding out what happened to the woman would be more important than playing pissing games with me."

"You can't speak to me—"

"Yes, I can," Veronika said, cutting Keegan off, but keeping her tone even. "If it's more convenient, I can come back in a squad car at home time." She gave him another smile. "I'm sure the children will love seeing a police car pulling up outside."

Unhealthy-looking blossoms formed on Keegan's cheeks, deep red patches that matched the veins that streaked his eyes and nose.

"You can speak to Hetty, but I'm only allowing this because I want to help find out what happened to Margaret Green," Keegan said, pushing back his chair. "But your approach is completely unwarranted and I will be making a complaint."

Veronika waited while the principal stomped towards the door and flung it open. She had no doubt he would make a complaint *and* she'd have to explain what had happened to her superintendent, but it was worth it to watch Keegan realise he wasn't all powerful and his tiny kingdom wasn't outside the law.

"You can wait in the staff room." He held the door wide, waiting for her to exit while taking care not to make eye contact.

Veronika took her time standing and straightening her jacket. As she passed Keegan, she paused in the doorway. At 175 centimetres, Veronika was almost on eye level with him and her closeness forced him to meet her gaze.

"I smell whiskey on your breath." She dropped her voice so it was barely above a whisper. "If I send a couple of uniformed officers back at home time, do you think you'll pass a breath test?"

The high colour drained from Keegan's face. "I don't... I've never..."

Veronika moved out of the doorway and headed down the short hallway. As she passed the reception area, she nodded to the woman seated behind the counter.

"Is that the staff room?" Veronika pointed to a door clearly marked *Staff Room*.

The receptionist, a fiftyish woman with blonde hair and dark brows pencilled above thick blue-rimmed glasses looked up from her post. Before answering, she gave Keegan a sidelong glance as he stomped out of the office.

"Yes." The receptionist stood and came around the counter. "I'll show you through. My name's Laura, by the way." She spoke over her shoulder as she led Veronika to the teachers' break room.

The room was dominated by a large white table surrounded by chairs that, like Keegan's attire, looked like they came from the seventies.

"Please feel free to make yourself a tea or a coffee." Laura gestured to the far corner where a commercial hot water dispenser sat near a kitchen unit.

Veronika thanked the woman and pulled out a chair. "Laura, did you know Margaret Green?"

If the question took the receptionist by surprise, she gave no indication. Instead, she let her hand rest on one of the padded chairs and pushed her glasses higher on her nose.

"I know almost all the parents in this school," she answered. "When I say parents, it's mostly the mothers that come in and out."

"So, Margaret came in and out," Veronika pushed, not sure what she expected the receptionist to add.

"Oh, yes. She came in and out." Laura raised one brow. "She wasn't a very happy person, always upset or angry about something."

Veronika was starting to get a pretty good picture of Margaret Green. Quick tempered and, according to her ex-husband, possibly suffering with depression or anxiety; she was a woman who was constantly looking to blame someone for her problems.

"Did she ever mention being angry with someone at this school?"

Laura rolled her eyes. "Yes, with whoever happened to be her daughter's teacher." The receptionist snatched a glance at the doorway. "I feel sorry for that little girl, but her mother tortured the teachers. Always hanging around before and after school, complaining. No one was ever good enough for Margaret."

"That must have made her very unpopular," Veronika commented.

"I don't know about that," Laura replied. "But she was one of those people that made you want to duck and hide when you saw her coming."

* * *

"Will this take long?" Hetty asked. "Only Dan's with my class and... I don't want to take too long."

"I'll be as quick as I can." Veronika gave the young teacher her standard comforting smile.

They were seated at the long table with their chairs pulled back so they could face each other. Behind them, the staff room door sat closed.

"When I was here the other day, you mentioned Jacqueline Winter having a run-in with Margaret Green on Monday the 18th of June. Can you go over what happened?"

Hetty frowned and glanced towards the door. "Um... As I said, Margaret was waiting for Jackie after school and I could see Jackie was trying to get away, so I sort of made out I needed her help." The young woman gave a mirthless chuckle. "I just wanted to help, because I know what Margaret was like. I wouldn't really call it a run-in, though."

Veronika could see the teacher was trying to be diplomatic, but she was sure there had been more to the encounter.

"Was that the only time you'd seen Jacqueline with Margaret Green?" Veronika asked.

Hetty's grimace suggested that this line of questioning had become painful. "No. I saw them together that morning before school. They were outside Jackie's classroom, but I didn't hear what they were saying."

"Okay." Veronika made a note on her pad. "You didn't hear what they were saying, but did you notice anything out of the ordinary?"

"Out of the ordinary?" Hetty repeated the question as she laced her fingers together.

Veronika put down her pen. "Yes, were they laughing or did it look like they were arguing? That sort of thing?"

The young woman's eyes were on the clock over the door. With her face in profile, Veronika noticed Hetty's lips were quivering.

"I saw Margaret sort of lunge forward." Hetty turned and made eye contact with Veronika. "Jackie looked scared. She dropped her keys."

So, Margaret was harassing Winter and Winter had lied about her conversations with Margaret being run-of-the-mill chats about the daughter's progress at school. Veronika let the information sink in before asking another question.

"Did Jacqueline say anything to you about Margaret Green?"

When she answered, Hetty Marsh's big dark eyes looked haunted. "She said she wished Margaret would vanish."

Somewhere on the other side of the staff room door a telephone was ringing, but to Veronika the alarm sounded like it was going off inside her head.

Chapter Thirteen

On her way back to the station, Veronika used the hands-free set to call her mother. She was surprised when the call was answered after only two rings. Usually her seventy-six-year-old mother either took an eternity to get to the phone or didn't answer at all. Not because she was slow in moving; far from it. Mary-Lynn Pope played golf three times a week and was more active than most women half her age, but hated being attached to a phone.

"Is everything all right?"

She always asked this question when her daughter called from work.

Veronika had been on the force for close to twenty years yet her mother still half expected her to call and report she'd been shot. After a few close calls that she'd kept to herself, Veronika had given up trying to convince her mother that policing wasn't as dangerous as it seemed on television.

"Yes, all good, Mum. I just want to ask you something about teaching."

There was a moment's silence on the line. Veronika could imagine her mother with her wire-rimmed spectacles resting at the end of her nose as she leaned on the kitchen counter. It was a comforting image, one that Veronika often called up when things got tough at work. Knowing her mother was at home waiting and sharing the responsibility for raising Veronika's now nineteen-year-old son made the long hours easier to bear.

"Don't tell me you're thinking of a career change?" Mary-Lynn's voice was deep for a woman, almost gravely.

"Don't get your hopes up." Veronika kept her tone light, not wanting to get into the familiar back and forth about finding a safer way to make a living.

"I just wondered if you ever had parents actually harass you." Veronika slowed at a stop sign. "You know, hanging around morning and afternoon, being a pest?"

Mary-Lynn answered without hesitation. "Yes, there's always one – one child in every class that makes teaching difficult and one parent in every group that doesn't understand the boundaries."

"Hm." Veronika's eyes were on the traffic and the smattering of rain dotting the windscreen, but her mind was focused on what her mother had said.

So, Margaret Green's behaviour wasn't that unusual, not for an experienced teacher like Jacqueline Winter. The whole idea of Winter killing Margaret because of the harassment seemed a little far-fetched, especially in light of what her mother was telling her.

"Did it ever get out of hand with any one parent in particular?" Veronika asked.

This time it took Mary-Lynn longer to answer. "There was one mother when I was a new graduate. She made my life hell." Her disembodied voice filled the car. "She got it in her head that I was picking on her little boy and just wouldn't let up. If it hadn't been close to the end of the school year, I probably would have quit."

* * *

"Jacqueline Winter's place belonged to her aunty." Jim was sitting across from her in the tiny room that passed for her office, his notebook on the desk in front of him.

"Yeah, the principal, Keegan, told me about the aunt," Veronika replied. "It would have been a bit more helpful if he'd given us that nugget of information the other day."

Jim was quiet for a moment before answering. "Do you think he's covering for Winter? Maybe there's something going on between them."

Veronika shook her head and picked up her coffee cup. "Doubtful. Keegan's an asshole – a bit of a megalomaniac. More likely he's trying to reassert his power by doling out information a bit at a time."

"There *is* something else." There was excitement in Jim's voice. "I tracked down the aunt's death certificate. It lists her death as the result of head trauma."

Veronika set down her cup and turned her attention on the window. Outside, the winter sky was heavy with dark clouds. They were on to something; she could feel it in her bones. The minute she learned Winter lived only streets away from where Margaret's body was found, there'd been a ticking in Veronika's brain. It was a strange feeling; a sense of focus and forward movement that only occurred when she was following a trail of evidence. With Winter there wasn't anything concrete, but that hadn't stopped the ticking.

There were other pressing lines of enquiry they could be chasing. Margaret Green's sister didn't have an alibi for the 23rd of June. And, according to the ex-husband, the two sisters' relationship was rocky. Then there was Margaret's oldest child, the son. Harris Green had telephoned his father at around eleven o'clock the night his mother went missing. It couldn't have been easy for a seventeen-year-old boy to live with a mother like Margaret. If they'd argued, maybe the son lashed out. All solid avenues, but none that couldn't be passed on for another team member to follow-up.

"What do you think?" Jim asked.

Veronika tipped her head to the side and narrowed her eyes. "I think we need to find out what happened to Helen Winter."

Chapter Fourteen

Rain rattled the window, but the constant patter barely registered. It felt like the world had stopped making sense. Everything Jackie knew was turned on its head and, no matter what she said, she couldn't put things right. And then there was that sense that life could be good. No, better than good; it could be great. Leaps forward kept coming in grabs of happiness: romance, success, and new-found financial security. Freedom from a job that had sucked the life out of her. All the tantalisingly shiny flashes were only made more tragic by the creeping knowledge that it could come crumbling down at any moment.

Jackie looked around the kitchen. There was an open bottle of wine and an empty glass next to the plate of uneaten eggs. She didn't remember drinking or how long she'd been sitting and holding her head. The light outside had changed and evening was drawing in. She'd been unmoving for almost two hours. Had she lost time again? The idea of not remembering her own actions was terrifying. She licked her lips and the bitter aftertaste of wine was cloying on her tongue.

She thought of going for a walk. The notion of rambling through the rain seemed more enticing than drinking herself to sleep, so Jackie grabbed her coat and keys.

There was a chill in the air and the icy rain on her hands and cheeks made her shiver, but rather than it driving her back, Jackie welcomed the cold shock. Not ready to face the river again, she turned left at the end of the street and headed towards the park.

A handful of cars passed her as she travelled the wet streets, but Jackie kept her eyes on the pavement, relishing the fresh scent of wet grass and damp tree bark. She had no plan in mind and only a drive to push through the muddy thoughts that taunted and terrified her.

Within ten minutes the side entrance to the park came in sight. As she dashed across the road, the patter of rain became a downpour. Jackie yelped and pulled up her hood, thankful she'd worn the puffer coat. Perth was a city that was dry, scorched by the sun for months at a time, but when it rained the wash was fierce in its intensity.

The downpour made the grass slippery and visibility almost impossible. With no shelter in the small square of open space, Jackie ducked under a tree and pressed her back to the trunk.

Watching the deluge saturate the park, her mind conjured up images of one of the last times she'd seen Aunt Helen before her fall. Helen had served her coffee on the back patio that overlooked the lawn and its kidney-shaped imprint from where the pool used to be. Like everything her aunt did, there was a certain flare to even such a simple thing as coffee: a silver tray and a coffee press together with tiny Florentines. Jackie remembered remarking on the rich taste of the coffee.

"It's Turkish," Helen said with a wave of her slender hand. "I picked up a taste for it when I was working on a story for Channel 12, and—"

Helen seemed to be about to say something else, but her mouth stopped moving and her eyes became fixed. It was an odd moment, like her aunt had just drifted away.

Jackie remembered calling Helen's name and when her aunt turned her gaze in her niece's direction, there was a cloudy look in her eyes. A look that terrified Jackie.

Jackie swiped at her cheek, brushing away tears and rain that mingled together and dripped from her lashes. She couldn't quite remember if that was the last time she'd spoken to Helen because there had been other instances in those final months. Instances where that cloudy look seemed to drop like a shutter over Helen's usually inquisitive eyes.

"I should have done something." She spoke to the empty park.

Why hadn't she said something or suggested for her aunt see a doctor? Jackie sniffed and jammed her hands in her pockets. She'd ignored those early symptoms that something was wrong just like she was trying to pretend she wasn't in deep trouble. Trouble seemed like a stupid word for what was happening in her life. A word so inadequate in the face of a lifetime in prison, it almost made Jackie laugh. As did the realisation that she was standing under a tree in a rainstorm laughing and crying.

She shook her head and felt her damp hair move beneath the hood. What did it matter if someone saw her? Jackie glanced out from the shelter of the tree and caught a glimpse of someone near the park's entrance. The sight of a dark shape stepping out of a cluster of shoulder-high shrubs made Jackie gasp.

The dark coat and hood looked slick and shiny like the scales on a snake's belly. Just like the time at the riverbank, the figure stood facing her, but remained motionless. Jackie's chest constricted, making it difficult to suck in air. How could Margaret Green still be following her? It was impossible, but unless she was seeing things, Margaret was standing less than thirty metres away. *She's closer this time.* So close that Jackie thought she could hear the rain drilling Margaret's dark coat. But that was insane. There was no way she could hear something so soft, not under the pounding rain. Not from thirty metres away.

Without planning to act, Jackie called out, "Margaret? What do you want?" The words were muted and doused with water.

The shape continued its sentinel, the coat flapping over a body that appeared as solid and unmoving as marble. Jackie's hands moved inside her pockets searching for her phone and then she remembered she'd only brought her keys.

And then, as if hearing a starter's pistol, the figure lunged forward. Jackie screamed and turned to run, only to lose her footing on the sodden grass. As her feet slipped out from under her, her heartbeat ratcheted up to a sickening barrage.

She hit the ground hard, sliding forward in a such way that her splayed hands did little to dull the impact. Her chin made contact with the grass, gnashing her teeth together with so much force she tasted blood on her tongue. Squirming, too panicked to find purchase on the slippery surface, Jackie twisted her head around trying to catch sight of the cloaked figure, but only managing to turn inside the hood.

The fall and climbing to her feet took less than five seconds, but seemed like an eternity where every moment could be the one where Margaret's dead hands took a hold of her. Shaking so badly her knees were clanging together, Jackie managed to hold her hood and look back.

The figure was gone. There was no one between her and the bushes, nothing but the rain now slowing to a light patter. For a moment she didn't believe her own eyes, but then a young woman in a yellow rain jacket and florescent jogging pants appeared at the entrance of the park. As Jackie watched the woman jog through the rain, she had the urge to call out and warn her about the dead woman hiding in the bushes, but instead clamped her lips together and rushed back to the entrance.

As Jackie half-walked, half-stumbled home, she couldn't shake the feeling she was being followed, being watched from between the dripping wet trees and over garden fences. It wasn't until she reached her street that the mud clinging to her legs, feet and hands even registered.

Shivering, she dragged the keys out of her pocket and jogged towards the house, only to come to a dead stop when she spotted the two detectives getting out of a car. Her first impulse was to turn and run in the opposite direction, but where would she go? She had no phone and no money with her. In the moment it took her to agonise over her next move, Detective Pope glanced sideways and spotted Jackie on the footpath.

Running would make her look guilty, yet being handcuffed and thrown in the back of the car seemed preferable to another round of questions. With Detective Pope waiting for her at the foot of Helen's driveway, Jackie had no option but to pass the police officers and enter her house.

"Are you all right?" Veronika asked, following Jackie up the path that led to the front door.

When Jackie didn't answer, Veronika continued. "Miss Winter, did something happen to you?"

There was concern on Detective Pope's face, but Jackie ducked her head and kept moving. She couldn't tell the detective what had happened at the park. How could she? She could hear the crazy ramblings in her head: *Margaret Green is following me.* If the detectives suspected her of Margaret's murder, insane stories of a dead woman stalking her would only add weight to their belief she was guilty.

When she reached the front door, Detective Pope was behind her. "Can we come in and talk to you? Just a few questions?" The detective wouldn't stop bombarding her.

Still holding the keys, Jackie turned and faced Detective Pope. "No." The word came out louder than she intended, but the detective didn't flinch.

Over Detective Pope's shoulder, the male detective, whose name she couldn't remember, took a step closer. With her hand shaking, the keys were jingling. Jackie had to get herself together and control the tears that were making her throat constrict.

"I got caught in the rain," Jackie said, holding out her muddy hands. "I slipped and fell, so as you can imagine I'm quite shaken up."

She noticed her hands were still out in an open-palmed pleading gesture, so she turned and tried to put the key in the lock. For a moment both officers watched her fumble.

"Miss Winter," Veronika said. "Let us come inside and talk. You look like you could use a hot drink. We could—"

"No, not now," Jackie answered without turning around. There was blood in her mouth, which she swallowed before continuing. "I... I can't at the moment. You'll have to come back another time."

When the key turned and the door opened, Jackie nearly let out a sob, only managing to hold it back by clamping her teeth together. With the female detective crowding the entrance, Jackie pushed the door open and slipped inside. Not bothering to turn around, she shoved the door closed and leaned against the heavy panel.

A few minutes later she heard a car start. It was only when she was sure the detectives had driven away that some of the stiffness left her body and she sank to the floor. With the immediate danger gone, tremors took hold, wracking her body. As she sat on the cold floor of the entrance, she could smell mud and grime, earthy like a grave on her hands and face.

When she was finally steady enough to stand, Jackie unzipped her coat and shrugged out of the sodden garment, letting it drop to the floor. Instead of stripping off her filthy jeans and standing under a hot shower, she moved to the study and pulled out Helen's notebooks. Jackie had read the volumes from cover to cover, but still couldn't let the stories go.

She sat on the colourful rug her aunt had bought in Marrakesh and began reading. For some reason she was drawn back to the final notebook, re-reading the chapters that revealed Elise and Dale's last night together and how their little boy wandered out of the house and into the midst of a battle zone. Jackie choked back tears as she read of Dale's wailing cries and how his tears fell on the little boy's lifeless head. Drinking in the beautiful yet tragic tale of love and loss, Jackie pushed all thoughts of dead women and prison out of her mind.

Chapter Fifteen

Veronika spread the photographs across her desk. There were identical copies on the board in the station, but having them at home gave her time to ponder the crime scene *and* Margaret Green's injuries in a way a busy police office didn't afford.

The images were stark and revealing, but for Veronika the pictures were less about horror and more akin to a personal connection to the crime and the victim. Details like Margaret's clothing helped Veronika get an image of the victim's final day. The dead woman was wearing a tracksuit, not the sort of thing a woman wears to meet a lover. Nor were the plain fleecy pants and hoodie the type of clothing women wore to the gym. Margaret was dressed like someone popping out to run an errand – someone who hadn't bothered to change or apply make-up. *She didn't care how she would be viewed.* Or, Veronika surmised, what the person she was going to see thought of her.

Veronika picked up the photo of the car, its door open, showing Margaret fully clothed and slumped in the driver's seat. The dead woman's phone sat in the console and her handbag was open on the floor on the passenger side. While nothing was out of question, Veronika discounted robbery or a crime of opportunity. However, the picture was all wrong.

Too restless to sit, she stood and bent over the images, intent on figuring out what bothered her about the picture. Close-up images of the victim's face showed a cut lip and scratches across her forehead suggesting she'd been beaten, while blood on the headrest of the driver's seat and stains from other bodily fluids indicated Margaret Green died in the car. The angle of the scratches and the cut on her lip didn't rule out a struggle inside the car, but were more likely to have happened outside the confines of the vehicle where her attacker could swing with enough force to split the woman's lip.

Then there was the angle of the head wound and the position of the body. The fatal wound came from Margaret's right, causing her body to slump left. The scratches on the victim's face had to have come from the left, yet the killing blow came from the right. Veronika blew out a tired breath and planted her hands on her hips.

The study door bust open, ushering in a gust of air that scattered the stack of photos on the floor beside Veronika's desk. Seeing her son in the doorway, she slid the photos on the desk into a pile, then turned them over. The urge to remind him to knock came and was quickly dismissed in favour of a calm interaction.

"I'm going to Rusty's house," Tony said, looking past her. "I'll be home late."

Veronika followed his gaze and realised he was staring at the post-mortem pictures of Margaret's naked body that littered the rug. In that moment she could almost see them through her son's nineteen-year-old eyes. The finality of death and the sterile examination of a being's remains was a gut-wrenching sight.

Stepping sideways, Veronika blocked the images with her body. "Okay. Drive carefully."

Tony nodded but remained in the doorway. It wasn't the first time he'd burst in and found her looking at such photos, but judging by the look on his face he was far from immune to their impact.

"Are you okay?" Veronika asked, not really expecting more than a monosyllabic response.

"Are those pictures of the woman on the news?" he asked, ignoring her question.

Veronika ran a hand through her jaw-length blonde hair. "Yes, you weren't supposed to see them, but if you'd knocked…" She wanted to bite her tongue, but the words were out before she could stop herself.

Tony frowned and Veronika waited for a sullen jerk of his chin, but instead he seemed unfazed by her admonishment.

"How can you do that?" he asked.

"Look, I'm sorry." Veronika wrapped her dressing gown around her. "I shouldn't have jumped down your throat like that, but—"

"No, not that," Tony said, pointing to her desk. "How can you stand to look at those photos?"

The question took her by surprise. It was the first time he'd really asked her about her job apart from the usual questions when he'd been a kid.

"It's my job." Even as the words came out, she knew they sounded hollow and almost trite. "I suppose I feel like I owe it to them," she tried again, doing her best to put her feelings into words. "Their voices have been stolen and I owe it to them to *really* see them and what was done to them." Veronika shrugged one shoulder. "I can't turn away or I'd be letting them down… Does that make any sense?"

"Yeah, it makes sense." He sounded unsure.

Tony was always a sensitive boy, empathetic and kind. Even the grumpy teenage thing he was still going through wasn't too bad. His sensitivity was one of the things Veronika loved about her son, but it also caused her pain. He'd never had a real girlfriend and, Veronika feared that when he did fall in love, he'd be too easy to hurt. The idea of some girl causing her son heartache made her chest constrict with dread.

"All right," she said, a little too brightly. "Go have a nice time." She made a shooing gesture. "I've got work to do."

"Yep. Okay." He turned to leave, but then he stopped.

To Veronika's surprise, he stooped down and kissed her on the forehead. "Don't work too hard, Mum."

As her son closed the study door behind him, Veronika felt tears prickle her eyes. It had been a while since he'd kissed her goodnight or goodbye; maybe the teen angst was over. It was a nice thought, but she suspected the kiss was more about empathy: the deeper and permanent part of his personality.

For a moment she stared at the door considering taking her son's advice and calling it a night, maybe even joining her mother in the lounge and watching some reality TV. There would always be a case that needed her attention. A puzzle to be solved. But the things she'd said to Tony about the victim having her voice stolen tugged at her thoughts.

Veronika turned back to her work, snatching up an image from the floor. It was a close-up picture of the wound that the medical examiner determined to be fatal. The semi-circular gash in the scalp just above Margaret's right ear had been washed clean of blood and the hair parted to give a clear view of the injury.

There was a neatness to the wound and a symmetry of impact that suggested the murder weapon wasn't a rock or any other jagged instrument. Whatever killed Margaret Green was heavy and weighty enough to cave in her skull while slicing a clear shape into her scalp. Veronika moved back to her desk and held up the picture that showed Margaret in her car alongside the post-mortem image of the wound.

In the car, blood matted the woman's hair and saturated her neck and shoulder. Margaret's body was slumped to the left. Veronika narrowed her eyes, trying to form a mental picture of the attack, but as her mind played over the details, something didn't quite fit.

She shuffled through the crime scene pictures until she found what she was looking for. She placed the four images on the desk. Veronika's pulse quickened as it always did when she began to see a clear picture of the crime.

Chapter Sixteen

Rather than plunge her deeper into despair, re-reading *Kiss the Wall* had soothed Jackie's nerves and allowed her to finally sleep. Now, sitting in Andrew Drake's office with the sun breaking through the clouds and casting crisp light across the solicitor's desk, she felt a measure of calm that she hadn't experienced since losing her aunt.

"Probate is progressing, but if you need access to more funds, I can write you a letter to present to the bank," Andrew said, looking down at the file in front of him.

"No." Jackie stretched the word out and waited for him to look up. "It's not about the will. It's another matter," she said and took a deep breath.

"I see." A look dropped over his face, one that made it difficult to tell if he did in fact see or was just being polite.

"It's the police…" Jackie had rehearsed what she was going to say but now the words were lost under Andrew's interested gaze. A gaze that made it difficult to know how to continue.

Andrew pulled a slab of paper out from the drawer on the side of his desk. "All right," he said picking up a pen. "What about the police?"

It took Jackie a little over half an hour to explain. She left out nothing except the part where Margaret confronted her at the river and Jackie's belief that Margaret had been following her. She hadn't meant to omit anything, but the idea of saying the words out loud made her gut constrict, so instead she'd jumped ahead to the police turning up on her doorstep with questions about her relationship with Margaret and her whereabouts on the night she was killed. She ended by telling him about her latest visit from Detective Pope and how the woman tried to talk her way into her home for a second time.

When she finished speaking, the air in Andrew Drake's spacious office felt warmer as though the heat of her words had filled the room. There was silence for a few moments, save the scratch of the solicitor's pen on the paper as he completed his notes. As the quiet stretched and Jackie watched Andrew's strong-looking hand moving over the page, she began to wonder if she'd made a mistake in coming to him for help. Had she revealed too much? Would he suspect her of holding something back?

The idea of Andrew's features twisted in suspicion made Jackie shift in her seat wishing she could get up and run for the door. She hadn't actually admitted anything, but the solicitor was an intelligent man. Maybe he could see through her story. It's not a story, she reminded herself. Everything she'd told the man was true.

"I haven't practiced criminal law in almost thirty years," Andrew said, placing his pen next to the notepad.

Jackie's stomach swooped like a dying bird. He was brushing her off, probably because he doubted her story. She could feel her emotions boiling up until tears were ready to fall. In a few seconds he'd be telling her to leave his office and the look of concern in his eyes would be replaced by disgust.

"But I'm glad you came to me with this. I've seen the reports on the news and this is shaping up to be a high-profile investigation," Andrew continued.

It took Jackie a few beats to make sense of what he was saying. Rather than condemning her, he was congratulating her on doing the right thing.

"I'd say the detectives that spoke to you are on a fishing trip." He flipped through the pages he'd just written. "Probably interviewing everyone Margaret Green knew, hoping to dig something up. If everything you've told me is true, you've nothing to worry about."

Was it her imagination or did something steely and questioning flash in the solicitor's eyes? Was Andrew asking her if she was guilty? Jackie swallowed and tried to keep her hand from creeping up and tugging at her hair.

"You don't have to speak to the police." He spread his hands wide. "Legally, there is nothing compelling you to talk to them. You've already answered their questions, so anything further would be going over old ground." He paused and held up a finger. "However, it helps to be cooperative. I suggest you send Detective... Um..." He looked down at his notes. "...Detective Pope. Send her a text confirming where you were on the 23rd."

He was waiting for her response as he picked up his pen and flipped the pages of his notepad.

"That's the thing," Jackie said, attempting to keep her tone casual. "I was home alone, so there's nothing really to tell... I mean... I don't have an alibi." She managed a dry chuckle. "It sounds ridiculous, like something out of a bad movie."

Andrew smiled, the expression softening his features so he seemed younger than his silver hair suggested. "Yes, but it's best to be as transparent as possible. No use clouding the situation. Just text the detective and tell her you were home alone, but keep it short and to the point. After that..." He shrugged. "If the police want to interview you again, give them my details and ask them to refer their request to me."

He was telling her she didn't have to talk to Detective Pope again. It was more than she could have hoped for, and the relief that swept through her made her want to weep with gratitude.

"Andrew… I… Thank you." She had managed to keep her emotions in check, but couldn't stop herself from spluttering.

He sat back in his chair. "No thanks needed. As I said, I no longer practice criminal law, but I'm happy to help. Especially after everything you've been through with Helen." He gave a wry smile. "You remind me of her, you know."

It would have been appropriate to just thank him, but after feeling alone for so long, his kindness made it difficult to keep up a veneer of strength.

"I wish I was like her, but I'm not," Jackie said, surprising herself with the honesty of her response. "She was so strong and independent, always knowing the right thing to do or say." Jackie looked up at the ceiling, blinking back tears. "She had more time for me than my own mother and now she's gone. I feel… I feel like I'm unravelling."

When she looked down, Andrew was watching her with concern. She might have been seeing what she wanted to, but there was no trace of judgement or pity in his gaze.

"Helen was a lot of things," he said, leaning forward. "Smart, capable and successful, but not perfect. She had her moments – tough times when I'm sure she had her share of self-doubt." When he continued, his tone was softer. "What you're going through is normal, particularly with the added pressure of the police investigation."

He was so understanding, Jackie wanted to tell him the truth. She could almost hear herself laying it all at his feet: the blackouts and the way she'd attacked Margaret Green. It was exhausting carrying around the weight of what she'd done. She imagined letting the truth out would be like taking off a heavy coat and standing in the sunshine.

"That's very kind of you to say." Jackie leaned down and picked up her handbag, worried that if she looked into his dark blue eyes she'd lose control and say too much. "I feel much better now that we've spoken."

* * *

On the drive home she played the conversation with Andrew over in her mind, agonising over how much she'd revealed and frightened by how opening up to him came so easily. By telling him she was unravelling, hadn't she almost admitted something was terribly wrong? *Unravelling.* Why had she used that word?

Once safely inside the house, Jackie went to the kitchen and found Detective Pope's card on the kitchen table. She kept the text brief just as Andrew had instructed. When it was sent there was no going back. By putting her whereabouts in the message, Jackie felt she'd committed to a course of action that would either take her to prison or a life of nagging guilt. The latter she decided would be easier to live with.

Still holding the phone, she wandered out the back door and onto the patio. It had only been a few months since Helen was last pottering around the garden, yet in that short time the weeds had found their way through every crack on the concrete. The lawn was almost knee-high, but somehow the shadow of the pool still left its mark on the turf.

Jackie wasn't much of a swimmer, but it would have been nice to splash around when the warm months arrived.

"I went off swimming pools in the eighties," Jackie said, repeating the words her aunt used every time she explained why the pool had been filled in.

Hearing herself speak the familiar words made her long for a few more minutes with Helen. She'd spent so much time with her aunt while she was growing up *and* as an adult, yet there were still so many questions left unasked.

Looking down, her gaze landed on the spot where Helen had fallen. Two steps down from the patio, the wide concrete stairs swooped right in a dramatic curve. The blood was gone but the image of Helen, semi-conscious and helpless, was carved into Jackie's brain like the wound that had ultimately taken her aunt's life.

"God." Jackie wrapped her arms around herself and looked up at the sky. "What a fucking mess."

Chapter Seventeen

"These pictures," Veronika said, pointing at the board where she'd stuck four images. "When they're put together, they tell a story."

They were in the meeting room adjacent to her office where she'd set-up a board beside a table littered with files. Five detectives were on Veronika's team but only Jim and a Detective Constable First Class with ten years of experience working homicide named Stacy were present. Margaret's ex-husband Nigel had given permission for his son to be interviewed. Two other members of the team were on their way to Nigel Green's house.

Veronika jabbed a finger at the first picture. "The cuts and scratches on the victim's face suggest she was struck at least twice, but not hard enough to cause any real damage save a cut lip. The angle of the injuries indicates the blows received on Margaret's left came from a right-handed attacker," she said, gesturing to the left side of her own face.

"So, there was a struggle and Margaret Green was knocked around a bit before the fatal blow," Jim offered.

"Yes, but if you look at this image..." Veronika pointed at the second picture showing Margaret slumped in the driver's seat. "You can see that the fatal blow came from the victim's right. That means if the struggle took place in the car, the attacker would have had to hit Margaret at least twice while sitting next to her in the passenger seat, and then they jumped out and ran around the car to the driver's side to deliver the killing blow."

"So, you're saying Green was attacked before she got in the car?" Stacy asked, a takeaway coffee cup dangling between her legs.

"Exactly." Veronika turned back to the board. "This third image was taken with the driver's door closed and the body still in situ. I couldn't work out what it was that bothered me about this photo until last night." Before continuing, she rapped on the image with her knuckle. "The window's up." She moved to the fourth photo, a picture of the inside of the driver's door. "Notice how the inside of the door is clean?"

"She wasn't hit through the window." There was excitement in Jim's voice, suggesting he'd already worked out where Veronika was heading.

"She had to have been hit while the attacker held the door open. And," Veronika said, "I think the blows that scratched Margaret's face and split her lip were delivered before she got in the car. The attacker needed space to swing with enough force to split Margaret's lip, yet there's no spatter in the car. In fact, the only blood we found apart from the back of the driver's seat was on the steering wheel, which suggests it came from Margaret's hand after she'd wiped her mouth."

Veronika faced the two detectives with her hands on her hips. "I think Margaret had an altercation with someone on the street. It escalated into a scuffle and the attacker followed Margaret to her car. While the driver's door was still open, the attacker struck the victim with a heavy object. When Margaret was dead, the killer closed the driver's door and walked away."

Veronika waited, giving the two younger detectives time to mull the story over. She already had a few ideas on what their next move should be, but she wanted to see what the other members of her team came up with. Experience had taught her no one person ever had all the answers, so it was wise to see what Jim and Stacy made of her account of the killing.

Stacy was the first to speak. "It makes sense."

Jim nodded. "If the killer had the car door open when they struck, the blood spatter would be on their clothes and shoes."

For a moment the three were silent, all knowing they would need something more than the tenuous link between Margaret Green and Jacqueline Winter to get a search warrant.

Veronika picked up another image from the file on the table. She didn't bother to stick this one on the board, but instead held it up for the other two detectives to see. It was the post-mortem image of the crescent-shaped wound on Margaret Green's scalp.

"Jim." Veronika jerked her chin in the detective's direction. "You said Jacqueline Winter's aunt died as a result of head trauma."

"Yes." Jim drew the word out. "That's what the death certificate says."

Veronika narrowed her eyes and tilted her head to the side. "Get the doctor's name. We need to pay him a visit."

* * *

Sorry about yesterday. Let me make it up to you by buying you dinner?

Jackie read the text from Rick while still standing on the patio. The late morning air was warmer than the previous day and the only sign of yesterday's rainstorm was the puddle at the bottom of the steps reflecting her image in wavering lines.

Only a day ago, Rick's touch brought her to life, but now spending an evening with him seemed like hard work. Was this see-sawing feeling part of losing her mind? First the blackouts, then the violent outbursts followed by emotional extremes and the inability to form normal relationships.

Jackie re-read the text trying to figure out how to respond, but in the end she shoved the phone in her pocket and wandered back inside the house. She was wandering a lot lately, drifting from room to room or going on long walks. Maybe it was because she'd quit her job and wasn't used to having so much time on her hands. *I'm unravelling.* That word kept coming back, dancing across her thoughts.

Wasn't the kitchen, filthy with its overflowing bin and stack of unwashed dishes and collection of empty wine bottles, an indication she was losing her ability to function? And wasn't the stench of alcohol proof enough she was spiralling downwards? All she needed was a few stray cats and the picture would become complete.

The phone buzzed in her pocket, making her jump. It was Rick again, asking if she was all right. How was she supposed to answer that question? *I'm losing my mind and I tell so many lies I can't remember what's true.* Jackie giggled. The laughter took her by surprise, so she covered her mouth just as tears started to well in her eyes.

Ten weeks ago she'd had a job and a reasonably nice home. Nothing as fancy as the place she was now standing in, but it was hers and when she closed the doors Jackie felt safe. She'd been lonely, maybe a little depressed, but there had been some measure of peace in her life. Now, all of that was gone and she couldn't quite identify where it had started to disintegrate.

Jackie dragged her fingers through her hair. Andrew had told her that she didn't have to talk to the police. If she kept her mouth shut, was it possible that her life could return to normal? It wasn't much, but the thin scrap of hope was something to cling to. And she was good at clinging. Hadn't she spent most of her life clinging to Aunt Helen? Wasn't that the reason she was still here in the house where Helen died?

Every stick of furniture was embedded with Helen's memory. The walls seemed to breathe her scent like giant lungs. Jackie rubbed her forefinger with her thumb, remembering a time when being in this house was an adventure. A chance to spend time with someone who didn't make her feel awkward or boring. With Aunt Helen she'd listen to music, go to restaurants, and stay up late.

For some reason known only to her mother, Jackie wasn't allowed to sleep over at her aunt's house until she was big enough to take care of herself. At least that's how her mother had put it. Looking around the kitchen, the mundane clutter seemed to lift and she could almost hear the echoes of the past. Echoes of a time when she'd raced through the house as a twelve-year-old.

"Slow down, Jacqueline," Aunt Helen called from the sitting room. "We have the whole weekend."

Jackie spun around, sure she'd heard Helen's voice like a ricochet from another time.

Chapter Eighteen

1986

"We'll have the whole weekend." Mike's voice sounded cracked and filtered by static, but the longing was unmistakable.

Helen held the telephone to her ear, wondering if she was really about to fall back into their old dance. A dance she'd told herself was over when heartache threatened to tear her chest in two.

"I have to see you." His voice was deeper than she remembered.

"You made a choice, Mike. This was what you wanted." Helen closed her eyes, knowing she'd give in, but at the same time determined to get the words out. Determined not to make it that easy for him.

"I can't go through this again." She could hear the pain in her own voice: pain *and* warning.

"I'm leaving her," he said, and the three words were enough to pull her back in.

Helen's hand tightened around the receiver. Mike West was many things, but a part of her still wanted to believe he wasn't a liar. Had he lied to her in the past? He'd lied to his wife; she was sure of that. Yet, he was still the only man Helen wanted or trusted. She'd been able to be vulnerable with him, shrugging off the tough veneer that made it possible for a female journalist to succeed in a man's world. And for his part, Mike had always been upfront with her.

"So, I'm supposed to just welcome you back with open arms?" Helen gave a joyless laugh and snatched a cigarette out of the packet on the nightstand.

"Yes."

There was finality in the word, and the way Mike said it had a lack of pretence that thrilled and angered her at the same time.

"I'll be back in Perth on Friday morning." She spoke around the still unlit cigarette. "Pick me up at the airport at ten o'clock."

She set the receiver back in its cradle without saying goodbye and picked up her lighter. Outside the hotel window she could see the outline of the Dayabumi Complex, its glittering lights tinting the night sky purple. She hadn't bothered to ask Mike how he'd tracked her to a hotel in Kuala Lumpur. He might have given up freelance photography, but he still had plenty of contacts.

How he'd found her wasn't important. What mattered was why now? They hadn't seen each other in almost four years and yet somehow he knew when to call. It seemed like he'd sensed her need for him even after all this time and all the miles between them. Helen blew out a plume of smoke and watched it drift around the shabby room.

She'd blamed Mike for the decisions he'd made when they both knew it was her that had pushed him away in favour of her career. A career that felt so important when she was in her thirties now seemed like an endless parade of crappy hotels and empty stories. A life spent chasing something that would make her feel valuable.

She grabbed her silk dressing gown off the bed and slipped it on. With the cigarette still clamped between her teeth, she began tossing clothes into her suitcase. There wasn't much to pack because she'd made travelling light a way of life in more ways than one. A lifestyle she was ready to abandon based on a single promise: Mike was leaving his wife. A wife he'd have never married if Helen hadn't refused to settle down. Or at least put their relationship before her career.

At forty-two-years-old she was finally ready and the idea both excited and terrified her. With the suitcase all but packed she stubbed out her cigarette in the ashtray on the desk and poured herself a shot of vodka. When she flew into Perth, he'd be waiting. He'd be older. Would he still be able to steal her breath away with a single touch?

Mike had once told her she made him feel like a kid on his first date. Would she still hold that much fascination? She paced the room while running her hand over her stomach where a ball of tension was building with a mixture of anticipation and doubt. Helen wasn't one for tears, but the idea of a second chance at love made her dizzy and emotional. Or maybe it was the vodka. Either way she was having a hard time keeping still.

In less than thirty-six hours she'd be back in Perth and then all her doubts would be laid bare. She finished the vodka then poured herself another, grimacing at the medicinal burn on her tongue. This time she told herself she'd be softer. Age and time had dulled her edges and for some reason she'd been given another chance. A chance Helen wouldn't mess up.

* * *

On her last press junket there'd been talk of the major airlines banning smoking. Helen lit a cigarette promising herself she'd cut back once things settled down. While the idea of flying without the aid of nicotine seemed almost cruel, she supposed it was inevitable that these small vices would eventually become controlled by the government. Maybe the change in attitudes was the universe's way of telling her the old type of journalism was over.

Smiling, Helen sipped her orange juice and craned her neck trying to get a look past the guy sitting next to her and out the window. She caught a glimpse of sandy and barren land and her heart did a weird flip-flop in her chest. She was nearly home. For so long home had meant nothing more than a short respite in an empty house, but now it signalled a new chapter in her life.

I'm acting like one of those lovesick women in romance novels. Later, when they were in each other's arms she'd tell Mike about her little flutters of nerves and they'd both laugh. She could almost hear his voice: sonorous yet somehow soft. Was it possible to miss someone so deeply and yet not realise what you'd given up until it was tantalisingly close?

With only half an hour until landing, she crawled out from the middle seat, apologising to the woman she had to step over to reach the aisle and access her hand luggage from the overhead compartment. Once inside the cramped toilet cubicle, she touched up her make-up and ran a comb through her hair, wishing she'd had time to get her wild curls trimmed.

Before returning to her seat Helen took a long look at her reflection, trying to see herself anew as Mike might see her. There were a few lines at the corners of her eyes that hadn't been there four years ago. Maybe a slight softening of the jaw line. Small changes that she'd never given much thought to until now. Mike wasn't a superficial man. She doubted he'd notice the signs of ageing, but she knew they were there. It was only a momentary lack of confidence, one she shrugged off with a toss of her head. When they saw each other, neither would be looking for crow's feet.

The idea of her and Mike peering at each other's flaws made Helen chuckle as she walked the aisle back to her seat. Somehow, even the recycled air filled with the smell of sweat and stale cigarettes seemed to lift as the aeroplane began its descent into Perth.

Chapter Nineteen

"Helen Winter's head injury was fatal in that it caused a great deal of swelling and bleeding which led to a series of strokes," Dr Tance said, indicating to the crescent-shaped drawing on the diagram showing patient injuries.

Veronika and Jim were in the doctor's office, a spacious set of rooms where a curious-looking sculpture of a giant head dominated the bookshelf that took up the entire side wall. A painting of white sand and salt bushes hung to the surgeon's right. It reminded Veronika of holidays at Rottnest Island when Tony was in primary school. Jim had managed to track down the neurosurgeon that had treated Helen Winter and had secured a meeting with the man between his consultations.

"I saw Miss Winter after she'd been admitted through Accident and Emergency and had been sent to the Critical Care Unit." Dr Tance's pale eyes danced between the detectives and the computer screen where he was looking at Helen Winter's file. "I informed the next of kin that while decompression surgery might help, given the patient's age and the extent of the damage it was unlikely Miss Winter would recover in any meaningful way."

Veronika couldn't help wondering if the surgeon had used a little more compassion when delivering the news to Jacqueline Winter. But then she reminded herself that if her suspicions were correct, Winter might have welcomed the diagnosis.

"So, you assessed Helen Winter's head wound as fatal?" Veronika asked.

Tance took a moment before answering. "Yes." He drew out the word. "Although it's never that simple. There are often other factors to consider, such as age and general health." He laced his fingers together and placed them on the desk. "If Helen Winter had been twenty or even ten years younger, I might have pressed the importance of surgical intervention."

Veronika noticed the surgeon's fingers were long and slender, the nails short and perfectly trimmed. They were hands that saved lives or, in Helen Winter's case, assessed the likelihood of death.

"So, you remember Helen Winter?" Veronika asked wondering how much of what Tance was telling them came from his notes and how much the surgeon actually recalled of the case.

"Yes, Detective," Dr Tance replied with a trace of irritation in his voice. "I remember Miss Winter. In fact, I'd met the woman years before at a press conference in Sydney where Dr Christiaan Barnard spoke. It was a memorable occasion and Miss Winter was a memorable woman." His voice softened on the last two words.

Veronika was thrown by the surgeon's connection to Helen Winter. It was definitely something she hadn't expected, but she kept the surprise out of her voice and pushed on. "So, you recall Miss Winter's head wound? I mean the shape of the injury and what it looked like?"

"Of course. It was an odd sort of wound," Tance said, narrowing his eyes. "When Detective Drommel asked for this meeting, I was led to believe it was because there was some doubt over Miss Winter's cause of death, so let me be quite clear." Tance leaned forward. "There is no doubt in my mind that the head trauma led to her death. And, I have patients waiting, so I'd appreciate it if you'd tell me what this is all about."

She still had questions but they could wait. What they really needed was an honest reaction from the doctor. Veronika nodded to Jim, signalling her partner to show Tance the photograph.

"We'd like you to take a look at this photograph and tell us what you see," Jim said, pulling out the post-mortem image of the wound on the side of Margaret Green's head from the package he'd brought with him and sliding it towards the surgeon.

Tance studied the photograph for a few seconds before picking it up and taking a closer look. Veronika watched the surgeon's face, but Tance gave nothing away.

"This wound looks remarkably similar to Helen Winter's." Tance tapped the picture. "You see this crescent shape. I remembered being puzzled by how it could have come from a fall, but Miss Winter's niece told me her aunt struck her head on a pot plant on the back patio."

The ticking in Veronika's brain intensified and with it grew the feeling that the case was gathering momentum. Out of the corner of her eye she caught Jim glancing her way. And, judging by Tance's reaction, he'd seen the younger detective's look.

For the first time since their meeting began, Tance appeared uncertain. "I had no reason to doubt her story. She seemed genuinely grief stricken by her aunt's condition."

"No. We're not suggesting there *was* any reason for you to doubt the niece's account of her aunt's injuries," Veronika said, scooping up the photo and handing it back to Jim. "We're just following a line of investigation and tying up loose ends, so it's important you don't discuss any of this with anyone."

The doctor was nodding. "I understand, but… That photograph, who is that woman?"

"As I said, it's an ongoing investigation," Veronika said, sidestepping the question. "We'll need you to make a statement detailing your conversation with Helen Winter's niece and your observations concerning the aunt's head injury."

At the mention of making a statement, the doctor's expression changed. Veronika noted a slight tightening of his jaw and jerk of his shoulders. She could have added that if there was ever a trial he could be issued with a subpoena and compelled to appear in court, but in her experience it was better to try diplomacy with a man like Dr Tance.

"I know you're very busy, but it really is vital to our investigation." Veronika pulled a business card out of the back pocket of her pants. "Sorry. It's a bit crushed."

* * *

"So, the doctor knew Helen Winter," Jim said, tossing his jacket over the chair and sliding in front of his computer. "I didn't expect that."

"Hm." Veronika was barely listening. Instead, her thoughts were on something else Dr Tance had mentioned.

"I want you to get the search warrant ready." Veronika was on her way back out of the office, but stopped and turned back to Jim. "We're looking for stained clothing and a crescent-shaped weapon."

"Will do," Jim said. "So, we're going ahead with the search?"

On the drive back to the station, Veronika had decided their next move should be getting a search warrant for Jacqueline Winter's place. While they couldn't force Winter to speak to them, they could search her house. And, under the Identification of Persons Act, they could force Winter to give a DNA sample and take her prints and photograph.

Maybe by showing the woman how serious they were, she'd rethink her decision to keep quiet.

"Let's just get the paperwork ready for now," Veronika said, checking her watch. "I'm going to give Winter one more chance to talk to me before we drop the warrant on her."

Jim frowned. "You going on your own, boss?" Under the florescent lights, the young detective's prematurely greying hair looked almost white.

Veronika nearly reminded him that she'd been doing this long enough to know how to take care of herself, but managed to bite back the reproach. Jim was a nice guy and a good detective. He was right to be concerned. Speaking to a suspect alone was always dicey, let alone a suspect that may have committed two murders.

"I'll be careful." She patted the side of her jacket, feeling the bulge of her gun against her ribs. "And call me Nika."

Chapter Twenty

Her phone buzzed, but Jackie ignored the sound. She'd meant to clean the kitchen, but all of a sudden sleep was the only thing she wanted. Still fully clothed, she crawled into bed and shut her eyes. As she fell into slumber, it wasn't Rick's face she saw but Andrew's. And, for a fleeting moment, Jackie wondered how – when her world was falling apart – she could be thinking about the solicitor and his dark blue eyes that reminded her of the night sky. She felt safe under his gaze. It seemed like a long time since she'd experienced that feeling.

The waters were grey and green, swirling and cold. Jackie wanted to turn away from the river and run, but the sound of the bubbling water dragged at her like an irresistible force. Around her, the trees were leaning in like bony fingers reaching to grasp her and thrust her into the watercourse.

Groaning with the effort, she pulled back only to see a figure dart out from between the trees. Jackie opened her mouth to scream, but her voice was strangled by terror. The thing in the black rain poncho jerked from tree to tree, jumping and shuddering with unnatural speed, its face hidden by the slick black hood.

When Jackie turned to flee, the water and the shrubbery opened into an arc where a hospital bed rested between twisted trunks atop a carpet of dead branches. She knew who was in the bed. She knew and didn't want to see, yet her feet were moving and the bed with its hospital wheels and blue sheets drew closer.

The covers hid an outline. Unmistakably human, the shape's chest rose and fell. The thing was alive and breathing. *Not a thing, I know who it is*. Without realising she was moving, Jackie was suddenly staring down at the covered shape, watching the hidden face suck the sheet in and out of its fabric-draped mouth with each frantic breath. The sound of breathing surrounded her, making it seem like the encircling woods were lungs.

"I don't want to see. I don't want to know." Her voice sounded small and childlike as the black trees crowding the bed towered over her.

Unbidden, her hand was reaching for the sheet and it felt like her own limbs were working against her. She snatched back the covers and howled as the black rain coated figure was revealed, only this time she could see the face. Aunt Helen's face, sunken and grey, and her eyes… Jackie's body jerked backwards as she found her voice and a scream bounced off the foliage.

It was too late. Aunt Helen was sitting up, her black eyes — viscous and mucky — ran like tar over her withered face as her mouth opened and closed making a *clopping* sound. Jackie's heels back-pedalled, but the sound grew louder until Helen's face was all she could see.

Jackie's eyes flew open while her fists were still tangled in the sheets. The clopping continued as she swivelled her head, searching for the nightmarish creature in the black poncho. There were no trees. No river. Only the guest room with its familiar pale blue walls and patchwork bedspread. The clopping was coming from the front of the house as someone banged on the door.

It's not real. None of it's real. But that wasn't right. The knocking was real and the figure in the black raincoat was real; she'd seen it. Was she still dreaming?

Untangling her fists from the bedding, Jackie dragged her legs over the side of the bed. Her hair was sticky with sweat, clinging to her forehead and neck as if she'd run a marathon. The knocking stopped and after a few minutes was replaced by ringing. Whoever was at her door was insistent, knocking and pressing the doorbell. *Is it the one in the black raincoat?* Maybe it's tired of just following and watching. Maybe it was on the other side of the front door waiting to pounce.

She could feel panic rising in her throat, cutting the air off from squeezing through to her lungs. Jackie could almost see the creature from her dream, its slippery black poncho flapping in the wind as its grey hand pressed the bell.

"I can't let it in." Her voice in the empty house sounded too loud. An invitation to the thing on the doorstep.

On heavy legs, she moved through the house trying to make as little noise as possible. In the hallway, a floorboard creaked under her weight. A small sound that seemed deafening in the silence between rings. Jackie pressed herself against the wall and waited.

One more ring and then nothing. She stayed in place, worried that the figure in the raincoat was testing her – waiting for her to move and reveal her location. But as the seconds ticked by, there was only quiet and the occasional hiss of tyres on the street.

It was another minute before she could force herself to push off the wall and walk to the front door. Standing facing the wood, Jackie reached out a hand and touched the panel, half expecting the wood to be icy like a corpse.

It could have been anyone. It could have been… Her thoughts floundered. *I'm unravelling.* The words slithered out of the darkness and across her mind. Maybe it would

120

be easier to go to the police and tell them what she'd done. Jackie pulled her hand back from the door. What had she done? Sometimes it was murky like a stagnant pool with the truth always churning just below the surface. *Not churning, slithering.*

In the kitchen, she turned on the lights even though the afternoon hadn't yet succumbed to evening. Needing a purpose, she boiled water and made tea. Her appetite, once voracious, was dwindling. Going without food was making her listless and jumpy. That was why she had the nightmare. Nodding to herself, she moved around the room, opening cupboards.

It had been too long since she'd bought groceries. There was precious little on offer apart from a few packets of noodles and six tins of tom yum soup: Helen's favourite. Jackie grabbed a packet of noodles and forced her eyes away from the tins only to find herself staring at the wine. She was down to seven bottles. There'd been sixteen when she moved in to look after Helen. She remembered being surprised that her aunt would drink wine that came with a screw top; it seemed lacking in flare.

What did it matter as long as it blurred the edges?

Jackie tossed the noodles on the table and snatched a bottle of wine. With the tea and food forgotten, she poured herself a drink.

Instead of retreating to the bedroom she went to the study. Jackie remembered finding a photo album in the cupboard under the bookshelf when she'd been searching for the lock that the key might fit, the night Helen died. At the time she hadn't given the album much thought, but now she was looking for something to block out the nightmare images still swirling around in her head.

The album was old with dark blue leather edged with gold. When she opened the cover, she caught a hint of tobacco, making Jackie wonder if the last time Helen looked through the pages she'd still been smoking. If that were true then no one had looked at this book in fifteen years.

On the first few pages she found the usual sort of snaps: aged images of her aunt as a child and one of Jackie's grandparents on their wedding day. Another was of Helen and Jackie's father sitting on an inflatable raft floating on what looked like a river. The black and white image made Jackie think of the churning waters in her nightmare, so she flipped the page.

The photos seemed to jump forward in time because these were coloured. Helen sitting in the deep frame of an open window, her hair tossed over one shoulder and a magazine open in her lap. Jackie traced her finger over the picture, marvelling at how effortlessly beautiful her aunt looked. Another more intimate image of Helen sitting up in bed, a cigarette in one hand while holding a sheet to her chest. There was a look in her aunt's eyes that was both relaxed and sultry, as if she were looking at her lover.

On the next page were a series of pictures of a man who looked to be in his thirties. Dark hair and a sharp jaw, he reminded Jackie of Gregory Peck, if the old-time actor had ever worn a leather jacket and baggy jeans. Was this the man who'd photographed Helen in bed? The idea made Jackie smile, except the expression on her face felt stiff, like wearing something that had grown too small.

Settling down on the rug, Jackie touched the photo of the man in the leather jacket. He was good-looking but obviously uncomfortable in front of the camera, and the street behind him looked dusty and crowded with bicycles and scooters. Squinting, Jackie made out a faded white building that looked like a hotel. The bustling street made her think of the Middle East – somewhere exotic and mysterious.

Jackie took another sip of wine and flipped the page. With the alcohol still in her mouth, she gulped and choked down the liquid. Staring at the photo put everything she thought she knew in doubt. The man from the previous shot stood in front of Helen's house. The leather jacket was gone, replaced by a blue cable-knit jumper. He was older in this image, his dark hair laced with grey, but the strength of his jawline was unchanged. But it wasn't that the man was photographed outside the very house where Jackie now sat that took her by surprise, it was the child in his arms.

A little boy of around three years of age. Dark curls and chubby legs below red shorts; the child bore a striking resemblance to the man. The casualness of the way the man held the boy confirmed him as the child's father. There was something gentle and protective in the man's posture as the child rested his head on his father's chest.

Jackie's mind jumped back to the child's shoe she'd found in the case with the notebooks. At the time she'd assumed Helen had a child and gave it up for adoption, but the photograph changed everything. The little boy wasn't a baby, but a small child, and he'd been at Helen's house with his father.

Before jumping to her feet, Jackie downed the last dregs of wine. She'd been so swamped by grief and self-pity she thought the shoe meant Helen had a baby, not taking in the obvious. The sandal had belonged to an older child. Now, dragging the case out from under the desk, she pulled out the little leather shoe and cursed under her breath. She had to be sure, so she hurried back to the photo album and dropped to her knees.

It matched. The little shoe, faded and aged now, was identical to the one the boy in the photo wore. Jackie's stomach fluttered in part with excitement, but mostly trepidation. Did this mean Helen and the man in the photo had a little boy? A boy that had lived in Helen's house? And if so, where was he now?

Jackie set the album down, trying to get her thoughts around what she'd discovered. *Why am I worrying about something that happened over thirty years ago?* Her mind should have been on the mess she was in instead of ancient history. But the thought was fleeting and quickly dismissed.

This time, when she stood, a wave of dizziness darkened her vision and for a second Jackie had trouble keeping her balance. With one hand on the side of her head she went in search of her phone.

The obvious course of action was to call her mother, but then it occurred to her that whatever the truth was about Helen's past, it had been kept from her. All the vague cautions about Jackie needing to know how to look after herself before being allowed to stay over at her aunt's place now seemed disturbing – veiled riddles that held implied warnings. Her parents had deliberately kept Helen's past a secret. For a moment she stared at her reflection in the phone's black shiny screen trying to remember what exactly it was that Andrew had said about Helen.

She had her moments. When he'd said it, Jackie assumed it was the solicitor's way of trying to make her feel better about her own failings, but maybe he knew more about Helen than he'd let on. Jackie went as far as bringing up Andrew's number, but hesitated over making the call. He was *her* solicitor now. If she had any hope of getting out of the mess with the police, she needed Andrew to believe in her. Demanding information on her aunt's past would only make her seem unstable.

No. Jackie decided it would be a mistake to start probing Andrew for answers. She lowered her hand and let the phone slip onto the kitchen counter. There had to be a better way, but with her brain beginning to fog over with a now-familiar sense of confusion, it was almost impossible to come up with a plan.

"I need air," Jackie mumbled over lips that felt thick and numb.

Wearing only jeans and a lightweight jumper, she grabbed her keys and headed for the door. It wasn't until she was outside that she noticed it was dark. For a second she couldn't quite remember where she was going and only that it was something important.

Standing on the path that led from the front door to the street with the night air lifting her hair, she tried to organise her thoughts. The chill made her shiver as the full moon painted the front yard in silver light and someone stepped out from the cover of the peppermint tree in the centre of the lawn.

Jackie let out a strangled shriek and clutched a hand to her throat. It was the figure, the one that had been following her even in her dreams. And now, like a living nightmare, it was rushing towards her as she backed up and almost lost her footing.

Chapter Twenty-one

1986

Travelling with one small suitcase had its advantages. As passengers crowded the conveyer belt wrestling with over-packed luggage, Helen retrieved her valise and headed for the customs desk. Twenty minutes later she removed her jacket, slung it over her shoulder and pushed open the double doors that led into the waiting area.

For a moment she could see nothing but a sea of eager faces – groups of people watching the doors for the moment their loved ones would appear. It was a singular scene, one that only occurred in airports and, to a lesser degree, train stations. No matter how many times she exited airports, Helen never tired of this moment. While she was usually only watching the reunions, the sense of anticipation and joy in the air always thrilled her.

Today, however, she wasn't just a spectator and the energy-charged air had her caught in its spell. Standing her ground, Helen skimmed the crowd until she caught sight of the face that was etched into her mind as clearly as her own reflection.

Four years had brought changes. Six years older than her and now approaching fifty, his dark hair was flecked with grey and even from ten metres away she could see the lines creasing his brow. But when their eyes met, there was still that connection. The connection that had nearly torn her in two when they'd parted.

Helen raised her hand, and as much as she'd promised herself she'd play it cool, she didn't try to stop herself as she let go of her case and ran forward. Home wasn't a place, it was a person, and for her that person would always be Mike.

Closing the gap until only a metre or so and a waist-high metal barrier separated them, the crowd parted and Helen's steps faltered. He wasn't alone. The child in his arms regarded her with the same blue eyes as his father.

"Mike?" The word came out as both a question and a greeting.

If he heard the uncertainty in her voice, he gave no indication. Leaning over the barricade, he pulled her close so she could smell his scent: clean and edged with the crisp scent of his cologne. A scent now mingled with another smell, milky and sweet; that of his child.

He kissed her. A gentle meeting of his lips to hers, but it was enough to take her breath away.

"Helen," he said pulling back. "This is Chrissy." As he spoke, Mike's fingers touched the little boy's hair, absently brushing back a strand that lay on the child's forehead.

With the shock of seeing the boy ebbing, Helen managed to muster a smile. The boy was so like his father that something in her stirred and she felt tears prickle her eyes, reminding her how different life could have been if she'd been the one to give Mike a child.

"Hi, Chrissy." Helen wanted to touch the boy, to run her hand over his little face. "I have a niece about your age. She likes chocolate ice cream."

The boy's previously sleepy eyes lit up. "I eat chocolate ice cream."

"I think I have some in my freezer." Helen glanced up at Mike. "If your daddy says it's okay, you can have some when we get to my house."

* * *

Ten minutes later with her case in the boot of Mike's car, Helen watched as the man she'd loved for almost ten years put his son in the child seat. This was a seldom revealed side to Mike, a part of his personality she'd always known, but one, for the most part, he'd kept hidden beneath a casual easy-going façade. Now as he settled his little boy in the car, she saw the gentle and sensitive man she'd missed for so long.

Mike slammed the door and for a moment they regarded each other across the car's roof. There was so much she wanted to say. So many questions forming in her mind. Questions about Mike's wife and what a future together might look like. About wanting to love his son and be, if not a mother, at least a loving figure in his child's life. But as aeroplanes roared above them, all her doubts seemed small.

"Are we really doing this?" she asked, almost afraid the feeling growing inside her was too joyful to be real.

"I love you." He'd said the words loud enough to drown out the noise of the jet engines overhead. "We've waited long enough."

With Chrissy napping in the back seat, Mike drove towards Regent Park. For a while the only sound was the little boy's soft breathing.

"Do you really have chocolate ice cream in your freezer?" Mike asked her with a sidelong glance.

The question was so unexpected Helen tipped her head back and laughed, only to clamp a hand over her mouth for fear of waking Chrissy.

"God, I've missed you," she said, shaking her head.

When Mike responded, all trace of humour had left his voice. "Thank you for agreeing to this. I know you weren't expecting me to have Chrissy with me, but…" His eyes were back on the road and Helen could see the muscles in his jaw tightening. "She's been sick. She's in hospital, so I'm taking care of him," Mike said, tilting his head towards the sleeping child.

Mike's wife Kathleen had been treated for depression after they lost their first baby. A loss that had nearly killed Mike and hospitalised his wife. For Helen's part, it was the tragedy that brought her back into Mike's life and to something she'd thought she'd never do: get involved with a married man.

"Is it the same as before?" Helen asked.

Mike didn't answer right away. Instead, he glanced in the rear vision mirror. "It's worse."

* * *

"Time for bed, mate." Mike hoisted the boy up into his arms. "Say goodnight to Helen."

They were in Helen's sitting room where a collection of small wooden trucks littered the rug. With Chrissy nestled in Mike's arms, the little boy held out his hands to Helen.

"I think he wants a goodnight kiss," Mike said around a chuckle.

The afternoon had flown by while Chrissy played with his trucks and Mike had made them dinner from the few ingredients he found in Helen's freezer. As promised, after dinner, Chrissy ate chocolate ice cream. It was a day unlike any Helen had experienced. She'd known a similar peacefulness years before when she and Mike spent weeks at a hotel in Turkey. Weeks of reading and waking late to drink dark sweet coffee in bed. But even then, there had been that nagging feeling that she should be in motion and that the world was waiting. Maybe she'd finally grown up because all Helen felt now was contentment.

She stood and came closer, enjoying the clean lemony scent of the little boy's skin washed clean and pink from his bath. As she leaned her head in and let Chrissy plant a wet kiss on her cheek, she recognised she really was ready to live the life Mike had wanted for them ten years earlier.

"Goodnight, sweetheart," she said, straightening the collar of the little boy's Superman pyjamas.

Chrissy reached out and took hold of a strand of Helen's hair, examining the copper curl.

"Night-night, Helen." Chrissy made her name sound like *Welen*.

A moment later she heard Mike's deep voice moving steadily over the words of a nursery rhyme as he went through his little boy's night-time ritual. The house she'd thought of more as a base than a home suddenly seemed full, not only of people but hope.

Resisting the urge to linger and listen to Mike's voice, Helen made her way to the kitchen and opened a bottle of wine. It would be an intense night. She was happier than she'd been in a long time, but Helen was no fool. They had things to talk about. Decisions had to be made, but for now she'd settle for a drink on the patio.

Chapter Twenty-two

"Jackie." The voice wasn't immediately familiar.

With her legs weak and unresponsive she tried to turn but the dark shape was on top of her, grabbing Jackie's arms and wrenching her forward. In that moment all her fears became reality as a bolt of panic shook her body.

"I've been calling and leaving messages all day." A shaft of moonlight fell on Rick's face. "I was knocking the door before, but you didn't answer. What the hell's going on?"

"Rick?" Jackie managed to get the name out, but was still torn between relief and the adrenaline that was driving her to break away from him and run.

"Why are you shutting me out?" Rick's voice was oddly high, almost petulant.

"Rick, I thought you were something else... I mean someone else." She was stammering now, trying to explain things she barely understood herself.

"What are you talking about?" Rick's voice was lower, but there was something tight and angry in the way he drew out his words. "Do you think it's okay to just pretend I don't exist?"

"What?" Jackie asked. A moment ago she'd been relieved to see him, but now she wasn't so sure. "You're hurting my arms, Rick."

He pulled her closer. "Oh, so you do have feelings?"

This close, his features were shadowed and dark, making it difficult for Jackie to make out his expression, but the smell of whiskey was unmistakable. As his fingers dug into her upper arms, she felt panic rising as she twisted her head, trying to see over his shoulder, hoping a passing car might see what was happening. The street beyond the front lawn was deserted and shiny under the moonlight.

"Rick, please." Jackie tried to keep the fear out of her voice, not wanting to escalate the situation. "I wasn't ignoring you. I'm just having a hard time and… and I—"

"Do you hear yourself?" he barked in her face. "It's all about you. You think because your aunt left you this house and all her money you don't need me?"

Rick let go of her right arm and Jackie let out a gasp of relief, only to wince as his hand snaked into the back of her hair, grabbing hold. He was pulling and forcing her backwards towards the house, the pace of his movements making her slip and stumble to stop herself from being bowled over as the skin on her scalp burned.

"Please, don't," Jackie begged as tears blurred her eyes.

"You're nothing but a spoilt, dressed-up slut," Rick said, slurring the last word. "You liked what I did to you, but don't want to share the money with me because—"

"What's going on there?" The voice was like a whip crack, loud and sharp.

Blessedly, the clench of his fingers on her hair released as Rick turned to search for the source of the voice. Between the darkness and the tears, all Jackie could make out was a shape on the lawn.

"Get away from that woman before I call the police." It was a woman's voice, strong and confident.

A light shone on Jackie's face making her squint and raise a hand to block the glare. Rick let go of Jackie's other arm and turned towards the light source.

"Piss off." His words were threatening, but his voice was losing its menace as he staggered to the right.

"I have my phone and I'm ready to call for help, so I suggest you clear off before this gets out of hand." The owner of the voice moved closer. "You've got three seconds before I start screaming. In a quiet suburb like this, neighbours will come running."

Still caught in the glare of light, Rick turned back to Jackie. Now his features were clear. She could see the unfocused look in his eyes and the stubborn angry pucker of his mouth. Once, his eyes had reminded her of honey and sunlight. Now, the glassy orbs made her think of vinegar, bitter and sharp. For a few beats he looked defiant, but to Jackie's relief his glassy gaze shifted and he turned to leave.

Like a snake, he lunged back her way and planted both hands on her chest, shoving her hard enough to knock the air out of her lungs. Jackie's feet skidded out from under her and before she could right herself she was on the lawn staring at the millions of flecks of light that filled the clear night sky.

Still stunned and struggling to get air into her lungs, Jackie turned her head and watched Rick jog towards the street as the damp grass soaked through her jeans.

"Are you all right?" A face appeared above her, female and vaguely familiar.

Jackie tried to speak but her chest felt weighed down, making speech almost impossible. The woman hooked a hand under Jackie's arm and wrenched her up into a sitting position.

"Come on," the woman said. "Let's get you inside before he decides to come back for round two."

A few minutes later they were in Jackie's kitchen and the woman was holding a glass up to the light, seeming to be inspecting it for cleanliness. Jackie slumped into a chair at the kitchen table, too exhausted and shaken to talk and too embarrassed to ask the woman to leave. Despite the shock of Rick's attack, Jackie couldn't help but see the house through her guest's eyes: dirty dishes, a bowl of mouldy fruit on the counter, empty wine bottles littering the table. Add to the mayhem the violent scene on the front lawn, and Jackie supposed the woman was wondering what sort of bogan she'd gotten herself mixed up with.

"Here," the woman said, setting a glass of water on the table. "Have a few sips and get your breath back. My name's Lena by the way. I live next door."

Jackie lifted the glass to her lips, trying to control the tremble in her hand. Aware that the woman, Lena, was standing over her, Jackie searched for something to say.

"Thank you for helping me, I'm Jackie," she finally said, putting the glass down in front of her.

"That's okay." Lena pulled out a chair and sat across from Jackie. "That man out there..." She jerked her chin towards the front of the house. "I'm guessing you know him?"

Jackie let out a dry chuckle. "Not as well as I thought."

Lena, obviously not seeing the humour in the situation, didn't so much as smile. Instead, she regarded Jackie with sombre brown eyes.

"Is this the first time he's been violent with you?" Lena asked.

It was a personal question, but one Jackie supposed Lena was entitled to ask. After all, the woman had put herself in harm's way by intervening. Lena was elderly, at least early sixties, yet she'd come to Jackie's aid. Thinking about the way her neighbour had stood up to Rick, Jackie felt a rush of gratitude towards the woman.

"Yes. I mean I don't know him that well. We've only been out a few times. I had no idea he could be like that." Jackie looked down at her hands. "I didn't know he was…" She trailed off, not really sure how to describe what Rick was.

"Men are full of surprises," Lena said with what sounded like a hint of anger.

"I think he's been following me." As the words came out, Jackie could feel her face colouring. "Every time I go out, he's watching me."

Lena remained silent for a moment, her eyes on something on the table. A moment ago Jackie wanted the woman to leave, but suddenly it seemed important to know what she was thinking.

"You should call the police." Lena tapped the table with her index finger. "If you don't put a stop to this, he'll be back."

At the mention of police, Jackie's stomach clenched. The last thing she wanted was another visit from Detective Pope.

"No." The word came out too loud and harsh so Jackie tried to explain. "I really don't want to get the police involved. I'm more embarrassed than hurt," Jackie continued, resisting the urge to rub her upper arms where Rick's fingers had dug into her flesh.

"All right then." Lena stood. "If you need anything just yell."

Jackie walked Lena to the door. Despite all the turmoil, Jackie's mind kept coming back to the photos she'd found in her aunt's study. As she thanked her neighbour once more, Jackie remembered something the nurse said on the day Helen died.

"Lena?" Jackie stood in the doorway, stopping the woman before she headed across the lawn and back to her house. "Did you know my aunt?"

Lena's face and body were clearly visible under the porch light and for the first time since meeting the woman, Jackie noticed the shabbiness of her neighbour's clothes: worn jeans and a frayed T-shirt. Not that Jackie was in a position to judge with her face streaked with tears and her pants damp and clinging. It was too dark to be gardening, so Jackie assumed Lena was working on her house – painting or cleaning.

"I only rented the place five months ago, so I never got the chance to do more than say hello." Lena tapped a finger on her bottom lip appearing to be thinking. "The woman next door on that side," she said, jerking a thumb over her shoulder and to Jackie's right, "her name's Ruth. She's lived here for years."

Jackie leaned out of the doorway, peering into the darkness. If what Lena was saying was correct, Ruth might be the one to provide answers about her aunt's past. Oddly, instead of exciting her, the prospect of discovering what became of the little boy in the photographs sent a shiver across Jackie's shoulders.

"You might have to wait a while, though," Lena continued. "She's gone to Europe for a month. I only know because I'm collecting her mail."

"Oh, okay." Jackie didn't know if she was disappointed or relieved, only that after everything that had happened, she wanted to be alone.

"Well, goodnight." Lena was already on the move, speaking over her shoulder. "Think about calling the police. A man like that shouldn't be walking around." Her last few words were caught by the breeze as the woman disappeared into the shadows.

Chapter Twenty-three

Jackie woke to a darkened room with no memory of going to bed. The last thing she recalled was saying goodnight to Lena and closing the front door. Now, staring at the clock and waiting for the first signs of morning to creep through the gap in the curtains, she tried to remember what she did after her neighbour had left.

The edges of her thoughts were draped in worry – worry over losing more time and the gnawing certainty that the police weren't done with her. At the forefront of her mind was the terrifying encounter with Rick and the growing belief that the man she'd slept with only a few days ago had been following her for weeks, terrorising her.

Jackie rolled over, trying not to imagine what would have happened if Lena hadn't shown up when she had. Would Rick have killed her? It seemed far-fetched, but after the things she'd been through over the last few weeks, she knew nothing was impossible when it came to human behaviour.

Finally giving up on sleep, she dragged herself out of bed and into the bathroom. After a hot shower and a strong cup of instant coffee she felt stronger and her brain less soupy. As always, there were things she could be doing. Cleaning the house for one, but her mind kept coming back to the little shoe and the photograph of the man holding the child. For some reason she couldn't quite fathom why it seemed important that she find out what happened to the child.

A growing part of her felt she owed it to her aunt to know her real story. After all, Helen had left her the house and all its contents. Didn't this meant she wanted Jackie to know the truth or at least had expected her to find the case and the photo album?

Once in the study, Jackie set the album and shoe on the desk and flipped through the pages, scouring each picture, but finding nothing more on the man and the little boy. Frustrated, she picked up the shoe and held it between her palms. When the doorbell rang, Jackie almost dropped the little sandal.

Standing in the hallway and listening as the bell chimed a second time, Jackie thought of Rick and the way he'd wrenched her hair. Even if he'd sobered up since last night, she didn't want to risk another scene. Or worse, another physical attack.

"Miss Winter, it's Detective Drommel. Please open the door."

She should have been relieved, but the urgency in the police officer's voice made her stomach clench with dread. They were back and they'd keep coming back until one day they'd drag her away in handcuffs. Would today be that day?

She considered ignoring the detective in the hope he'd give up and go away, but she quickly dismissed the idea knowing it would make her look guilty.

When Jackie opened the door, she was surprised to see the younger detective wasn't unaided. A quick glance over his shoulder told her the officer was in fact far from alone. Parked behind the detective's dark Sedan were two other police vehicles.

"Miss Winter, I have a warrant to search this house," Drommel said, holding out a sheet of paper. "This document allows us to search the entire residence, including sheds, outbuildings, and vehicles. We may also seize any items listed in the warrant or items we believe relevant and pertaining to the murder of Margaret Green." He paused for a second before adding, "I'd also like to ask you a few questions about Detective Pope."

Jackie took the paper from the detective's hand, not sure what she was supposed to do with it while still trying to process what he was telling her.

"Do you understand what I'm telling you, Miss Winter?" Drommel asked.

"I... Yes, I think so," Jackie said, looking over the detective's shoulder to the vehicles parked on the street and watching as uniformed officers climbed out of a car and van. At a glance she counted at least five cops heading towards her house.

Drommel turned his back on Jackie and waved the officers forward.

"It might be easier if you go back inside and take a seat," Drommel said, stepping forward.

Still holding the sheet of paper, Jackie backed up and let Drommel enter. It was only when uniformed officers began streaming in through the open door that her mind kicked back into gear and she grasped what was actually happening.

"I'm calling my solicitor." She wasn't sure where she found the strength to get the words out, but once spoken she was in action.

Jackie pulled the phone out of her pocket and called Andrew's number. Leaning against the wall just inside the front door, she listened to the phone ring while Drommel stood with his arms folded less than a metre away. To her relief, Andrew answered on the second ring.

"Jackie." He sounded surprised and pleased. "Good news. Probate was granted yesterday, so I should have all the paperwork—"

"No. It's not about probate," Jackie said, turning her back on Drommel and facing the wall. "The police are here with a search warrant." She lowered her voice to a whisper. "I... I really need your help."

There was silence on the line and for one dreadful second she thought Andrew had hung up on her.

"Okay. I'm in the car now, on my way to the office," Andrew answered. "I'll be there in..." There was another pause. "Give me fifteen minutes and don't say anything until I get there."

He was coming. She wasn't alone. Jackie put the phone back in her pocket and let her head drop forward so she was looking at her bare feet. Tears, which she didn't bother to wipe away, welled in her eyes as around her people came and went, opening and closing doors and cupboards. She kept her gaze on her feet; silent and unmoving, hoping she'd go unnoticed until Andrew arrived.

The notion was quickly wiped away as a hand reached under her arm and yanked her back from the wall. It was Drommel, marching her into the sitting room.

"In there and sit down," he said, and thrust her towards the sofa hard enough to make her stumble.

It was the second time in less than twelve hours that a man had pushed her around and made her feel helpless and terrified. While part of her wanted to protest and to stand up for herself, there was another darker part that wanted to accept the abuse as nothing more than what she deserved. If the uniformed officers that filled her house noticed the detective's rough treatment, none of them intervened or even glanced her way.

Jackie seated herself on the sofa and used her forearm to wipe the tears off her cheeks, telling herself that

Drommel wouldn't go too far, not with a house full of police and her solicitor on his way.

Drommel stood over her and for the first time she noticed the change in the man. His clothes were crumpled like he'd slept in them and his face was darkened with stubble.

"Where's Detective Pope?" he asked.

The question took Jackie by surprise and for a few seconds she wasn't sure what he meant.

"I don't know," Jackie said, glancing towards the hall. "Is she with the others?"

For a moment Drommel didn't speak and only stared at her as if trying to see through her. The power of the man's gaze made Jackie shift in her seat. Something had changed since the last time the detective had called on her. She could see it in the detective's appearance and hear it in the barely concealed anger in his voice.

Drommel dropped to one knee so his eyes were level with hers. The suddenness of his movements made her flinch back into the sofa.

"Don't fuck me about, Winter. Where is she?" The last three words came out slowly as if he was speaking to a child.

"I don't know." Jackie hated the whinging tone in her voice, but couldn't stop herself. "I don't understand any of this. Why are you asking me about Detective Pope?"

Drommel leaned closer. "Detective Pope left the office at around four o'clock yesterday with the intention of coming here to speak to you." He jabbed a finger in her direction, not quite touching her. "She didn't return to work and her family reported her missing late last night."

"Oh, no!" Jackie looked down and noticed she was still holding the search warrant.

Suddenly, everything made more sense and, as it did, she understood how out of control things had become. The police believed she'd killed Margaret Green and now

Detective Pope was missing and she had become the obvious suspect.

"What happened yesterday? Did Detective Pope say something that made you angry? Did you hit her like you hit Margaret Green and your aunty?" Drommel fired the questions at her so quickly she could barely keep up with what he was saying.

Jackie tried to answer, but the saliva in her mouth had evaporated, turning her tongue to cardboard. Her mind was darting in different directions, trying to sort through what he was saying. The only thing she could grasp on to was her aunt. Had he said she'd hit Aunt Helen?

"My aunt?" She repeated the words, as though by saying them aloud she might understand what he meant.

Drommel's face was closer now; so close she could see the red veins in his eyes. "Tell me where Detective Pope is or this isn't going to go well for you."

In that moment he reminded her of Margaret Green and the way the woman had invaded her space. Jackie had the urge to push him away, but instead squeezed at the paper in her hand.

"The last time I saw Detective Pope was when she was with you." Jackie didn't know how she managed to keep her tone level. "The day I came back from my walk and I'd had a fall. That's the last time I saw her." She shook her head. "She didn't come here yesterday," she said.

Drommel sat back on his heels, his face unreadable. "So, no one visited you yesterday afternoon?"

Her mind jumped back to the day before and how she'd been roused from her nightmare by someone knocking the door. The knocking had continued for a few minutes and then there was a gap before the bell was rung. She'd assumed it was Rick, but now it occurred to her that it could have been Detective Pope. Pope might have knocked and then when she left maybe Rick rang the bell.

Drommel was watching her, waiting for her to speak. Andrew had warned her not to say anything, but how could it hurt to tell the truth for a change?

"Someone knocked my door, but I didn't answer," Jackie answered. "Then shortly after that someone rang the bell. I was afraid to open the door, so I just—"

"Why were you afraid?" Drommel was still in front of her, but no longer in her face.

Jackie hesitated, not sure how much to reveal. If she told the detective she was afraid it was the police, she'd look guilty. If she told him about the figure in the black raincoat, she'd sound crazy.

Still torn between the need to explain, to make him understand she hadn't hurt Detective Pope and the impulse to lie and protect herself, she clamped her lips together, refusing to meet Drommel's gaze. It was then that Andrew appeared in the hallway and Jackie felt her body slacken with relief.

It was a different Andrew Drake that entered the sitting room and took charge of the situation. Gone was the relaxed friendly man she'd met only a few weeks ago, replaced by someone imposing – almost larger than life.

To Drommel, Andrew said, "I'm Miss Winter's solicitor. I'd like to see your warrant and then speak with my client." To Jackie, he used a softer tone. "Are you okay, Jackie?"

Jackie wanted to leap from the sofa and throw herself into his arms. Instead, she nodded and swiped at the tears that dripped off her chin.

It was Jackie who handed Andrew the warrant then waited in silence while he read the document. Before Andrew finished, a uniformed officer appeared and jerked his chin, signalling Drommel out of the room.

With Drommel gone, Andrew sat down beside her. For a moment she thought he meant to take her hand, but then she realised he moved next to her so no one would overhear what he was about to say.

"I don't want you to say anything until we've had time to talk. If they had anything, they'd have arrested you already. Keep that in mind," he said quickly, his voice barely above a whisper.

A moment later Drommel returned with the uniformed officer on his heels.

"Miss Winter, please stand," Drommel said, crossing the floor in a few steps. "I'm taking you to Central Processing where you'll be fingerprinted, photographed, and required to give a DNA sample."

Chapter Twenty-four

She was aware of darkness and pain. The only two things Veronika could fully identify were that her eyes were open. She could feel her lids blinking and she could feel pain. Crippling pain that tore across her brain like a fire searing through her thoughts and motions. Movement, even the smallest amount, not only rocked her head with agony but sent her stomach roiling.

A stream of vomit bubbled up in her throat, giving her no choice but to turn her head to the side as the sour liquid poured over her lips. Groaning at the jolt of agony in her head, Veronika couldn't bring herself to move a second time. Instead, she let her face rest against what she assumed was a tiled floor while the smell of vomit added to her misery.

There was some light, a slash of white that was distant and cold. As her eyes adjusted, she could make out the bottom of a door and what she now understood was a wedge of light shining from another room. Room or cell, she had no memory of entering the dark space she now inhabited. Or maybe nothing was real and what she was experiencing was death. Could it be that the light was the world slipping away as the pain swallowed her?

With each breath, the stench of bile and stomach juices filled her nose. *The smell is real.* The pain *is* real. She was alive, of this she was sure. Alive was something she could cling to. To stay alive she needed help; this much she could fathom even in her current state of confusion.

As if discovering her limbs for the first time, Veronika found she had to focus in order to make her right hand move. Her left, the side she rested on, was numb from her weight or perhaps injured beyond use. Panic and fear competed with the pain and nausea, but she fought to keep herself calm. Staying calm was important if she was to find a way out of the darkness. She could do calm.

Her fingers moved up and over her hip, searching for the bulge of her phone in her pants pocket, but found only the curve of her leg. The phone was gone. In the silence there was only her breathing. That was good; breathing was good – regular and unimpeded. How many things was she aware of now? Six. Veronika was aware of six things now: her eyes were open, the smell of vomit in her nostrils, the sound of her breathing, the movement of her right hand, the light under the door, and the pain. She couldn't forget the pain.

Progress. She'd gone from knowing only two things to an awareness of six facts. That was progress. Calm and progress, the two words were at the forefront of her thoughts. Her phone was gone, but she was calm and making progress. It didn't matter that she couldn't remember as long as she was making progress. That meant the case was moving forward and...

Veronika let out a breath. A case had brought her to this dark cell of pain. But there had been so many cases, all of them crowding her mind. Sharp images of bloody crime scenes and stark photos, so much suffering that her brain couldn't sift through the memories. Confusion was a new state of being, one that threatened to take over. She could feel herself falling. Falling into a grey web of panic and oblivion.

As much as she battled to focus her thoughts, Veronika's body won the fight and her eyes closed.

* * *

Jackie tried to keep warm by wrapping her arms around herself. Still at the police station and wearing only a light jumper and jeans, she followed a police officer, a woman that had hair the colour of mud and thick arms that swung loosely at the sides. The female officer, her name was Treeborn, walked slowly as if she had all the time in the world. Tripping along on the woman's heels, Jackie wondered what the officer would do if she stopped walking and sat down on the floor. Would Officer Treeborn drag her to her feet? Call for backup or whatever it was cops did when someone refused to cooperate? Or would she simply keep sauntering along the endless hallway, not even aware that she'd lost her charge?

It was a ridiculous thought, but in the two hours she'd been at the station her mind had begun to take strange pathways. While being photographed, Jackie had considered sticking her tongue out. Maybe it was an avoidance technique, a way of ignoring the predicament she was in that drove her to these ideas. Throwing up crazy scenarios as a means of changing the gravity of the situation?

"In there," Treeborn said, opening a door and standing aside.

Jackie hesitated. She'd been moved from room to room, someone always telling her to wait but never giving any timeframe. Each new officer she encountered treated her with stinging contempt that skirted the edges of outright aggression. They were people used to dealing with criminals, but she supposed in their minds she was the lowest form of offender because they believed she'd harmed one of their own.

The idea of another half an hour in limbo, not knowing what was going to happen to her next or if she'd ever be free to return home was as frightening as it was exhausting.

Still standing beside the open door, Treeborn rolled her eyes. Jackie wished she was brave enough to make a stand, to point out that she'd cooperated and should now be entitled to leave. Instead, she shuffled through the door like an obedient dog.

"Andrew," Jackie said, rushing into the small windowless room.

Seeing him sitting at the small table after hours in what felt like a hostile environment was like coming out of the dark and into a patch of light. Warm light.

"Are you okay?" he asked, gesturing to the chair opposite him.

Jackie nodded and dragged a hand through her hair as she folded herself into the seat. The room smelled of polony meat and coffee. The combination of odours was so strong that it almost made her gag.

"I told Detective Drommel you'd be willing to share any information you have on Detective Pope's whereabouts." Andrew paused. "Do you know anything about what happened to her?"

Jackie pressed a hand to her stomach and closed her eyes, determined to keep her emotions under control. He was actually asking her if she'd done something to the policewoman. Only hours ago he'd been on her side and now he was treating her like she was as guilty as everyone believed.

"How can you ask me that?" She tried to keep the hurt out of her voice, but couldn't stop the tremor. "Do you really think I'm capable of what they're suggesting?"

The solicitor's blue eyes looked almost black under the florescent lights. "I'm sorry if you don't like the questions, but they're ones I have to ask," he said with no trace of an apology. "In five minutes Drommel will walk through that door expecting answers. And," – he pointed to the camera positioned high up in the corner – "that light will come on. So, if you want to walk out of here today, tell me what happened yesterday evening."

His terseness took her by surprise, but what choice did she have but to do as he said and trust him? Helen had trusted him enough to put her estate in his hands. Besides, there was no one else.

"I was asleep," Jackie said. "I heard someone knocking the door. I didn't want to answer. You see, I'd had a nightmare and I thought..." She put her hands on the table and spread her fingers wide. "I don't know what I thought, but I didn't want to open the door."

She spoke quickly, trying to get it all out before the detective returned. When she reached the part where Rick attacked her, she thought she saw Andrew's expression stiffen, but it could have been the shadows cast by the unforgiving lights.

Five minutes later Detective Drommel opened the door. If possible, he looked more dishevelled than he had when he had arrived at her home. Flecks of grey in the man's stubble gave him a haggard look. Despite her situation and Drommel's obvious dislike for her, Jackie felt a stab of sympathy towards him. Whatever she thought of him, Drommel was clearly distressed about his missing partner. When he approached the table, Andrew stood and moved to Jackie's side so he was sitting next to her as they both faced the detective.

Andrew was the first to speak. "My client has agreed to give you a statement, but only as it pertains to the search for Detective Pope. Miss Winter wants to cooperate, but she won't be answering any questions relating to the death of Margaret Green," Andrew said, and held the detective's gaze for a second. "Are we clear?"

"Perfectly," Drommel said, and turned to Jackie. "Okay, let's hear it."

He was angry; she could see it in the upward tilt of his chin and the clench of his jaw.

Nervous at first, Jackie began recounting events from the previous afternoon, how she woke from a nightmare to the sound of knocking. As she spoke, retelling the humiliating encounter with Rick, she began to find some confidence. Not much, but enough for her to garner the strength to meet Drommel's eyes as she recounted the things Rick had said and how Lena came to her rescue.

"Can you tell me why Detective Pope's car was parked a few streets from your home in the exact spot where Margaret Green's car and body were found?" Drommel asked, never taking his eyes off Jackie's face.

Shocked, Jackie sucked in a breath. "I don't—"

"That's it," Andrew said, leaning forward. "We agreed there'd be no questions concerning Margaret Green." He looked at his watch. "This has gone on long enough. I'm taking my client home."

Rather than protest, Drommel sat back in his seat, his hands raised in surrender. "By all means, feel free to leave, but we will be in touch." There was a challenge in the detective's voice, one that chilled Jackie to the bone. Andrew, however, simply shrugged and took hold of Jackie's arm, leading her out of the room and, in a few minutes, out of the building.

Andrew's car had been parked in the sun, so when Jackie sat in the passenger seat, she did so soaking in the warmth. Pushing away the questions that swarmed her mind, she closed her eyes and let the sun shine on her lids, trying to imagine she was somewhere far from the grey building that she'd just exited, somewhere clean and grassy while lying on her back under the afternoon sun.

"We're going to my office." Andrew's voice cut through her reverie.

"No." Jackie sat forward, her hand reaching for the door. "I want to go home."

"I'll take you home, but not until we've had time to talk. If you don't want to go to my office, we'll go somewhere else, but not your house, not yet," he insisted.

Jackie began to protest, but Andrew raised a hand to silence her.

"It's not unusual for the police to install listening devices. God knows they've had plenty of time to do it while they made a big song and dance of fingerprinting and photographing you."

"Can they do that?" Jackie asked, appalled at the idea of someone listening to her every movement when she thought she was alone in her home.

"Yes, and not just in the house," he said, starting the car. "From now on you need to be careful what you say on the phone."

If the gravity of the situation hadn't fully hit her during the hours she'd spent at Central Processing, the idea of faceless men monitoring her phone and house drove the magnitude of her predicament home, making the warmth she'd enjoyed only a moment ago slip away until she was shivering.

"I want to help you, Jackie," Andrew said. "But you need to be honest with me. I know you're holding something back. Whatever it is, it's time to level with me."

Chapter Twenty-five

1986

Summer nights in Perth always pulsated with the songs of sandgropers and crickets, an insectile music that caught on the sea breeze under unblemished skies. Helen had missed those nights, not because she'd been away too often but because when she *was* home, the next story always dominated her thoughts. Now, with Mike settling his child in her guest bedroom and the radio playing softly, she could imagine nowhere she'd rather be.

"He's out like a light," Mike said, stepping onto the patio.

Helen took a sip of her wine and watched him pour himself a glass.

"I see you still drink the cheap stuff," Mike said with a wry smile, then held up his glass and regarded the pale liquid.

"Australian wine is underrated," Helen said. It was a familiar response, one that came almost absent-mindedly.

Instead of turning on the outside lights, she'd lit candles around the pool, enjoying the way the soft yellow light turned her suburban garden into a dreamy oasis. As much as she loved the eighties with its swiftly evolving technology and changing political climate, part of her longed for the early seventies and a more naïve way of life. The music was sweeter and the clothes soft and feminine, and love was fearless, not deadly.

"What's wrong?" Mike asked, coming towards her. "I've overwhelmed you, haven't I? I shouldn't have put so much on you so quickly."

"No. No." Helen blinked back tears. "It's nothing like that, really. I don't know why, but I'm feeling sentimental." She laughed, not because it was funny but because sentimentality was something she'd always thought was a luxury of the old, and at forty-two she didn't feel old.

He took her hand and led her to the table. Feeling his skin against hers brought with it a flood of memories and for a moment she thought he might be right, that all this *was* too much. Too many emotions, too many memories both good and bad between them. Needing something to do with her hands, she pulled a cigarette out of the packet and put it between her lips. As she moved, he picked up her lighter and held the flame for her. In response, she dipped her head to the light, cupping his hand.

It was a small thing, something they'd done hundreds of times over the years, a movement so familiar and somehow intimate that the connection couldn't be denied. They were like magnetised pieces fitting into place so perfectly that she knew she had to be honest and forget her romantic notions of a happily ever after. If she wasn't honest now, those pieces would become jagged and broken.

"I don't want to be responsible for breaking up your marriage," Helen said, blowing out a plume of smoke. "I don't want your son to grow up hating us both for what we're thinking of doing. I'd rather be alone than cause misery or hatred."

"My marriage is already over," Mike said with a bitter laugh. "I should have seen that long ago. I did see it, but..."

There was sorrow in his voice. Hearing him like this made her want to weep, but she had to be strong. Helen wouldn't let herself be his solace, not again.

"So, what's changed?" She sounded callous, but didn't want to pull her punches, not with him. "Why now?"

He scrubbed a hand over his face. "Nothing. Everything. God knows I'm not perfect, but Kathleen just keeps getting worse. I've only stayed this long out of guilt, and for Chrissy."

He didn't need to explain his feelings of guilt; they both knew what they'd done. Helen had always been upfront about putting her career first, but when she refused to marry him, Mike took it hard. They argued and made up, then argued some more. The bitter feelings and resentment grew until Helen couldn't take it anymore. She walked away and cut him out of her life.

Mike met Kathleen when he was in England covering Wimbledon. Kathleen was a talented young tennis player with a promising future. While Helen had never wanted to know the details of Mike's relationship, she knew from friends in the industry that only a few months into their relationship Kathleen became pregnant. Hearing of Mike's marriage had nearly broken Helen. His newfound happiness was a double-edged sword, making her both happy that he finally had what he wanted but at the same time grief-stricken because Kathleen was younger – so much younger and able to give him something Helen never could.

Then, only months after Mike and Kathleen were married, Kathleen had a minor car accident and lost the baby. When Mike turned up on Helen's doorstep late one night, Helen meant to turn him away. She tried to steel herself and send him back to his young wife, but seeing him so wracked with pain, Helen couldn't let him go. While Kathleen was in hospital struggling with depression, Mike was in Helen's bed. Cheating was too small a word for what they did. They fell in love again, or so Helen thought.

Mike returned to Kathleen, intent on ending their marriage, but five weeks later he phoned Helen and told her Kathleen was pregnant again. The memory of that phone call, the way his voice cracked as he said the words was like a tidal wave crashing over her. Even now, four years later, listening to him tell her his marriage was over, Helen could still feel the weight of those words and how they had almost destroyed her.

"I knew something was wrong with her right from the beginning, but I tried to blame her behaviour on her pregnancy," Mike said, staring at the pool. "Then after she lost the baby, I thought it was grief and depression, but I think she's sick. She's always been… unwell." He shook his head. "She told me there never was a baby, not in the first place."

"What?" Helen sat forward not sure she'd heard him correctly. "You mean she lied about being pregnant and losing the baby?"

"Not just then but also the second time," Mike answered. "When I left you to tell her it was over, I had a few drinks that first night and the next morning she was in bed next to me. I couldn't remember anything from the night before." He shrugged. "A few weeks later she told me she was pregnant, only none of it was true. I only slept with her once after that. She begged and I thought she was having my baby, so… And that's when she truly fell pregnant."

Helen felt unable to move. The things he was telling her were like punches, each blow hitting harder until her whole body felt numb. For years she believed Mike had betrayed her by going back to Kathleen and sleeping with her. A small dark part of Helen thought he might have lied to her about ever wanting to leave his wife. Lied and used her in the worst possible way, leaving her to languish in guilt and uncertainty. Telling herself that she had no right to feel cheated, not when she was the other woman, had been her only way to deal with it. Now, if what he was telling her was true, both she and Mike had been cheated.

"How... When did you find out?" Helen asked, still unsure of what to believe.

"About a year after Chrissy was born." He was looking at her now, the candlelight casting his face in shadows. "She was off her medication. One minute she'd be happy – too happy. The next she'd be paranoid and convinced I was seeing other women or... or the mailman was watching her and reporting back to the doctors at the hospital where she'd been treated. Out of the blue, she told me about the lies." He gave a bitter laugh. "She thought it was funny, a big joke and I was the idiot who fell for it. She can be so cruel, so single-minded."

Listening to him, hearing the anguish in his voice, Helen felt a sudden and fierce anger towards the woman who had played with their lives. For so long Helen had punished herself, believing she'd wronged a young innocent woman. There'd been opportunities for Helen to find happiness over the last four years. Not the sort of consuming passion she felt for Mike, but maybe a degree of contentment. Opportunities she turned her back on, believing she'd forfeited her right to happiness.

"If you knew, why did you stay?" she asked, wanting to say more. *Why didn't you tell me? Come back to me?*

"For Chrissy." His voice was flat, exhausted.

For the first time she noticed how tired he looked. How aged his face had become in just a few years. Any resentment she felt for him melted into concern. Helen reached out and took his hand. In response, Mike raised her fingers to his lips.

"All that's over now," he said, still holding her hand. "I've made an appointment with a solicitor. I know it's unusual for a father to be granted custody, but Kathleen's mental state will prohibit her from keeping Chrissy." He paused. "I don't expect you to jump back in, but maybe over time there's a chance we can start again?"

Time, Helen thought, had not been kind to them. She had no intention of leaving her fate in the hands of time ever again.

"I don't need to jump back in. I've never been out. You know that," Helen said. "We're in this together now."

She felt a small surge of fear, but also joy. A dizzy feeling of hope. There were many emotions, but not surprise because from the moment she heard Mike's voice on the telephone she'd known she was always in.

On the radio, a familiar tune caught her attention. One they'd danced to ten years earlier in an ancient city where they'd posed as a married couple so they could share a hotel room.

"Dance with me?" Mike said, walking rather awkwardly to the middle of the patio.

Helen laughed and shook her head even as she stood and moved into his arms. She'd almost forgotten how much he loved to dance, but not how wonderful it felt as she put her head on his shoulder and swayed. Still slightly dizzy, Helen relaxed and enjoyed the music and the feeling of being in another time and place. Maybe they'd hurt each other enough and now it was time to heal. She had no illusions that the road ahead would be easy, but for tonight she wanted nothing more than the feeling of his body against hers.

Chapter Twenty-six

Leaving the hulking city buildings behind, she wondered what Andrew was thinking and if he believed she was a killer. But for most of the drive Jackie was just grateful to be out of the police station and contented herself with listening to the radio and watching the city give way to the suburbs as the afternoon sun snaked in and out of a curtain of clouds.

With no idea where they were going, Jackie spotted the ocean and realised they were heading for the boardwalk and boat harbour.

"We need somewhere quiet where we don't have to worry about being overheard," he said, gesturing to the rows of boats crowding the grey jetty. "It's not as formal as the office, but it's a good place to talk."

He pulled into the nearly empty parking lot, drawing into a spot facing the circular bay. Even under the grey clouds the small stretch of sand gleamed impossibly white against the dark green of the Indian Ocean.

Stepping out of the car, the wind whipped Jackie's jumper against her body, but unlike the cold of the police station the sea air felt clean on her skin as the taste of salt touched her lips. The ocean always re-energised her. Even as a child it seemed like a place of healing. Why was it, she wondered, that she'd not thought of coming back to the beach after Helen died?

"Are you cold?" Andrew asked.

"No," Jackie said. "I feel awake." She turned to look at him. "Which one's yours?" She nodded to the row of crafts moored at the jetty.

Andrew's boat, *Long Daze*, was an ageing blue and white yacht that looked like it hadn't seen a lick of paint since the seventies. When he offered Jackie a steadying hand and led her below deck and into the shadows, she caught a whiff of diesel and damp.

"Take a seat," Andrew said, gesturing to the bench seat and table opposite the tiny galley kitchen, barely visible by the light from the overhead hatch. "As I said, it's not as formal as the office and as you can see, not as spacious either, but it's private."

"It's nice," Jackie said, sliding into the bench. "I haven't been on a boat in years. My father used to take me out in his boat. Nothing as big as this, just a half cabin, but he loved it. Some of my happiest memories were on that vessel." Jackie couldn't help smiling as she recalled the feeling of freedom that came with dropping anchor and plunging into the cold ocean.

"It must be nice," she began, "to be able to just pick up and head out to sea whenever you want."

"That's the plan." He pulled a cord over the sink and the cabin flooded with yellow light. "It's still a work in progress, so I haven't ventured far, but she's definitely seaworthy. With any luck and a bit of free time, I'll have her ready by the end of summer."

As he spoke, Andrew looked around the narrow space. There was an expression on his face, one of contentment and pride. Jackie would have never picked him as an outdoorsy type, but she saw that the setting suited him.

She found herself wishing they could just chat like this; pretend they were friends setting out on a sailing trip with nothing to worry about but the swell and where the day would take them. It was a nice dream but that's not why they were on the *Long Daze*. They weren't friends and this was never going to be a pleasure cruise.

He opened a panelled door next to the sink, revealing a compact fridge. "It's not running, but if you're happy with room temperature, I can offer you a cola?"

A few minutes later and with glasses of cola, they faced each other over the small table.

"Tell me what happened between you and Margaret Green?" he asked.

Jackie knew the question was coming, but suddenly she felt unprepared. With less than half a metre between them, the closeness of the cabin made the conversation seem intimate. Andrew looked larger in the small space; his shoulders almost blocked the rest of the cabin from view. Her practiced story about not seeing Margaret after that last day at school died on her lips.

"I killed her." Jackie didn't want to look him in the eyes and see horror, so she kept her gaze on the glass of cola.

For a moment there was silence. Maybe he was too shocked to speak or perhaps he was still processing her confession. Whatever it was, she wished he'd say something. Anything that would fill the silence.

"All right." Andrew spoke slowly, his tone calm. "Tell me how it happened."

Jackie let out a long breath and began speaking. Surprisingly, the words came easily, tumbling out in a steady stream. As she spoke, the weight of the truth lightened and she realised how much she'd longed to share her story. How liberating it was to finally let it all out.

She talked for almost half an hour, only stopping to sip cola when her throat became dry. In that time Andrew sat unmoving with his eyes on her face. If he was repulsed by what she told him, he gave no sign. The only time his expression changed was when she recounted the moment at the river when she'd lost her temper and began hitting

Margaret. His eyes narrowed as though they were straining to see the confrontation in his mind.

"I left," Jackie said. "Just ran home and tried to forget it ever happened. I almost convinced myself it was just a nightmare... Until the police showed up."

She could feel the boat moving, a gentle motion, but the shifting reminded her of the moment she'd opened the front door to two detectives. After a second she became aware of Andrew's silence and wondered if he was trying to find a way to tell her she'd have to find another solicitor. Not that she'd blame him. He was supposed to be dealing with her aunt's estate and now he was sitting across from a murderer. No, she corrected herself. She hadn't meant to kill Margaret. That had to count for something, didn't it?

"Say something." Jackie tried to keep the desperation out of her voice, but sitting facing him after bearing her soul was like being naked. She felt exposed in the most unbearable way.

"You said you hit her?" Andrew spoke slowly. "With your hand? Your fist?"

He was asking for details – details she hated thinking about, but it was better than anger or disgust.

"I... I slapped her, hard," Jackie said, closing her eyes. "Then..." She dropped her face into her hands and rubbed her fingertips over her eyes trying to scrub the image of Margaret's face away.

"What did you hit her with?" Andrew's voice was sharp – urgent.

"I punched her." Jackie didn't want to cry, but could feel her throat tightening. "I punched her in the mouth and... and she fell. There was blood on her lips. I'd never punched anyone before. I never thought I was capable of that sort of violence, but she wouldn't leave me alone. And... and Margaret just sat on the grass staring up at me, so I ran."

"So, she was alive the last time you saw her?" he asked.

Jackie nodded, knowing that didn't mean that the blows hadn't killed the woman.

"She was alive," Jackie said, "But the police said they found her in her car, so she must have staggered back to her vehicle and then…" It was difficult to say the words. "She died in her car alone because of me."

The tears she'd been holding back fell. With nothing to mop them away with, she used the heels of her hands.

Andrew stood and rummaged through one of the cupboards over the sink. "Here." He handed her a handful of paper napkins.

He was still being kind, even after hearing what she'd done. Jackie felt a pathetic sense of gratitude and a fresh stream of tears ran down her cheeks.

"Look at this." Andrew sat down and pulled the search warrant from the inside pocket of his jacket. "They've listed certain items such as coats and jackets." He placed the document on the table and turned it in Jackie's direction.

"That tells me," he continued, "that they're looking for something you wore that might have traces of Margaret's blood or DNA. But they've also listed tools – a kitchen mallet and lengths of pipe or solid cylindrical items."

He was excited. She could hear it in his voice, but so far she wasn't sure what he was getting at.

"They're looking for a murder weapon. Something solid and heavy." He tapped the page.

Jackie wiped her eyes and looked from Andrew's face to the paper. Her pulse jumped as she began to understand what he was telling her.

"You may have had a physical altercation with Margaret Green," Andrew began, "but you didn't kill her."

Chapter Twenty-seven

Unable to stomach another mouthful of coffee, Jim Drommel sat at his desk swirling the dregs of his fifth cup in one hand while replaying the interview with Jacqueline Winter in his mind. The two uniforms he'd sent to speak to the neighbour said the old lady confirmed Winter's story. But Winter hadn't told him everything; of that he was sure. Yet, when he told her Veronika was missing, Winter's surprise seemed genuine; *or* lack of sleep was clouding his judgement.

Grimacing with disgust, he set the almost empty cup down on his desk. So far, the only trace they'd found of Veronika was her car. And the most telling part about discovering the detective's vehicle was finding her phone in the console. Leaving your phone behind while on duty was unheard of. Even off the clock most cops kept their phones within reach at all times. He was certain Veronika wouldn't have gone anywhere without her phone. Not willingly.

"Marclowe's still not answering," Stacy said, approaching his desk. "I tried his work number, but they haven't seen or heard from him in a few days. Marclowe's uncle owns the business and I got the impression that it's

163

not unusual for his nephew to disappear. In fact, the uncle didn't seem surprised to hear from the police."

Jim stood and grabbed his jacket. "Let's drop by the undertaker's house and see why he's too busy to answer his phone."

* * *

Fredrick Marclowe's house was on a quiet street on the edge of an industrial area. Like Jacqueline Winter's place, the home was long-standing. But, Jim noted, age was where the similarity between the houses ended. Marclowe's home was in disrepair and the dusty front yard overlooked an ageing warehouse and an auto repair shop's side wall where graffiti had been sprayed over with uneven splats of black paint. The half-hearted clean-up job added to the area's derelict appearance, giving the place an inhospitable feel.

Fredrick Marclowe had two previous convictions, one for assault and the other for dangerous driving. One look at the detective's dark sedan might tip the man off and send him running out the back door. With this in mind, Jim was careful to park one house back from the corner so if Marclowe happened to look out the front window, he wouldn't see the vehicle.

"What do you think?" Stacy asked from the passenger's seat.

"I think I'm not going to waste time getting a search warrant," Jim said, unbuckling his seat belt. "Once we get inside, I need you to keep an eye on Marclowe while I look around."

He knew he was asking her to bend the rules, but they both liked and admired Veronika. If she was in Marclowe's house, they owed it to her to do everything they could to find her. *No*, Jim corrected himself. He owed it to her. He should have been with her when she went to talk to Winter. Even though dropping by Jacqueline Winter's house seemed a low risk, she was still a suspect in a murder investigation. It didn't matter that Veronika was the lead officer. Jim should have voiced his concerns. With each passing hour it seemed like he'd have to live with the guilt of not speaking up.

"Got it," Stacy said without hesitation.

After a few minutes of knocking, a bleary-eyed Marclowe opened the front door. A look crossed the man's face, one Jim had seen countless times before – calculation. The expression told Jim that Marclowe wasn't surprised to see two cops on his doorstep. Maybe he'd even been expecting a visit.

"I'm Detective Drommel and this is Detective Newport," Jim said, holding up his ID. "Can we come in and ask you a few questions about Jacqueline Winter?"

As Marclowe's gaze bounced between the two detectives, Jim placed his free hand on the door and took a half-step forward. If the undertaker tried to shut the door, Jim was more than ready to force his way in. But rather than try to keep them out, Marclowe's shoulders slumped and his hand fell away from the door.

"Okay, come in if you want," Marclowe said, standing aside.

Beyond the entrance was a shabby sitting room dominated by a large screen TV. Judging by the collection of beer cans and crusty-looking takeaway tubs littering the coffee table, the undertaker had been on quite a bender.

"I didn't do anything to her," Marclowe said, slumping down onto the sofa. "I just didn't like the way she brushed me off. I only wanted to talk to her."

Jim took up a position, standing over the man while Stacy remained near the now closed front door. Every time Marclowe opened his mouth, Jim got a blast of beer-soaked breath.

"Is that why you were hanging around Jacqueline Winter's house yesterday evening?" Jim asked, looking down at the man. "Is that why you were angry?"

Marclowe's chin jerked up so he was staring up at Jim with wide wounded eyes. "It's not like that. I didn't do anything." The man's voice was high and petulant, his words slushy and running together. "Whatever she's saying is... is. Did she tell you how she couldn't wait to jump into bed with me?" Marclowe laughed. "No, I bet she forgot to mention that."

Jim put his hands on his hips trying to bite back the wave of disgust he felt towards the man. "We've got a statement from Miss Winter's neighbour. She says you attacked Jacqueline and tried to force your way inside her house."

Marclowe ran a shaky hand through his hair. Under the right circumstances, Jim supposed the man could have been considered quite attractive. But wearing stained jeans, a ripped T-shirt and stinking of alcohol, Fredrick Marclowe looked like someone struggling to hold himself together. It wasn't a great leap to imagine that a man whose life was falling apart might do something desperate – something out of character. Jim didn't have Veronika's instincts for the truth, but she had taught him that the most obvious person isn't always the guilty one. Maybe they were off-base about Winter and it was Fredrick Marclowe who had something to do with what happened to Margaret Green. But with the clock ticking, Jim's focus was on finding his partner.

Jim also knew that Veronika didn't allow intimidation tactics, but when he spoke to Mary-Lynn and heard the barely concealed terror in Veronika's mother's voice, he'd made the decision to do whatever it took to find his partner.

"Tell me about Detective Pope?" Jim lowered his voice and bent forward so his face was looming over Fredrick. "You were angry when you saw her at Jacqueline's house. Jacqueline had rejected you and the old lady next door told you to piss off. That must have made you want to hurt someone. Maybe you were sick of women telling you what to do. Is that what happened? Is that why you attacked Detective Pope?"

"No. No, I didn't attack anyone." Marclowe's voice was clearer, as if the gravity of the situation was sobering him up. "I don't know who you're talking about... I wouldn't—"

"Where is she, Fredrick?" Drommel asked, using the man's first name. "This will go easier for you if you tell me where she is."

It wasn't until that moment, while waiting for Marclowe to tell them where he'd dumped Veronika's body, that Jim let himself consider that she might be dead. The idea of Veronika, a brilliant detective and possibly the best partner he'd ever worked with, snuffed out by a weasel like Marclowe made him want to hurt the man. Fury made him want to smash his fist into Marclowe's pretty boy face. A feeling Jim had never encountered in all his twelve years on the force. But it was one that was so powerful he could almost see himself grabbing the man's T-shirt and wrenching him off the couch.

"No, I don't know where she is." Marclowe was crying now and shrinking back into the sofa, as if he could sense Jim's thoughts. "I swear I haven't hurt anyone."

Jim straightened up and jerked his chin at Stacy, indicating for her to step forward. Marclowe, maybe sensing the tenseness of the situation, didn't object while the detective exited the sitting room and began searching the house.

Ten minutes later Jim returned to find Marclowe had recovered some of his composure and was sitting on the edge of the sofa speaking to Stacy in a hushed voice.

"Why's that room off the sleep-out locked?" Jim asked.

He could feel the blood rushing in his ears and the adrenaline coursing through his body, making him jumpy. On finding the locked room, his first instinct was to try and kick the door in, but he'd forced himself to calm down and think through his next move.

If Veronika was in the room, she could be on the other side of the door. Breaking through by force might injure her. Pushing his earlier thoughts aside, Jim was determined he would find his partner alive. Until he had proof otherwise, he would operate under the assumption Veronika was very much alive and in need of assistance.

For a moment Marclowe simply stared and Jim noticed the look of calculation creeping back into the undertaker's bleary eyes. The confused drunk seemed to be slipping away, replaced by a man that was watchful and almost hyper-alert.

"Do you have a search warrant?" Marclowe spoke slowly with almost forced confidence.

Before Jim could respond, Stacy grabbed the man under the arm and jerked him off the sofa.

"Where's the fucking key?" Stacy demanded. She was shorter than Marclowe, but broad shouldered and muscular from hours spent in the gym. She easily managed to pull the man to his feet.

Marclowe tried to shrug Stacy off, but when she clung onto the undertaker's shoulder, he looked over her head towards Jim.

"Call your dyke partner off and come back with a warrant." He sounded less confident now as Stacy reached behind her back and produced a pair of handcuffs.

Despite the urgency of the situation, Jim couldn't help being impressed by Stacy's ability to handle the man. This was the first time he'd worked with the detective constable, and while he had no doubt she was smart and capable, he was surprised by how effortlessly she took control of the situation.

With Marclowe's hands secured behind his back, Stacy pushed the man back down onto the sofa. "Key." She snapped her fingers in front of the man's face. "Don't make me ask again."

"You can't do this. I want you both out of my house." Marclowe turned to Jim, hoping he would intervene as

Stacy took hold of the undertaker's chin and wrenched his face back in her direction.

"Don't look at him." Stacy's voice was like ice. "Look at me and understand what's about to happen."

Jim merely shrugged. He was doing his best to look unfazed, but every muscle in his body was itching to return to the locked door and kick it in. And something else was beginning to dawn on him – a smell.

Chapter Twenty-eight

Lucidity moved with quicksilver speed. Clarity came in and dropped out at a terrifying pace until the only thing Veronika was sure of was the bar of light under the door. She tried to remember what she'd been sure of before everything went dark, but that area was like a misty forest: a place of shadows and fog and not a place she wanted to revisit.

There was pain. She remembered the pain. It was still there, not as bad, but threatening to flare up at the slightest movement. But for now the light was under the door and her eyes were open. Veronika took a breath, letting the air slip over her papery tongue. She needed water. Water and medical help. Her mind was clearer and better able to understand her predicament. How she came to be in this hell and who put her here was still hidden in the forest that was her memory.

It seemed like she'd been staring at the light for hours when she heard the voices. Not even voices at first and more of a ripple under water. Then louder, morphing into a man's voice. A familiar voice joined by a woman.

Veronika lifted her right hand, groping at the darkness and the sound of voices. They were close and moving towards her, but not on the other side of the door. Maybe a room away. The idea of help made her jolt and instantly regret the movement.

"Help me," Veronika shouted, realising the words were loud inside her head but little more than a rush of air on her lips.

She mouthed the words a second time, tears filling her eyes and blurring the light. *Please, I'm all alone.* Blinking away the stream that filled her vision, she thought she heard her name being uttered.

"Pope."

The word was so clear it made her tears flow harder. *I'm here.* She thought she managed to put more strength into the words but couldn't be sure. Had they heard her? She wanted to scream. She wanted to call her son's name and let whoever was nearby know she was a mother. Still listening to the voices, she remembered something else. Something swinging into view like the moon. Something silvery moving with speed. And then a door slammed or maybe thunder clapped and the lucidity she'd been clinging to slipped from her grasp.

* * *

She wasn't responsible for Margaret's death. At least Andrew didn't believe she'd delivered the killing blow. If what he'd told her was correct, the nightmare she'd been living since the police first arrived on her doorstep might soon be over. Jackie watched Andrew talking to the waiter and couldn't help smiling.

"You look a lot brighter," Andrew said when the waiter left their table with their order.

With his jacket draped over the back of his chair and his sleeves rolled up, he looked more relaxed than he'd been when talking about the case. Now, Jackie could imagine Andrew working on his boat or sailing into the harbour.

"I feel like I've been given a second chance at life. All this time believing I'd…" She hesitated, glanced around the almost empty restaurant and lowered her voice. "Believing I'd killed someone. I can't explain what it means to me. I'm so grateful to you," she said.

Andrew gave a tight smile. "It's not over yet. We still have to prepare a statement for the police. And," he said, matching Jackie's guarded tone, "someone killed Margaret Green. It could be that that someone is the person who's been following you. As if that wasn't enough, now the lead detective on the case is missing. Until we know exactly what's going on, you need to be very cautious. Cautious with your safety *and* with what you say to the police."

He was right. Something very strange was going on. With Detective Pope still missing, Jackie felt a jolt of guilt. She'd been so relieved when Andrew told her she hadn't killed Margaret, she hadn't stopped to think about the detective and what her family must be going through.

For a moment neither of them spoke. Instead, Jackie let her gaze travel around the small bistro. Whoever killed Margaret and abducted Detective Pope could be watching them right now. Jackie's mind went to the figure in the black raincoat. He could have followed them along the boardwalk from Andrew's boat to the restaurant. She told herself she was being paranoid. The jetty had been deserted. Surely they would have spotted someone watching them.

"I'm sorry if I've upset you," Andrew said. "But it's my job to make you aware of all aspects of this case."

Before Jackie could respond, the waiter arrived and set their food on the table. Just as Andrew had promised, the cosy bistro served excellent pasta. Despite the day's tumultuous events, Jackie found herself really hungry for the first time in weeks and was content to eat without conversation for a few minutes.

"Do you think any of what's going on has anything to do with my aunt?" she asked.

Jackie watched Andrew lift his fork then set it back down on his plate. There was a crease between his dark brows, suggesting he was thinking.

"With Helen?" Andrew's navy eyes were thoughtful. "How do you mean?"

Jackie wasn't quite sure what she meant, only that despite everything that was going on, she still felt that the photos and the child's shoe were important somehow. And now, thinking over what Andrew had said about her aunt, something strange occurred to her.

"I'm not sure." Jackie set down her fork. "You said you knew Helen from years ago."

Andrew leaned forward, his chin jerked up and down in agreement. There was something attentive and concerned in the way he regarded her that sparked a surge of affection towards him. Maybe it was because he'd come to her aid earlier when the police were searching her house, or it could have been because he'd told her she wasn't a killer. Whatever the reason, she liked being in his company. More than liked it. She felt safe and at ease with him in a way she hadn't experienced before.

"You said you knew my aunt when you were young and then you mentioned not practicing criminal law since your younger days. Is that how you first met Helen?" Jackie asked. "Was it on a criminal case?"

For a moment Andrew held her gaze but didn't answer, making Jackie wonder if he was trying to decide how much he should reveal.

"I don't see how it could have anything to do with what's going on now." He spread his hands wide. "It was a long time ago, Jackie. Your aunt was going through some really painful stuff. I don't think she'd want it all dredged up again."

Even though Helen was gone, Andrew still felt the need to protect her. Jackie couldn't help but admire the solicitor's loyalty, even if it did make it difficult for her to find out what she needed to know.

"I know," Jackie tried again. "But I've found some things in the house. Photos and a child's shoe."

At the mention of the shoe she thought she saw Andrew's posture change, or maybe he was just tired. It had been a long day for both of them. Perhaps she was asking too much.

"I'm sorry," Jackie said and set her napkin on the table. "You've already done so much for me, but I've no one else to ask. My mother is never around and even when she is… Well, she's not that interested. I loved Aunt Helen so much. I just want to understand her life."

She was babbling now, revealing more about herself and her situation than she'd intended.

"If she had a child, I don't understand why she never told me. I wouldn't have judged her. I just wish…" She stopped herself, knowing if she went on there'd be tears.

"She didn't have a child," Andrew said and ran his hand over the back of his neck. "My guess is the shoe belonged to a little boy named Christopher West. Helen was in love with the boy's father."

At some points in the story, Andrew's voice was thick with emotion. By the time he finished, his eyes were shiny. Perhaps from fatigue but more likely because the things he revealed were still difficult for him to talk about. And for Jackie, the details of her aunt's heartbreak were crushing. As she listened, she wished she'd never found the shoe or the photos.

Chapter Twenty-nine

1986

It had been years since she'd woken up with someone in her bed. There had been men in her life, but they were brief episodes, meaningless encounters where Helen was always careful to extricate herself before dawn; walking dim hallways and silent hotel lobbies, head held high despite the emptiness in her chest.

Today she allowed herself time to luxuriate in the shared warmth of their bodies while listening to a charm of restless magpies warbling their morning song. The noise was so bound to her childhood and life in the West that sometimes, in strange cities, she dreamed of the sound.

Mike was asleep on his stomach. While there was more grey in his hair and deeper lines on his once flawless face, sleep had erased many of the signs of ageing, returning his face to that of a younger, untroubled man. Watching him, Helen felt an almost physical ache. An aching need to touch him and also to protect him.

As if sensing her gaze, Mike woke and gave a slow smile. It was an expression she'd missed and one that made her laugh.

"What time is it?" he asked, reaching out and running his fingers over her bare shoulder.

Helen grabbed her watch from the nightstand. "Almost seven o'clock."

For a moment Mike seemed confused. "Jesus! Chrissy will be up."

He flung back the covers and snatched his jeans off the floor, pushing his feet into the trousers and almost stumbling as he stood. Helen watched him, surprised by his sudden jolt into wakefulness. In her experience, Mike liked to take his time waking up and was more inclined to fall back to sleep, then spend hours reading the newspaper and sipping coffee after finally getting up.

Before dashing from the room, he paused and planted a kiss on her head. "Three-year-olds don't sleep in."

This new life would be a learning experience, Helen told herself. Still smiling, she heard Mike calling to his son. At first his voice was gentle, lighthearted, but then the tenor changed and became urgent.

"Chrissy? Chrissy, where are you?" Mike's calls echoed through the house in a way that set Helen's nerves on edge.

"Mike?" Helen was out of bed and pulling on her robe. "Is everything okay?"

Mike didn't lose his cool easily, so when he appeared in the doorway, hair wild and a look of panic on his face, Helen's heart took a sickening leap.

"I can't find him. He's not..." Before Mike could finish, he was already turning and rushing towards the kitchen.

As she followed, Helen could hear Mike's footfalls across the kitchen floor. *He's fine. He's okay and just playing somewhere. Just hiding.* The reassurances kept tumbling through her mind even as a sense of dread squeezed at her chest.

The back door slammed open. Helen raced into the kitchen just in time to see Mike barrelling out the back door. *The back door, was it locked?* Did they even remember to close it? The night before was a blur of music, wine and sex.

Helen stopped just short of the doorway. The morning sun was streaming into the kitchen and somewhere outside birds were still singing. The birdsong and the golden light seemed threatening now, somehow sinister. The idea of passing through that doorway and seeing what was on the other side made Helen's stomach churn.

"Chrissy!" Mike's voice was a roar of panic.

Helen made herself keep moving. She forced her feet to step out onto the patio. When a thunderous splash exploded from the pool, the spell that slowed her progress vanished and Helen was running.

Mike was in the water. For a moment Helen thought he was carrying a bag and then her mind recognised the stupidity of her misconception. It wasn't a bag hanging limply in Mike's arms like a bundle of sodden cloth, but a child. A child draped in dripping wet Superman pyjamas.

"Call an ambulance!" Mike screamed, his voice hoarse and terrified.

Before she turned to run back into the house, Helen caught a glimpse of Chrissy's face. As she ran for the study, the little boy's blue skin and slack mouth filled her mind.

Speaking to the operator was like trying to shout into wind. Helen's breathing was so ragged that the words were difficult to form and the receiver shook in her hand. With instructions to find out if Chrissy was breathing, Helen left the phone off the hook and jogged back outside.

Mike was on the ground, his son cradled in his arms. "Come on Chrissy. Come on, love. Chrissy, come on." Mike spoke the words over and over, his voice cracked and raw.

"Is he breathing?" Helen began approaching but hesitated.

"Come on, sweetheart, open your eyes." Mike was patting his son's cheek.

"Mike!" Helen screamed the name. "Is he breathing?"

He didn't answer but when he looked up there was anguish in his eyes, dark and horrific. A look of agony. A look Helen had seen in war-torn countries and on the faces of those left behind after the worst natural disasters had struck. It was an expression of living death.

* * *

They didn't talk to each other; there was nothing to say. No words could adequately sum up what they'd experienced. Mike had shown little movement since the police and ambulance arrived. When it was time for them to take Chrissy, Mike exploded, howling like a wounded animal and refusing to let his son go. It was then that Helen had wrapped her arms around him, running her hands over his hair and face. She whispered in his ear, nonsense words. Reassurances that meant nothing. Maybe it was the cadence of her voice or it could have been exhaustion, but finally Mike had let go of Chrissy's little body. Since then, he'd remained on the sofa in the sitting room, holding one of Chrissy's shoes. She couldn't remember seeing Mike go to the spare room, but somehow the tiny sandal was in his hand.

There were questions to be answered, explanations required. Helen did her best to give the police officers all the details while casting glances at Mike and the little blue shoe. Watching with anguish as the man who had been so alive with hope last night slipped out of the world and into a place where he was beyond reach.

She wanted the ordeal to end so she could hold Mike, do what little she could to comfort him. But as the day wore on and the police officers departed, Helen understood that Mike was beyond comfort.

She sat beside him and ran her fingers over his back, only to feel his muscles stiffen under her touch as his hand clamped over the shoe, squeezing the leather between his large fingers.

"Mike?" Speaking to him felt like an intrusion, but she had to try. "Do you want to lie down for a while, try to sleep?"

Her throat was tight, plugged with emotion. She couldn't let her grief or shock out. Grief was Mike's right. Any tears should be his.

"I should have made sure the door was locked," Mike said, staring at the shoe. "Why didn't I make sure the door was locked?"

When he turned his head and looked at her, it was worse than watching him stare at the shoe. His eyes were empty, devoid of light and hope.

Helen grappled for an answer. "It was an accident... Just a stupid accident." As she said the words, Helen heard how weak and hollow they sounded.

"I'm his father." Mike looked down at the shoe. "I *was* his father. I'm supposed to keep him safe." His shoulders shook. "I should have kept him safe."

Helen tried again to touch him, but he shrugged her off and stood. Still clutching the shoe, he headed for the door.

"I have to go and tell his mother. I can't let her hear it from someone else," he said without stopping.

Helen followed him to the front door, wanting to touch him but afraid he'd jerk away from her again. Afraid that if he looked at her, she'd see accusation in his eyes. After everything that had happened, that was the one thing she couldn't take. Mike's hatred would be the thing that would break her.

"Wait," she trailed after him. "You shouldn't be driving, let me..." She stopped herself, knowing how ridiculous the idea of her driving Mike to his wife would be. How harmful and callous it would be for them to show up together.

Mike stopped a moment with the front door open. "It's all right," he said, turning to look at her. "I have to do this, but I'll be back." His voice was calm, almost normal, and he seemed to be seeing her clearly for the first time since they woke that morning.

To Helen's relief there was no anger or recrimination in his voice. Before leaving he touched her face and she noticed how cold his hand was against her skin.

* * *

In the week that followed, Helen saw Mike only twice. Once when he returned to her the next day and spent a few fleeting minutes standing in the kitchen. In those moments his eyes were always moving, darting from her face to the back door then to the window. Searching out the pool, wanting to see it or maybe desperate to never view it again.

"I'm going to stay with Kathleen for a while," Mike said, pulling his gaze away from the back door. "Her mother's flying in from Sydney, but I can't leave her on her own." He folded his arms over his chest. "Not now."

"Yes, of course," Helen said, lighting another cigarette. "How are you feeling? Can I do—"

"I should go. She'll be wondering where I am. There's so much to take care of." Mike stopped, seeming to have lost his train of thought. "He was so little," he said. "His body was almost weightless in my arms." He held out his hands and Helen noticed they were shaking.

Without thinking, she stepped into his arms and pulled him into an embrace. For a second his body was rigid as though he meant to push her away, but instead he melted into her. For a while they stayed unmoving, Mike clinging to her while sobs wracked his body. Helen held him without speaking, trying to absorb some of his pain so it might be lessened in some way.

A moment later he stepped back and made an excuse to leave. Helen didn't try stop him. When he left, she let her own tears fall. Tears for Mike and the life they'd almost had, but mostly for the little boy she'd known for less than twelve hours.

Chapter Thirty

Jim hadn't noticed the stench when they first entered the house. Probably because the odour of beer and fried food permeated the air, but now the smell was unmistakable: blood and urine.

"Smell that?" Jim addressed the question to Stacy who frowned and nodded.

"Tell me where the fucking key is or I'll use the butt of my gun to knock your front teeth down your throat," she said, still holding Marclowe's chin.

Despite the urgency of the situation, Jim was alarmed by Stacy's ferociousness. Alarmed and also relieved she was on his side. If not for the raw anger in her voice, Jim would have laughed.

Marclowe, maybe picking up on Jim's uneasiness, began sputtering. "The key's in the kitchen under the kettle. But… but it wasn't my idea. I didn't want the bitch here." He pulled his face out of Stacy's grip. "I'm sorry I didn't do anything. I wanted to get rid of her. You have to believe me."

"Watch him," Jim said to Stacy.

His legs were heavy. Jogging the few steps back to the kitchen, his heart beat so hard that Jim pressed his hand to his chest. The smell was stronger now, a thick cloying odour that made him want to gag.

As Marclowe had said, the key was under the electric kettle. Jim snatched it up and stepped out to the annex. As he approached the locked door, he heard a sound. Faint at first, but clearly a whimper.

Despite the smell and the pained cry, Jim felt a moment's relief. Whatever shape she was in, whatever had been done to her, Veronika was alive. No matter how horrific her ordeal, they would deal with it. He'd help his partner deal with it.

His hands were shaking when he slid the key into the lock. There was another noise from beyond the door – scraping.

"Veronika," Jim said, turning the key and pushing the door open. "It's Jim, you're safe."

There were opaque louvre windows on the left wall draped in a length of faded green fabric. In the half-light of the window, the mess on the floor was in shadows. In the few seconds it took Jim's eyes to adjust to the gloom and comprehend what he was seeing, his racing heart gave an uncomfortable lurch.

"Oh, Jesus," Jim whispered as he let go of the door and clamped a hand over his mouth.

"Jim?" Stacy called from the other room. "You okay?"

"I'm okay." Jim realised he was whispering and raised his voice. "I need you to call for a couple of uniforms and the RSPCA."

Jim turned back to the room and lowered his voice as he entered. "It's okay, girl. I won't hurt you."

The female golden retriever, at least that's what Jim guessed the dog might be, lowered her head, pressing her ears close to her skull. As she moved, her chin covered the pup closest to her chest. There was terror in the dog's eyes as she twitched and whimpered, trying to cover her pup and preparing to receive a blow.

An injured bitch severely emaciated and with a litter of new-born pups wasn't what he'd expected to find. Part of him was relieved it wasn't Veronika lying in the filthy room, but the fear in the dog's eyes and the weeping cuts and wounds on her head and body struck at his heart in a way he wasn't prepared for.

As he crouched low still talking to the retriever, tears prickled his eyes. He'd seen a lot of shitty things in his career. Battered women, neglected children, even dead bodies, but something in the dog's eyes reached into his soul and stabbed at the place that still believed there was good in the world. In her panicked brown eyes, Jim could see all the beatings and neglect the animal had suffered while her tail wagged nervously and responded to the kindness in his voice. In that moment he'd never hated anyone in the way he felt about Fredrick Marclowe.

* * *

"What now?" Stacy asked, starting the car.

It had taken almost an hour to arrest Marclowe for animal cruelty and wait for the RSPCA officers to arrive and assess the dog and her pups. In that time Jim had managed to get himself together, but the incident had left him shaken in a way he hadn't experienced in years.

"We're back to square one," Jim said, rubbing his eyes. "It's almost five o'clock. Drop me back at the office and you can knock off for the day."

When Stacy pulled away from Marclowe's house, Jim let out a tired breath. He wanted to be as far away from the undertaker's house as possible before the sun went down. It wasn't fear but more a crawling feeling on his skin that he couldn't quite shake. A sense that he'd just encountered something truly evil that made him want to wash all of its traces away.

"You okay?" Stacy asked, turning onto the highway.

He was touched by her concern and at the same time he could tell by the way she gripped the wheel that seeing the dog in that condition had upset her, too.

"I'll be better after a shower." *And crawling into bed with my wife's arms around me*, he thought but didn't add. "How about you?"

"Sick to my stomach," she answered. "I know it happens, but I'll never understand how someone can do those things to a defenceless animal. I've got two dogs of my own." She glanced his way and he could see the tension in her face. "A Labradoodle and a Blue Heeler. When I think about what that dog has been through…" She tapped the steering wheel with her index finger. "I don't know, Jim. Maybe this job isn't for me."

He knew what she meant. He'd had more than a few moments where he'd wondered if he wanted to spend the rest of his working life seeing what the worst of humanity was capable of, but in the end didn't both their reactions to what they'd seen at Marclowe's house mean they were still human enough to make a real difference? Didn't it prove they could still feel for the victim?

Jim thought about telling Stacy that feeling sick meant they were still, to some degree, untainted. Instead, he went for gallows humour.

"That's funny. An hour ago you were ready to do some medieval dentistry on our friend, the undertaker," he said, raising his eyebrows.

Stacy let out a surprised bark of laughter and after a second Jim couldn't help but join in. There was release in the laughter as well as humour. It felt good to let some of the tension go, if only for a few minutes.

"Seriously," Stacy said. "I saw that thing about the teeth and the gun butt in a movie. It was the best I could come up with on the spot." She was half-smiling, half-grimacing as she watched the road. "Was it too much?"

The look on her face made Jim laugh harder. "You had *me* convinced."

***

With a cup of coffee sitting untouched on his desk, Jim tried to focus his eyes on the invoice of items seized from Jacqueline Winter's property. As far as he could see, the only thing close to a match for the murder weapon was an egg-shaped marble paperweight found in the study. But it didn't take an expert to see that the wound on Margaret Green's temple wasn't caused by something with smooth edges. Frustrated, he pushed back his chair and stood with his hands on the small of his back.

The lights in the other workrooms were off, leaving Jim's area a circle of illumination in the darkened offices. He'd assured Stacy he was leaving after he finished the paperwork on Fredrick Marclowe, but instead of heading home at 5:30 p.m., Jim had called his wife to let her know he'd be late. Just how late he hadn't said. And Julie, understanding that Veronika's disappearance was something he couldn't just switch off and put on hold until the following day, didn't ask. Nor had she pushed for information on the search. They'd been married for seven years and worry was evident in her voice. Not just concern for Veronika's safety. Jim knew the worry was for him and how he'd handle losing another partner.

Restless, he walked over to the windows and stared down at the lights of the city. Darkness came early in winter. He remembered Veronika once telling him that at night Perth seemed less civilised and that being so isolated made anything possible. He supposed that was true of most cities, yet none were as lonely as Perth. To drive to another capital city would take days and in between there was a lot of desert. So many places to lose someone. *Or get rid of a body.*

His phone vibrated in his pocket, pulling him out of his reverie. It was only twenty-four hours since Veronika was last seen and already every call held its own threat.

"Just wanted to update you on the mother and pups." The voice was unfamiliar but when the caller mentioned pups, Jim understood he was talking to RSPCA Inspector Rodney Edgerton.

"How's she going?" Jim asked, watching the dark streets below.

"Well," Rodney said, drawing out the word. "As you know two of the six pups were dead at the scene. Unfortunately, another died before we reached the vet's emergency rooms."

Jim shook his head, grateful he was alone. "Shit."

"Yeah. But the other three are still hanging in there and the mother's receiving treatment. Judging by her wounds and old scar tissue, the vet reckons she was used as bait for fighting dogs." The inspector sounded exhausted. "We've taken plenty of photos... Despite what she's been through, that Golden Retriever still has a very sweet disposition, so there's hope for her."

"Hope is good," Jim said, turning away from the window. "You've got my card so flick those photos to me and keep me updated on the dog."

"No worries." Rodney took a breath. "It's a good thing you found her when you did. The vet says much longer and we'd have lost her and all the pups."

A moment later, Jim hung up and put the phone on his desk. There really wasn't much left for him to do in terms of new leads. The case against Fredrick Marclowe for animal cruelty was solid and he'd all but admitted to being involved in a dog fighting ring. Now, the sensible thing for Jim to do would be to go home, eat, and get some rest. But the sensible thing didn't appeal to him. Not tonight. Not with Rodney's words still ringing in his ears: *It's a good thing you found her when you did, much longer and we'd have lost her.*

Jim picked up the now room-temperature coffee and took a gulp, grimacing as the bitter liquid filled his mouth. There had to be something he'd missed. Any little scrap of information that might move things forward. In that moment he wished he could work the case the way Veronika did, turning the pieces in her mind, sometimes staring at photos until nuances became ideas that clicked. She once mentioned a sense of ticking in her brain that intensified as the case progressed. All Jim could hear was the blood pounding in his ears.

Determined to keep going, he sat down at his desk and opened a new document. Maybe recounting everything that had happened since Veronika left the office the night before would clarify the course of events and shake something loose.

He'd received the call about Veronika not returning home at eleven last night and since then Jim hadn't slept. Now staring at the screen, he closed his eyes, willing the weariness away. After a few seconds he returned his gaze to the page and started typing.

Chapter Thirty-one

With so many unanswered texts, Jackie couldn't ignore the fact that she'd been operating in a fog of alcohol, guilt and fear for weeks. Back in her aunt's house amidst the mess of open drawers and cupboards left in the wake of the police search, she wondered if there really was a way out of the chaos she'd fallen into. It was only when she entered her bedroom and saw the laundry basket upended with its contents spilling onto the rug that she experienced a sense of reality like a jarring punch to the gut.

Cops – strangers – had picked through her dirty laundry. They'd handled her personal items, taking what they thought relevant. A flush of humiliation burned her skin. The time for lies and evasion was over. Tomorrow she would make a frank and honest statement to the police. While the idea of facing Detective Drommel again made her nervous, her worries were lessened by the knowledge that Andrew would be there to support her. And this time she would tell the truth.

She'd been a fool to think she could start a new life based on deceit, and reading the unanswered texts from Lisa made her realise there was something else she had to put right.

In the study, Jackie turned on her laptop and accessed her mailbox, finding amongst a flood of mail two unanswered emails from Jason at Thorn Publishing. The first was an offer to publish with a request for Jackie to call him as soon as possible to discuss the details. Jackie rubbed a hand across her lips and frowned. It would have been easier if Jason had decided to pass on the manuscript, then she wouldn't have to admit she'd tried to take credit for someone else's work. It would be even easier to face with a glass of wine. Almost as soon as her thoughts turned to how she could avoid the truth, Jackie stopped herself.

If she had any hope of putting everything that was wrong in her life right, wiggling out of the lies had to stop and so did the drinking. Since moving into Helen's house, drinking had become a way of hiding from the world – a destructive buttress that led to blackouts and, if she was honest with herself, a change in her behaviour. Thinking about her episode with Rick Marclowe made her shudder with repulsion towards the man she'd slept with, and for her own actions.

"No more," she said under her breath and clicked on the second email.

This time Jason suggested a time for her to call and hinted at the possibility of an advance. The publisher's enthusiasm was both exciting and overwhelming. Not giving herself time to overthink what she was about to do, Jackie fired off an email letting Jason know that the manuscript belonged to her late aunt and apologised for any misunderstanding. Before hitting *send*, she pressed her lips together and took a deep breath. It was still a half-wiggle – calling a lie a misunderstanding – but at least the truth about the ownership of the manuscript was out there.

Once the email was sent, she sat back in her chair and thought about Lisa. They'd been friends for a long time, yet Jackie had lied to Lisa and then had shut her out of her life. Sorting things out with her friend wouldn't be as easy as sending a quick email. The temptation to push the unpleasant thoughts from her mind took hold, but Jackie held fast to her determination to start putting her life in order. After what Andrew revealed about her aunt's life, Jackie realised a few things: she had to hold on to those she loved at all costs because nothing was guaranteed.

Feeling more focused than she had in months, she sent her friend a text apologising for not responding, and promised to explain everything in a few days.

To her surprise, Lisa responded almost immediately.

I'm worried about you. Just tell me you're okay?

Jackie stared at her friend's text, moved by the concern. Why, she wondered, did she keep cutting herself off from people? When Helen died, Jackie hadn't reached out to her best friend or even her mother. What did that say about her? Could it be that her feelings of abandonment were more about her own behaviour and her belief that her mother didn't care? Had Jackie distanced herself from the people closest to her so she didn't have to deal with perceived rejection? Could it be that her own feelings had isolated her more than anything her mother had actually done?

Her mother wasn't perfect, but she did the best she could. Wasn't that all anyone could do? Also, believing Lisa was the sort of fair-weather friend that wouldn't want to be involved when things got heavy, wasn't that just another way she had separated herself from anyone who could hurt her?

Still holding the phone, Jackie couldn't help but wonder about her brief but disastrous relationship with Rick; why had she turned to him and not the people in her life who really cared about her? Or maybe she turned to Rick because she could use him, take what she needed from him and keep him at arm's length. Rick was an asshole, but the idea of using him made Jackie sick with guilt. Contacting a man as unstable as Rick was too risky, but that didn't mean she couldn't make amends closer to home.

> *I'm sorry for worrying you, and knowing you care means so much. Just give me a few days and I promise we'll talk.*

Jackie sent the text to Lisa hoping that she really could make everything okay again. Then, tossing her phone on the desk, she went through the house and turned on the backyard lights.

With the moon only a faint crescent of silver draped in clouds, Jackie stepped onto the patio and surveyed the long grass. As always, the outline of the pool was visible. Only now, the kidney-shaped gouge seemed more like a ghostly reminder of the property's tragic past. Why, she wondered, did Helen stay in this place? How could she bear the constant reminder of so much loss?

She couldn't. That's why she had the pool filled in. Jackie wrapped her arms around herself and shivered. On the steps leading down to the pool was the spot where Helen had fallen, so close to the place where Christopher West lost his young life. Standing in the circle of illumination cast by the outside spotlight, Jackie thought she understood why Helen wrote *Kiss the Wall* and what the story really meant.

Helen had taken her pain and transformed it into something beautiful. Every hopeful and tragic page was a testament to her aunt's strength and belief that people are more than their actions, particularly the things they do in their darkest hours. Jackie hoped, for once, she could live up to her aunt's example and be more than the lies she told, and better than the screwed-up choices she'd made.

"I'm so sorry, Aunt Helen," Jackie whispered into the darkness.

Almost as soon as the words were out, the telephone rang. Not the familiar electronic sound of her mobile's ring tone, but an actual ring; an old-fashioned shrill, bell-like sound. Recognising the noise as the old push-button landline in the kitchen, Jackie rushed back inside.

The cream-coloured handset was mounted on the wall next to the fridge. It had been there as long as she could remember, but how long had it been since anyone had called on this number? As she approached the telephone, Jackie experienced a sense of disquiet — a feeling that something was off kilter. As she reached for the hand piece, the idea that she would hear her aunt's voice jumped into her mind. A strange notion that maybe by speaking to her under the moonlight, Jackie had somehow summoned her spirit.

"Hello, Jackie."

Hearing a woman's voice threw Jackie off balance. For a second she just stood there holding the receiver and staring at the shadow of the outside light as it fell on the kitchen window.

"It's Lena from next door."

Jackie let out a breath and slumped against the fridge. If she wasn't so rattled, she would have laughed out loud.

"Are you there?" Lena asked.

"Yes, I'm sorry," Jackie said, trying to get her nerves under control. "I just don't get many calls on the landline."

"Well, I wanted to talk to you about my visit from the police." There was ice in Lena's voice. "Can you come over?"

Until now, she hadn't thought about her neighbour being dragged into her mess. And, judging by Lena's voice, she wasn't happy about the situation.

"Look, I'm really sorry that you've been involved in this..." Jackie fumbled for the appropriate words to extricate herself from the situation. "I'm grateful for what you did last night, I really am, but—"

"There's something I have to tell you." The coldness had warmed a little. "It's about something one of the police officers said."

There was an urgency in Lena's voice that made Jackie wonder if she really was out of the woods. Maybe the police had found something in her house. Jackie's mind jumped to the puffer coat. After she'd seen the raincoat figure and she fell, Jackie recalled returning home and peeling off the puffer. It was the coat she'd worn when she had the confrontation with Margaret. Was Lena calling to tell her the police had found Margaret's blood on her coat?

"What did he say?" Jackie asked, trying to sound less afraid than she felt.

"Look, I can't explain on the phone. Come over." Lena huffed out a breath. "Or don't. It's up to you. I'm just trying to help."

Jackie recognised the finality in Lena's tone. It was clear she wanted to tell her the news face-to-face.

After a slight pause, Jackie answered. "Okay. I'll be there in five minutes."

Chapter Thirty-two

Tony was calling for her, but she'd not long come off a late shift and found it almost impossible to lift her head from the pillow. Still, he persevered, his childish voice pained and afraid. She could tell by the woeful tone of his cries that the ear infection which had persisted for weeks was back. Briefly, she wondered why her mother hadn't intervened so Veronika could catch up on her sleep. But almost as soon as the thought occurred to her, a rush of guilt followed.

Tony was her son. It didn't matter she was only nineteen when he'd been born. The responsibility was hers. Her mother had done more than anyone could ask by allowing Veronika to stay at home so they could share the job of raising Tony together. Because of Mary-Lynn, Veronika was able to enter the police academy and work at a job she loved – a job that called for punishing shifts and late hours. Yet, sometimes – just sometimes – Veronika wished she could be like other twenty-three-year-olds and think only of herself.

What she couldn't understand was why she was having such a hard time opening her eyes and sitting up. Another cry for help propelled her into action and Veronika opened her eyes. When the slash of light under the door came into view, she experienced a sensation of falling that was like the world pulling away then crashing back into place.

When the crashing stopped, she remembered and let out a cry that was equal parts despair and pain. Tony was nineteen and almost a grown man and she was hurt and trapped in the dark.

The passage of time no longer meant much. She'd been lying injured for what felt like days, but now she suspected it was closer to a day or two at most. The pain was still jarring in her head, and also the shoulder she rested on. That was good. Her arm had been numb before. Pain meant she could feel her left arm again.

Slowly, Veronika rolled onto her back. A scream of static seared through her ears and into her brain – a jarring noise that reminded her of the screech that came from holding a microphone close to a speaker. Mercifully, the static in her brain eased to a dim buzz. There was also relief in changing positions and taking the weight off her injured shoulder. And it *was* her shoulder; she could almost see the site of the injury in her mind's eye, the socket where the head of the humerus bone sits in the cavity.

Tipping back her head, she let out a hiss of breath and explored her left shoulder with her right hand. The shoulder was dislocated. As the information clarified in her mind, the misty forest of her memory began to slip away.

Veronika recalled bending over to inspect something and then turning. It wasn't as she'd remembered before, a silvery moon swinging towards her, but a weapon – shiny and solid. She'd been struck, once in the head and then on the shoulder. The details were still out of reach but she was making progress. Calm progress. That was good.

Still exploring her injuries, she touched her head and her fingers came away sticky. The extent of the wound was anyone's guess, but Veronika couldn't discount a fracture or at the very least a severe concussion. Passing out again could be deadly, but how long could she hold herself together?

She needed water and medical help – urgent medical help. If she worked on those two goals, the rest would fall into place and she'd recall who had attacked her. With another push, she rolled onto her right side and raised her head. The light under the door doubled and moved in a kaleidoscope of colours as her stomach rocked with a sickening dip.

"Help." She tried to put force into the word, but stopped herself before calling again.

The part of her brain that had seen her through so many harrowing situations was coming back to life. She had to think. She'd taken stock of her injuries. Now it was imperative that she consider her situation.

The spinning light settled. Staring at the bottom of the door, she considered whether or not her attacker thought she was dead.

If whoever attacked and left her for dead was nearby, would calling out be wise? The light was on and she was in a house. She squinted, trying to remember if it *was* a house she'd entered, but for the moment that nugget of information was still out of reach.

"It doesn't matter," she whispered into the dark.

If her attacker was on the other side of the door, calling out would either bring them to finish the job of killing her, or be useless. Better to focus what little energy she had on reaching the door and trying to get out.

Veronika used her right arm to push herself up into a half-sitting position and began edging towards the light.

* * *

The lights were on inside Lena's house, shining out from behind drawn curtains. Yet, the outside of the building was in darkness, making it difficult for Jackie to navigate the garden path that led to the front porch. From memory she recalled there wasn't much in Lena's front yard apart from a few bare rose bushes. Thinking about the garden made Jackie wonder why the woman seemed to spend so much time gardening in a yard that consisted of so little, but the thought was fleeting, forgotten almost as soon as it fully materialised.

Before knocking, Jackie stuffed her keys in her pocket and drew her baggy cardigan over her chest. As she raised her hand, the door swung open.

Dim light from the hall set the area in shadows and turned Lena into a dark outline. Seeing her in that light ignited a spark of recognition, but Jackie couldn't quite put her finger on what it was that seemed so familiar.

"Come on in." Lena's voice was more relaxed than it had been on the phone. "I'll make us some tea," she said and stepped back, throwing her arm out in a welcoming gesture.

Once inside the house, Jackie glanced around, noticing a kitchen at the end of the hallway. As Lena closed the door and led her into a sitting room, Jackie couldn't help but notice the echoey quality of their footsteps on the bare boards. The sound suggested an empty house, but as Lena had pointed out, she hadn't lived there long.

"Have a seat." Lena gestured to a worn sofa under the front window.

Jackie seated herself and waited while her neighbour took her time settling into an equally aged armchair. There was very little in the way of furnishings inside this room apart from the sofa, an armchair, and a wood veneer display cabinet.

"Are you still unpacking?" Jackie asked.

Lena frowned and looked around the room as if unsure what Jackie meant. As the moment stretched out, Jackie shifted in her seat, wishing she could take the clumsy question back.

Desperate to fill the silence, Jackie stumbled on. "I mean... I like that cabinet. It's very... It's nice."

"Is it?" Lena shrugged and leaned back in her chair. "It came with the house."

Somewhere in the house a clock ticked. As the uncomfortable silence stretched, Jackie restrained herself from saying anything further for fear it would come out sounding as awkward as her initial question. Lena, on the other hand, looked relaxed in thick woollen pants and a loose grey jumper.

"I'm actually packing up," Lena said and swiped at something on her leg. "Time to move on." She chuckled as though she'd made a joke. Jackie smiled, unsure what was so funny.

"So, you wanted to tell me about the police," Jackie inquired, trying to move the conversation along so she could extract herself from the uncomfortable visit.

"Would you like some tea?" Lena asked, ignoring the question. Her eyes were wide, the irises a peculiar shade of grey.

"Oh, no." Jackie waved a hand. "Please don't go to any trouble."

"It's no trouble at all." Lena jumped to her feet so suddenly that Jackie lurched back in her seat.

Lena gave another one of her no-joke laughs and dashed out of the room.

Left alone, Jackie's shoulders slumped. It had been an emotional and exhausting day, and now it seemed there was more to come. How long, she wondered, would her neighbour keep the visit going? Almost as soon as the thought crossed her mind, Jackie felt a jab of guilt. Lena had come to her rescue last night. It had taken guts for an elderly woman to get involved in such a violent scene, and in doing so she had most likely saved Jackie from something horrendous. All Lena wanted in return was a little company. Would it kill Jackie to give her half an hour?

As the sound of water running and cups clattering echoed down the hall, Jackie forced herself to relax. What a lonely life the woman must lead, Jackie thought. Moving from place to place with her few belongings. Lena was obviously socially inept. Maybe she was trying to strike up a friendship in her own off-key way.

As her mind wandered, Jackie's gaze fell on the display cabinet and the small collection of items it housed. Without thinking, she stood and moved across the room to take a closer look.

A few trophies with faded engravings, a couple of photos, and a small trinket box; an almost pathetic assortment of memories for someone Lena's age, which Jackie estimated to be early sixties. *This could be me*. It was a familiar fear: being old and alone. But at least Jackie had her house, so there would be no moving in and out of rented places. And maybe, if she let people get close to her, she might not end up completely alone.

"What are you doing?"

Startled, Jackie span around to find Lena standing in the doorway holding a tray.

"I… I was just admiring your trophies and photographs." She hadn't really done more than glance at the items, but now Jackie picked up a framed image. "Is this your wedding photo?"

With nowhere else to unburden her hands, Lena set the tray down on the floor next to the armchair and came and stood at Jackie's side.

"Yes," Lena said, taking the picture out of Jackie's hand. "I was only twenty-three when I was married. I thought I was the luckiest girl in the world." She ran her thick fingers over the glass. "But it was a stupid dream and I soon learned to toughen up."

Jackie watched Lena's features as she stared at the old photograph. There was a strange expression on her face, not quite anger but more like hunger. The look made Jackie nervous. She wondered if that was the countenance on the woman's face in the dark the night before when she told Rick to leave. The idea gave Jackie goosebumps.

"These," Lena continued, "are my trophies." She set the photo down and picked up a heavy-looking statuette of a woman on a semi-circular base holding a tennis racket. "I was good. Really good." She turned and held the trophy up at shoulder height. "I don't have much left, but I still have my backhand," she said, swinging the statue like a tennis racket.

Lena's hand froze in mid-swing while her eyes became fixed on something over Jackie's shoulder. Lonely or not, Jackie decided she didn't want to be in the woman's house any longer than necessary.

"What did the police say?" Jackie asked, trying to keep her voice pleasant.

Lena let out a sudden gust of breath and placed the trophy down next to the photo.

"Let's have our tea," Lena said. A smile lifted her narrow lips, revealing a row of yellowing teeth.

Chapter Thirty-three

It was full dark when Jim exited the building and headed for his car. Putting the chain of events on paper hadn't done much to spark any new ideas. With reluctance he had decided to head home.

With peak hour over, traffic flowed smoothly as he passed the Swan River and rounded the turn-off for Stirling Highway. The dark water reminded him of Helen Winter and her house so close to the banks of the Swan. Somehow, everything was tied to Winter. It had to be. Nothing else made sense. Yet, when he'd interviewed her, she seemed genuine in her lack of knowledge about Veronika's disappearance. He didn't have Veronika's gut for liars, but he'd interviewed enough suspects to know when he was being manipulated, and he didn't get that from Jacqueline Winter. In fact, he felt a bit sorry for the woman.

Jim rubbed at his aching neck then turned on the radio hoping some mindless pop music would clear his brain. What he really needed was sleep. Sleep and food, then just maybe he'd come up with a new angle. As it was now, he was hitting a wall of exhaustion. Food would have to take second place because as he turned off the highway, his lids drooped dangerously close to closing.

Lowering the window and letting the stinging night air into the car helped, but not much. He was still fifteen minutes from home, so he decided to pull into a service station. He'd had more than his fill of coffee, so he opted for a can of fizzy, which he drank standing next to his vehicle.

Watching customers shuffle in and out of the service station clutching their purchases made him think of a movie he'd once watched in which a woman entered a large service station and disappeared. In the movie, the woman was never seen again. Would that be Veronika's fate?

Jim drained the can, crushed it, and tossed it in the rubbish bin. Maybe it was the shot of sugar or perhaps the memory of the tragic movie, but suddenly he felt energised. Maybe Winter wasn't directly responsible for Veronika's disappearance, but she was somehow at the centre of everything that had happened, including her aunt's death *and* Margaret Green's murder.

Whether Winter knew it or not, she was connected to Veronika. Jim was certain that with a little prompting he might get something from her. Even a small detail could help. The solicitor Andrew Drake had made it clear that Jim wasn't to approach her without speaking to him first, but what if she approached Jim? There was a chance that if Winter saw him, she might feel compelled to speak to him. It was a very slim possibility but better than trying to sleep while Veronika was still out there somewhere.

With a plan of action forming in mind, he got back in the car, exited the service station, then turned back onto the highway. The two uniforms he'd sent to talk to the neighbour reported that she had confirmed Winter's story about Marclowe. While the two officers had done their job, Jim doubted they'd dug very deep. In fact, he was sure they'd only asked about Marclowe. Turning up on the neighbour's doorstep with a few follow-up questions would serve two purposes. One, give Winter an opportunity to see him outside her house and maybe prompt a conversation and, two, give him the chance to really question the neighbour on what comings and goings she'd seen. The two times he'd been to Winter's house with Veronika, the old lady was always in the front yard. She must have seen something.

* * *

The tea was served in long narrow mugs set on gold saucers; the liquid smelled of cloves mixed with something fruity. When Jackie took a swallow, the taste was sour and slightly chalky, an unpleasant combination that reminded her of mouthwash.

"These are lovely cups," Jackie said, more out of politeness than any real interest in the crockery.

"They were my mother's." Lena had her cup balanced on her knee. "The tea is my own recipe. I use peaches. This time of year they're difficult to get so I had to make do with canned fruit. I don't think you can tell the difference."

As her neighbour prattled on about the tea, Jackie couldn't stop thinking about the way Lena zoned out while holding the trophy and the disturbing look in her eyes when she held her wedding photo. Had Lena made up the story about having something important to tell her? It was beginning to feel like the woman was deliberately stalling.

"You look like her." Lena turned the cup around on its saucer. "When she was younger."

"What?" Jackie was thrown off balance by Lena's sudden change of direction. "What do you mean?"

"You're not drinking your tea," Lena said, lifting her own cup to her lips.

"I'm really not thirsty." Jackie set the cup down in the saucer. "It's been a long day. I think I'll just—"

"I know what I forgot," Lena said, setting her cup and saucer down on the floor with a clatter loud enough to make Jackie wince. "I have some wafer fingers in the pantry. They're delicious with peach tea."

Before Jackie could object, her neighbour was on her feet and hurrying out of the room.

Alone again, Jackie ran through what had just occurred, wondering if Lena was just a lonely oddball or if something strange was happening. The thing with the tennis trophy was unsettling and then Jackie was sure she'd said she looked like someone. Who was Lena talking about? None of what was going on made sense.

On impulse, she put her cup down and stood up, deciding it was time to leave. No matter how awkward or rude it would seem if she just walked out, it couldn't be any worse than spending another minute inside Lena's house.

With the decision made, Jackie felt relieved, but before turning away she took one last look at the cabinet. Was it her imagination or did the man in the wedding photo look familiar? Snatching a quick glance over her shoulder, she moved towards the cabinet.

The wedding photo looked old and the clothing dated, but it was the groom that held Jackie's attention. His face was half-turned. Not towards the bride but away, as though he was staring at something off to the side. Lena, on the other hand, was looking into the camera and, although she was much younger, her tall frame and broad shoulders were unmistakable. She'd had longer hair as a young woman: shoulder length and brown, not the closely cropped iron grey style she now sported, but the smile hadn't changed.

Jackie stared at the photo for a few seconds before she realised what she was seeing. Mike West. Jackie stepped back and then something else fell into place. When Andrew told her about her aunt, he mentioned Mike's wife being a tennis player.

With her mind whirling, Jackie whirled around and as she did, the room tilted. The sensation of being off balance lasted only a second before she found her equilibrium and headed for the front door.

Moving quickly while trying to make as little noise as possible, Jackie grabbed the doorknob only to find it locked. Another wave of dizziness hit and with it came real fear. The knob had a keyhole where it could be dead-locked. Lena must have locked the door when she let Jackie in.

"Shit," Jackie muttered, trying to suppress the urge to rattle the handle.

With her back braced against the front door for support and her eyes fixed on the kitchen at the end of the hall, she reached into her pocket feeling the bulge of the keys and remembering she'd left her phone on the desk in the study. Unsure what to do next, her mind went back to the trophy.

If Lena was Mike's wife, how did that fit with Margaret's murder and the disappearance of the detective? How would Lena even know Margaret and what possible reason could she have for doing something to Detective Pope? What reason could the woman have for harming people she didn't know?

With the questions piling up in her mind, time ticked away and she knew any minute Lena would return. But what about Helen? Detective Drommel's words resonated in her head. *Did you hit her like you hit your aunt?* After what Andrew told her, Jackie realised Lena might believe she had a very good reason for killing Helen.

The dizziness had subsided as a cold prickling of sweat gathered at the base of her neck. All the unanswered questions could wait. What Jackie needed was to get out of Lena's house, get to her phone, and call the police.

She glanced sideways to the wall near the front door and her eyes fell on the coatrack. Jackie blinked, trying to take in what she was seeing. The black raincoat, like slick reptilian skin, hung next to the door.

"Jackie?" Lena called from the kitchen. "Could you help me with something?"

Chapter Thirty-four

"That's an impressive trophy," Veronika set her tea down on the bare boards and crossed the room.

The idea of questioning Winter's neighbour was a spur of the moment decision and until she'd spotted the statuette it seemed one that would be a waste of time.

"There's not much more I can tell you," Lena said from her position in the armchair. "I keep to myself and stay out of other people's business."

"Hm. It has a very distinctive shape." Veronika studied the trophy, but refrained from touching it. "Does Jacqueline Winter ever pop in for visits?"

"She might have." Lena was on her feet now. Veronika could hear the woman's movements as she crossed the room. "Has she done something wrong?"

When Veronika turned, a wave of dizziness took her by surprise, as did the woman's closeness. Veronika wanted to tell Lena to step back but was having a difficult time keeping her balance.

"Are you all right, Detective?" Lena's face swam in front of Veronika's eyes.

"Yes," Veronika answered. "Just a little dip in blood sugar. I skipped lunch. Would you mind if I took the trophy with me? I can give you a receipt for it and make sure it's returned to you."

The woman's lips pursed, suggesting she wasn't happy with the request. The chances were slim that the neighbour's trophy was the weapon used to kill Margaret Green, but if Winter had access to Lena's house she might have taken the trophy and returned it later. The idea seemed unlikely but the statuette's crescent-shaped base was too close to the shape embedded on Green's temple to ignore.

"Okay, if it will help," Lena said, picking up the trophy.

Veronika suppressed a wince as she watched the woman handling the statuette. "Would you mind putting it down while I run out to my car and get a bag to put it in?"

"No need," Lena said over her shoulder as she headed for the door. "I've got some bags in the kitchen. I'll pop it in one and while I'm there I'll find us some biscuits to go with our tea."

Veronika followed the woman, cursing under her breath. By handling the item, Lena might be smearing prints and removing vital evidence, but without a warrant Veronika couldn't force the woman to hand over the trophy.

Unlike the sparseness of the front part of the house, the kitchen was a jumble of boxes and unwashed dishes. Veronika noticed there were pill bottles and packets lined up on the draining board amidst a cluster of dead flies. *Jesus, I drank tea she made in this mess.*

Still holding the trophy, Lena flung open the cupboard under the sink. "Sit down, Detective. You look as pale as chalk," Lena said, rummaging through the clutter.

Veronika had no desire to spend any unnecessary time in the clutter, but suddenly, standing felt exhausting and the smell of rotten food combined with the knowledge she'd drunk tea made in the filthy kitchen made her stomach roil.

Grateful to be sitting, Veronika surveyed the chaos littering the kitchen table. Crusty plates, mouldering bread, and more medication packets. How, she wondered, did the woman live like this? It was difficult to imagine Jacqueline Winter voluntarily entering this house for cosy visits.

"Damn." Lena made a clicking sound with her tongue. "I know I have some bags here somewhere." As she spoke, she moved around the room, opening and closing drawers and cupboards.

"Please don't bother," Veronika said. "I can grab a…" The words petered out as her eyes landed on one of the packets of tablets.

Even reading upside-down, the name Margaret Green was clearly legible. It took Veronika only a second's hesitation to reclaim her composure and make sense of what she'd seen. In that second, she understood that she might be in danger.

"As I said, I have plenty of evidence bags in my car." Veronika spoke slowly as she reached into her jacket and touched the butt of her gun.

"That woman…" Lena spoke from behind Veronika. "I saw Jackie arguing with her. It was never my plan to hurt her, but it was an opportunity I couldn't pass up."

Veronika unclipped the strap holding her gun in place and wrapped her fingers around the butt. She could hear the woman behind her, but didn't want to make a move until she'd finished confessing to murder.

"You see, Helen Winter killed my son. She took away the only part of me that was good. Helen loved Jackie like I loved my boy. Only the police wouldn't listen. They wouldn't put Helen in prison where she belonged, so I knew I had to make it so Jackie would rot in prison. She looks just like her aunt, you know."

A flicker of movement out of her left eye caught Veronika's attention. She turned in time to see the trophy swinging towards her and managed to duck her head and raise her left shoulder in time to avoid being struck in the head. When the weapon hit, the force knocked her forward and something in her shoulder gave an audible *pop*. Veronika grunted, staggered to the right and out of her chair still grappling for her gun. As she stood, her left arm dropped with an agonising jerk. At the same time, Lena kept coming, the statuette drawn back across her body.

"Drop the weapon!" Veronika put as much force as she could gather into the words while trying to move out of the woman's reach.

For an elderly woman, Lena's reflexes were lightning fast. Feigning one way and then stepping the other, she closed the gap between her and Veronika. As the heavy trophy swung towards her head, Veronika reacted with equal speed by diving forward. She felt the statuette bounce off her skull, but only for an instant. When she landed on the floor, Veronika was already unconscious.

* * *

Still in the dark but almost close enough to the bar of light that she could reach the wood, Veronika recalled the moment when Lena attacked her with almost perfect clarity. There were still vague spots. She had no memory of being moved or how she came to be in the dark. At first, she'd had no idea where she was, but the smell of rotten food coming from under the door told her she was still inside Lena's house. And the sound of voices told her she wasn't alone.

The pain in Veronika's head had lessened, but each shuffle forward set off sparks of agony and waves of dizziness. Weary of losing consciousness again, she forced herself to move slowly and not try and stand.

There were other sounds now, dishes clattering and cupboards opening. Someone was close on the other side of the door. What Veronika couldn't tell was if that someone was just Lena or if Lena had company. Rather than use what might be her last burst of strength opening the door only to encounter Lena, Veronika waited and listened.

Chapter Thirty-five

With no other choice available, Jackie walked down the hall, pausing in the kitchen doorway. The room was a pigsty and the smell of rotting food hung in the air. The filth and the stench only added to Jackie's growing fear and desperation to get out of the house.

Her neighbour was bent over the sink. When Jackie entered the room, Lena straightened and turned her way. There was something in her hand. Jackie took an involuntary step backwards before she realised the woman was holding a packet of biscuits.

"Here they are," Lena chimed. "Now, we need to put these on a nice plate."

"No." The word came out louder than Jackie had intended, making Lena frown. "I can't stay. Would you mind unlocking the front door so I can leave," Jackie said, hoping she sounded more in control of the situation than she felt.

Lena fished a stained plate out of the sink and set it on the table, then used her fingers to pull biscuits out of the open packet. Either she hadn't heard Jackie's request or she was deliberately ignoring her.

"You look pale, Jackie. Why don't you sit down for a minute?" Lena pointed to the chair at the end of the kitchen table. "I've made you some more tea."

Jackie glanced at the back door, noticing the bolt at the top was drawn. If she tried to unlock it, would it spark some sort of physical confrontation?

When she glanced back in Lena's direction, the woman was watching her with the same hungry expression Jackie had witnessed when Lena had been staring at her wedding photo. Unsure how to react, Jackie snatched a look at the door on the right of the exit. It was closed. Probably a pantry or a washroom and no use as a way out.

Lena stepped forward and pulled out the chair. "Come on. Take a seat." There was a hard edge to the woman's voice, making her words more of a command than a suggestion.

This is ridiculous, Jackie told herself. *She has to be thirty years older than me.* Was she really going to let an elderly woman intimidate her? But Lena wasn't just an ageing woman; she was a murderer – someone capable of anything.

For a moment neither woman spoke or moved. Finally, Jackie decided it might be safer to just go along with Lena for now and wait for an opportunity to get out the back door. If that didn't work, she could always ask to use the bathroom and climb out of a window.

"All right," Jackie said and sat at the table.

The frown eased and Lena's face relaxed. She returned to the sink area and picked up a mug, which she placed in front of Jackie. Without having to look, Jackie could smell the cloves and knew it was more of the sour tasting tea.

While Lena settled herself at the table, Jackie's mind worked on calculating the time it would take her to reach the back door and shift the bolt.

"Do you know how they used to make patients behave and cooperate in psychiatric hospitals?" Lena asked, her tone conversational.

Jackie had no idea what the woman was talking about and shook her head.

"A chemical straitjacket they called it." Lena's eyes were wide and eager. "I suppose they still do it that way because it's very effective. But things *have* changed. Now, they like to send patients home and treat them as out-patients. If they appear to be taking their medication and turn up for their weekly appointments…" She shrugged her wide shoulders. "Everyone's happy."

Jackie didn't know what she was supposed to say and remained silent.

"Drink your tea." Lena jerked her chin towards the mug.

"I'm not thirsty." Jackie dropped her hands into her lap and sat back.

Lena nodded and reached under the table. When she raised her hand, she was holding a gun. Jackie gasped and pushed her chair back from the table.

Lena chuckled. "No need to get in a state." She placed the gun on the table beside her right hand. "Not as long as you drink your tea. I've become a bit of an expert on chemical straitjackets over the years."

Jackie was beginning to understand the dizziness and the sour taste of the tea. This was Lena's way of subduing her – making her manageable, but for what reason?

"You killed my aunt," Jackie said, ignoring Lena's demand. "But why Margaret Green? Why Detective Pope?" She shook her head. "Why are you doing this?"

Lena smiled her toothy grin; she seemed to be enjoying herself. "I've been driving by your aunt's house for more than thirty years. Every year I park out there on the anniversary of my son's murder." Her voice dropped slightly. "I'd just sit in my car and stare at the house. Years spent just sitting and thinking about my boy."

Despite everything she'd done, Jackie couldn't help pitying the woman. She could only imagine what it must have been like to lose her child and how that tragedy had taken over Lena's entire life.

"Lena, I don't know what you must have gone through, but this isn't—"

"Then," Lena continued as if Jackie hadn't spoken, "this year something different happened. There was a *For Lease* sign on this house. But I knew," Lena said tapping her forehead. "It was a sign just for me. A sign inviting me in. When Christopher was killed, I went to the police, but Helen got herself a high-priced solicitor who helped her worm out of taking any responsibility. But that sign, it told me now was the time to put things right."

By "putting things right" Jackie understood Lena was talking about killing Helen. Believing that her aunt had fallen was painful enough, but knowing she had been bashed over the head was gut-wrenching. Jackie swallowed and looked at the gun, wondering what Lena's plan was for her. Was she to be shot or bludgeoned? While Lena continued to talk, her words were almost blocked out by the whooshing of blood in Jackie's ears.

"Helen was always sloppy. That's why my boy is dead." Lena was still talking, but now Jackie's attention was on the gun.

"She didn't bother to lock her back door when she went out, so it was easy for me to slip inside. And..." – Lena snapped her fingers, making Jackie jump – "...true to form she still drank that cheap screw-top wine. The same slop she'd been drinking when my boy drowned. It was in the police report. Time for the chemical straitjacket." Lena's voice took on a sing-song quality.

"You put something in the wine?" Jackie asked, already knowing that was exactly what Lena meant.

The woman raised her eyebrows and shrugged. "For a while it was enough to watch the batty old thing floundering around. Helen Winter, the big-time reporter. So clever, so stylish. So much more interesting than boring little Kathleen. She didn't look so smart wandering back and forth between her house and the car with her cardigan on inside out." Lena gave a girlish giggle that turned Jackie's blood cold.

The idea that Lena had enjoyed watching Helen's growing confusion was like a slap in the face. Knowing that the woman had revelled in her aunt's misery made Jackie want to leap across the table and grab Lena by the throat. Anger eclipsed her fear as Jackie realised her blackouts and forgetfulness weren't a symptom of excessive drinking. She now understood that she, too, had been a victim of Lena's brand of justice.

"But in the end," Lena continued. "I decided I couldn't move on until she paid for what she did. Until Helen paid for killing my son *and* my husband."

Chapter Thirty-six

1986

"Kathleen called me a murderer," Mike whispered. "In a way, she's right."

They were sitting on a bench near the river because Mike couldn't bear to enter Helen's house.

"No." Helen pulled his head onto her shoulder. "You're not to blame. Don't do this to yourself. She doesn't mean it. She's just hurting. You're a good man, Mike. A good father. It was a tragic accident, but no one's fault."

Mike was silent, making Helen wonder if he could hear her or if he was inside his own head reliving the moment he pulled Chrissy's little body out of the water. It was only six days since it happened, but already Mike seemed older – wasted.

Helen turned and kissed his forehead. "I'll rent a cottage down south. Somewhere far away from here in a place where the grass is long and we can't hear the cars going by. We'll go for long walks in the mornings. In the evening, we'll watch the roos eating the grass as the sun goes down." She continued to talk, spinning an idyllic future while his breathing evened out and became more relaxed.

Sometime later, they walked back to Mike's car and he drove the few streets back to her place. For a moment they sat staring at the house. The funeral was planned for the following day and while it hadn't been discussed, they both understood that Helen couldn't attend.

Before she climbed out of the car, Mike pressed his lips to hers. It was the first time he'd kissed her lips since Chrissy's death. A kiss that felt desperate, leaving her breathless, but not with passion, only sorrow.

"Who would have thought it would come to this?" he said when he pulled back.

Despite the warm breeze ruffling her hair, Helen felt cold as she watched him drive away. Tomorrow would be one of the worst days of Mike's life. A day he would have to endure before entering into years of grief. Wrapping her arms around her body, she turned back to the house.

* * *

The news of Mike's suicide came from an old friend, Jack Lyon, a fellow journalist Helen hadn't spoken to in over a year. A courtesy call to someone Jack believed to be an old flame.

"Just wanted to let you know before it hits the newspapers," Jack said with equal amounts of sympathy and tiredness.

"That's very sweet of you," Helen said standing in the kitchen holding the phone. As she listened to the details, Helen stared out the window, almost surprised that the sun could be shining when her world was turning black.

"I know you and Mike were close once upon a time, so I didn't want you reading about it."

"Yes." Helen squeezed the receiver, determined to keep all emotion out of her voice. "Once upon a time we were very close."

When she hung up, Helen remained standing next to the wall-mounted phone trying to picture a world where Mike West no longer existed. Even when they were apart, knowing he was somewhere living his life made things okay. And all the time that passed didn't matter because she knew they would come back together one day.

She stayed there in the kitchen for a long time. Or maybe it was only minutes; Helen had no idea how much time had passed. When she did move, it was to the spare room where she sat on the bed that Chrissy had slept in.

It was then, in a trance, she spotted the other shoe peeking out from the gap between the bed and the nightstand. Just as Mike had done a little over a week ago, Helen took the little shoe and held it in her hands, squeezing the leather like it had the power to transport her back to another time. A time when Chrissy was eating chocolate ice cream while Mike ran his fingers over the back of Helen's neck.

When she laid down and closed her eyes, all she could see were images her mind conjured up. Stark pictures she'd never seen, yet they were so clear in her mind's eye: Chrissy's body floating in the water; Mike hanging from a rafter in his garage.

The pillow was cold under her cheek. Chrissy's baby scent had faded, leaving nothing but the shoe as a reminder of the little boy and his father. Helen's tears were running across her cheek and pooling under her face. There would be years of grieving, but the grief would be hers alone now. There would be no cottage in the long grass, only a lifetime of regret.

Over the next few weeks, Helen held herself together by picturing that cottage. She made it through the police investigation into Chrissy and Mike's deaths by picturing Mike and Chrissy holding hands and standing in the grass as it turned gold in the late afternoon sun. She made it through the next thirty-three years by picturing the boy and his father waiting for her in that field of gold.

Chapter Thirty-seven

"My aunt didn't kill your husband or your son." Jackie knew she was provoking the woman, but couldn't allow Lena's lies to go unchallenged even if it was only Jackie who heard them. "Helen loved your husband and your son. She was a victim, not a murderer. You," Jackie said, pointing at the woman, "you're the murderer."

Lena's mouth puckered. She slammed her palm down on the table with enough force to make the cups and pill bottles jump. Despite her best efforts, Jackie couldn't stop herself from wincing.

"That's a lie!" Lena's voice was a shrill. "A wicked lie. That woman didn't care about anyone but herself. She took everything from me, and now," she said, her voice shaking, "I'm taking everything from her."

Jackie could see Lena was getting worked up, so she dropped her hands below the table and took hold of the table legs on either side. If she had any chance of getting out of her neighbour's house alive, she'd have to act fast.

As Jackie tensed the muscles in her arms and gathered her nerve, a rattle came from behind her. Judging from the startled look on Lena's face, she'd heard it, too.

As both women looked towards the sound, the door Jackie had assumed led to a pantry swung inwards. For a beat, Jackie couldn't take in what she was seeing. Detective Pope, her face streaked with blood and her eyes wide, was slumped half-kneeling in the open door. The moment was so shocking, it took Jackie's breath away and almost snatched her resolve.

"Winter..." Pope's voice was little more than a croak. "Run."

While her first instinct was to run *to* the detective, Jackie stayed glued to her chair and turned her focus on the gun still sitting on Lena's right. Lena's attention, Jackie noted, was on Detective Pope. And, judging by the way her neighbour's eyes were blinking and her chin moved up and down, the situation was spiralling out of Lena's control.

There were two people's lives at stake now. If Jackie hesitated, Lena might snap back to life and decide the easiest course of action would be to shoot both Detective Pope and her. She swallowed and as her heartbeat stuttered, Jackie used all the strength in her left arm to lift one side of the table and flip it.

As the kitchen table slammed onto its side, the gun as well as the litter of plates and cups clattered across the kitchen floor. The upturned table blocked the passage between Lena and the sink.

Almost as soon as the table hit the floor, Lena was out of her chair and coming around the other side of the upturned piece of furniture. With equal speed, Jackie was also already standing and took hold of her chair. She tried to lift the wooden seat, planning to use it to swipe at the woman, but the chair was too heavy. Instead, Jackie settled for kicking it forward so as Lena rushed towards her, it collided with her knees.

The move worked, knocking Lena off balance and sending her sprawling to the floor. Breathless and unsure what to do next, Jackie froze for a second watching Lena scrabbling to her feet.

With Lena on her knees and her eyes wild with rage, Jackie kicked the chair again sending it smashing into the woman's chin. Lena let out a cry and fell to the side.

"Go," Detective Pope tried to yell from the doorway. "Get help."

Ignoring the cop's instructions, Jackie rushed over and crouched in front of Detective Pope. "Can you stand?" she asked.

Detective Pope shook her head and almost fell forward. "Go call for help." Her words were losing conviction.

"I'm not leaving you with her," Jackie said and slipped her arm under Detective Pope's. "Get up."

When Jackie's hand clasped on the detective's side, she groaned but managed to get her feet under her. Glancing over her shoulder, Jackie noted that Lena was still on the floor, her mouth smeared with blood.

"Don't you fucking move," Jackie spat at Lena as she hauled the detective to her feet. "I don't care how old you are. If you try anything, I'll kill you."

If Lena understood what Jackie was saying, she gave no indication. Instead, she sat on the kitchen floor, her eyes trained on the two women as they struggled to move. While Jackie meant what she said, Lena's gaze was predatory, blank and focused at the same time. If she survived this night, Jackie knew she would see those pale eyes in her nightmares.

"Lean against the wall," Jackie said to Detective Pope while shuffling a few steps to the right.

As gently as possible, Jackie set the detective against the wall and turned to the back door. Stretching up, Jackie threw back the bolt and turned the knob. As she did so, Detective Pope called her name and Jackie heard a rush of movement.

When she turned back from the door, Lena was barrelling towards her with something shiny in her hand.

* * *

As Jim pulled up, he noticed the lights were on in Winter's house. The plan was to speak to the neighbour and maybe in the process Jacqueline Winter would see or hear him pulling up. Maybe his presence would prompt her to come out and speak to him. However, with the curtains drawn, the possibility of her coming outside in the dark to confront him seemed ridiculous. The plan itself, he realised, was ridiculous.

Jim turned off the engine and scrubbed a hand over his eyes. Whatever he'd told himself, the reality was there was only ever one plan: question Winter until he got some answers. Turning up on her doorstep after her solicitor told him to keep away could see him charged with harassment. After a few seconds hesitation, Jim decided he'd gladly risk suspension if it got him closer to finding Detective Pope.

There was no sound coming from inside of Winter's house and no answer when Jim pounded on the door. Maybe she had heard his car and was on the phone to her solicitor, but he'd gone this far and didn't intend to back down now.

"Jackie?" Jim stepped back from the door and called the woman's name again. "I just want to ask you a few questions." He paused then added, "Please, Jackie. I need to find my partner."

After a few minutes with no response, Jim walked back along the path to his car. Instead of getting in the vehicle, he pulled out his phone and called Winter's number only to listen to it ring until it went to voicemail.

"Jesus, Winter," he said with disgust and hung up without leaving a message.

Short of breaking into Winter's house, there wasn't much more he could do, but instead of driving away he decided that while he was there, he might as well talk to the neighbour. Jamming his phone back in his pocket, he headed for the old lady's house.

Apart from the light coming from the front window, the neighbour's front yard was in darkness, forcing him to slow his pace and strain to see the garden path. Halfway between the house and the street, a scream tore through the night, shattering the silence and sending Jim running for the front door.

Chapter Thirty-eight

In the time it took Jackie to spot the knife, Lena was already in front of her with the blade held high. As the woman plunged the knife towards her neck, Jackie instinctively raised her left hand, trying to block the blow.

The blade sliced through the flesh between Jackie's thumb and forefinger. Pain was immediate, tearing through her hand like fire. Jackie let out an agonised scream as she felt the tip of the blade gouge bone. At the same time, Detective Pope was shouting something as Lena dragged the knife back through Jackie's torn flesh.

Before Lena had time to draw the blade back for another strike, Jackie used her uninjured hand to grab the woman's wrist. As Lena struggled to free herself, Jackie stumbled forward, knocking the older woman against the kitchen counter.

"You ruined everything! You killed my boy!" Lena was screaming in Jackie's face, her pale eyes huge with outrage.

Jackie was aware of movement around her, but she hung on to Lena's wrist as the blade waved closer to her body. With her left hand clutched to her chest, blood ran down her forearm and splattered the floor making it difficult for Jackie stop her feet from sliding out from under her.

As the struggle continued, Jackie's vision darkened and the room jolted sideways. She was weakening as Lena seemed to be gathering momentum. The woman pushed Jackie backwards, trying to force the tip of the knife into her stomach. Jackie gritted her teeth, crying out with the effort of holding off the attack. As her vision dimmed then cleared, Jackie caught sight of Detective Pope moving behind Lena with her shoulder hunched over.

Jackie wanted to shout at the policewoman, ask for help, but it was no use. Lena's face filled her field of vision, her mouth wide with yellowed teeth that gritted as the tip of the knife scraped the flesh on Jackie's belly. At any second the blade would sink into her stomach and she'd be left to bleed out on the filthy floor.

Something shattered and the pressure of Lena's hand released. Still gripping the older woman's wrist, Jackie was pulled forward as Lena sunk to the floor. Confused, Jackie let go and looked up to where Detective Pope stood holding a broken piece of what appeared to be a plate.

It took Jackie a few seconds to realise what had happened. Detective Pope had smashed a plate over Lena's head. Before Jackie could speak, the detective staggered and dropped the shard of crockery.

"Here." Jackie grabbed Detective Pope with her right hand. "Put your arm around my neck."

The detective did as instructed and together they moved to the back door. Struggling to cradle her injured hand and reach around Detective Pope with her good hand, Jackie managed to get the back door open. The cold night air was a welcome shock, a jolt which gave Jackie a burst of energy, allowing her to shoulder some of Detective Pope's weight as they limped outside.

"Let her go and get on the ground!" A man's voice roared out of the darkness.

Still reeling from what had happened in the house, Jackie squinted as a light came on and shone in her eyes. Next to her, Detective Pope was trying to speak.

"Winter, get on the ground!" the man demanded.

"Jim," Detective Pope croaked out. "Jim it's…"

"Get away from her! Drop it or I'll shoot!"

Jackie realised the voice belonged to Detective Drommel.

"I didn't," Jackie began.

An explosion of sound blocked out her words as a flash lit up the darkness.

Without realising she was falling, Jackie found herself on the ground with her face resting on the damp grass. Echoes of the blast bounced around in her head, blocking out all other sound. Someone touched her shoulder, making her jump. Was she shot? There was no pain other than her hand, but maybe she was too numb to feel the wound.

Noise came rushing back, Drommel yelling and Detective Pope's calm voice, weak but steady. Jackie sat up still clutching her hand to her chest. That's when she saw Lena lying just outside the back door in a shaft of light. Even from a few metres away Jackie could see the woman's jumper was almost completely coated in blood.

Drommel was kicking something away from Lena's reach, which Jackie realised was a gun. Next to Jackie, Detective Pope sat hunched forward, wavering slightly, but still upright.

"Jim's calling an ambulance," Detective Pope said, her teeth chattering. "Are you okay?"

"I should be asking you that question," Jackie answered, surprised by how normal her own voice sounded.

They both watched as Detective Drommel tore off his jacket and pressed it to Lena's chest. The woman's eyes were open. As Drommel moved around Lena, her head rolled to the side and she locked eyes with Jackie.

There was pain in the older woman's gaze, but something more: hatred, hard and unwavering. Staring into those seething eyes made Jackie realise that for Lena the lines between Jackie and Helen had become blurred. Despite everything Lena had done, Jackie could feel only pity for her. Pity and sadness because both Lena and Helen had lost everything they loved. And, while Helen had found a way to go on and turn the pain into something beautiful with her books, Lena had let bitterness rob her of any hope of happiness.

By the time the first ambulance arrived, Jackie was shivering but able to keep standing, while Detective Pope remained on the grass wrapped in a shock blanket. She watched as Lena was placed on a stretcher and lifted into the vehicle. She was alive. If she survived the gunshot wound, Jackie doubted she would ever be released from prison or hospital, whichever the authorities decided.

In the few moments before the second ambulance arrived, Detective Pope slumped to the side. Jackie wanted to do something to help her, but Drommel was kneeling beside her, calling her name.

"Is she…" Jackie asked, standing over the two detectives.

"She's unconscious," Drommel said, holding Detective Pope's hand. He dragged his gaze off his partner and looked Jackie's way. "Thanks for getting her out." His eyes were red-rimmed and raw looking.

Before Jackie could say anything, two paramedics came charging into the backyard, pushing a trolley. In minutes Detective Pope was loaded into an ambulance, accompanied by her partner.

It was only after Jackie's hand had been wrapped and a paramedic helped her into a third ambulance that what had happened hit her. The shock of being stabbed and fighting for her life fell on Jackie like a hammer, and suddenly she was shaking uncontrollably. As the tears started to fall, she found herself engulfed in sorrow. Sorrow for her aunt and for Margaret Green, the two women who had lost their lives because of a tragic accident more than thirty years ago.

Blood loss, shock and grief sapped Jackie's strength until calmed by sedatives and numbed with a local anaesthetic. Her wound was cleaned and stitched, and then finally she was allowed to sleep.

In the early hours of the morning she awoke to see Andrew sitting beside her bed. For a moment, in the seconds before he noticed her eyes were open, she watched the solicitor, noticing how tanned the skin on his forearms looked against the white of his rolled-up sleeves.

"How are you feeling?" Andrew asked, leaning forward with his elbows on his knees.

"Tired." Jackie pushed herself up in the bed. "A bit sore, but okay. How did you know I was here?"

Before answering, Andrew stood and settled the pillows at her back. "Detective Drommel called and filled me in."

He must have noted her stunned expression because when he sat down, he was nodding. "I have to say, I'm as surprised as you. But Drommel was sincerely concerned about you and didn't want you to be discharged without someone to help you get home."

For a moment Jackie didn't know what to say. Drommel had been hard on her. More than hard, but she reminded herself the man believed she'd killed two people and had abducted his partner. Learning that he was worried about her was touching.

"Any news on Detective Pope?" Jackie asked.

"She's come through her surgery and is in a serious but stable condition, or so I'm told."

Jackie let out a relieved sigh. "And Lena?" Just saying the woman's name jolted Jackie back into the moment when the knife sliced through her flesh.

He hesitated and rubbed a hand across his chin. "Your neighbour, Kathleen 'Lena' West, has also survived surgery." Andrew's voice was tight and clipped as he recounted Lena's condition. "At some point a decision will be made on her fitness to stand trial, but that's nothing for you to worry about just yet."

Jackie wondered if the woman would ever face charges over what she'd done to Helen and Margaret. Part of her wanted justice for the two people who'd lost their lives to Lena's insatiable appetite for revenge, but there was another part of Jackie that just wanted to put the whole nightmare behind her and start living again.

"What did Detective Drommel tell you?" she asked, trying to remember if Detective Pope had had the chance to tell her partner any of what had happened.

"Just a few highlights," Andrew answered. "They'll be plenty of questions, but I doubt Drommel will be involved. After a shooting, he'll be facing an internal investigation, so my best guess is another detective will be assigned to take your statement."

Jackie looked down at her hand. It was almost unrecognisable as a human limb under the thick wad of bandaging. If Detective Drommel hadn't acted fast and stopped Lena, Jackie might have suffered a much worse fate than fourteen stitches.

"He saved my life," Jackie said. "Probably both mine and Detective Pope's, and now *he's* under investigation?" She shook her head, feeling frustrated and weary at the same time.

"I know." Andrew leaned forward and for a second she thought he meant to take her hand, but instead he touched the side of the bed. "Drommel knows how these things work. He'll be fine. Things might be tough for a while, but it will be okay."

With just a few words Andrew managed to make her feel better. And instead of fretting and storing up her concerns, Jackie chose to believe him when he said everything would be all right. It was a feeling she was unused to, a sense of trust and one she wanted to embrace.

"Any chance of a lift home?" Jackie asked.

Chapter Thirty-nine

Veronika switched channels, not really taking in the chain of banal talk shows and daytime soap operas. With the curtains closed, dim light turned the pile of laundry on the nearest armchair into a slouching shadow, a shape, which in the half-light, nearly resembled an elderly woman.

For a moment Veronika stared at the laundry and as she did so, a headache materialised behind her eyes. Not the blinding pain of a few months ago, but still enough to make her want to rub at the once shaved spot on her scalp – a patch now filled in by hair that was beginning to settle into the rest of her blonde locks.

Dragging her gaze away from the pile of towels and sheets, she tried to focus on the day ahead. Or half-day ahead. The first part of her day had vanished into a mist of sleep and television. The only reason she'd bothered to dress in track pants and a stretched-out T-shirt was because she'd promised her mother she'd go outside and take a look at the reticulation timer. A promise she now regretted.

The idea of going back to bed danced across her thoughts, but instead she rolled off the sofa and shuffled into the kitchen, only pausing to swipe at the laundry pile, sending linens fluttering to the carpet.

How many cups of tea had she consumed over the last four months? As she filled the kettle and set it to boil, Veronika did a quick calculation. Eight cups a day for four months equalled one-hundred-and-twenty.

"Jesus," Veronika mumbled and rolled her left shoulder, trying to ease some of the stiffness.

After pouring milk in her tea, she stood for a while, staring at the honey-coloured liquid. Her body had healed. Not completely, but to a point where she was for the most part pain free. She should've been back at work a month ago, so why was she still wandering around the house half-asleep making endless cups of tea?

The answer niggled at the edge of her thoughts like a mosquito dancing annoyingly out of reach. Maybe it was time to accept that she couldn't go back. Time to call it quits and find something else to do with the rest of her life. Tony was almost a grown man and her mother had friends and a busy social life. All Veronika had was her job. *I had my job.*

Picking up the cup, she headed back to the lounge room. If she hurried, she'd be in time to watch Judge Judy tell some poor idiot that they weren't smart enough to pull the wool over her eyes. She could either do that or sit on the back deck and watch the neighbour's cat stalking birds on the back lawn.

When the doorbell chimed, she ignored it and continued on her journey back to the safety of the couch. It was only after the third ring that she decided to put an end to the intrusion and tell whoever couldn't keep their finger off the bell that whatever they were selling, she wasn't interested.

"Why haven't you answered your phone?" Jim didn't bother with a greeting.

"Hello to you, too," Veronika said, trying to cover her embarrassment with sarcasm – something she'd never been good at.

Ignoring her attempt at humour, Jim simply stood on the doorstep and waited. It was only when the dog whimpered that Veronika noticed the Golden Retriever sitting at his side.

"Can we come in?" he asked, stepping over the threshold before she could answer.

Seeing the dimly lit messy lounge through Jim's eyes, Veronika felt a spike of not only embarrassment but also misery. This, she recognised, had become her life. Daytime television and an inability to get even the simplest of task, like folding the laundry, done.

"Take a seat." Veronika picked up the last few towels, clearing a space on the armchair.

After a moment's hesitation she bent and gathered up the laundry from the floor. While Jim settled himself, she dashed down the hall and dumped the pile on top of the washing machine. When she returned to the lounge, she noticed Jim had pulled the curtains so the room was flooded with light.

"What's going on, Nika?" Jim was seated in the armchair with the dog at his side. In front of him on the coffee table was a green manila file.

Veronika flopped down on the couch. "Nothing. I just knocked the laundry pile over because—"

"That's not what I'm talking about and you know it." The gravity in his voice took her by surprise. "I've been calling and leaving messages for weeks. The superintendent is asking me why you're not answering his calls and emails." Jim hesitated. "Jacqueline Winter has been texting me wanting to know if you're all right. Everyone is worried about you."

Hearing Winter's name set off a reel of images, grim snapshots of watching the bar of light while struggling with pain and confusion.

"You don't have to be worried. I'm okay." Veronika rubbed her hands on her thighs. "I'm just taking some time and… Talking to people, rehashing what happened to me. I'm not ready for all that."

Jim nodded. "I get it, really I do. If you don't want to talk about it that's fine, just don't shut everyone out." As he spoke, his hand dropped onto the dog's head and began stroking its golden fur.

With the sunlight streaming in, Veronika noticed the thick lines of grey scar tissue criss-crossing the dog's head and muzzle. The tip of her left ear was missing and a pink scar ran across her black snout. While the animal's face told a story of brutality, incredibly, the retriever seemed to be smiling as her warm brown eyes regarded Jim.

The scene touched a nerve. Pain that Veronika knew existed but thought she'd buried so deep it could no longer hurt, reared up, and suddenly there were tears in her eyes.

"Is she…" The question caught in her throat.

"Yes," Jim said, scratching behind the dog's ragged ear. "This is Hope. No one knows what her original name was or if she ever had one, so I decided she needed a new name to go with a fresh start. I was only supposed to be fostering her, but…" He shrugged. "Julie's too attached to her to let her go, so she's staying."

There was an expression on Jim's face when he looked at the dog, one Veronika didn't think she'd ever seen before: adoration. It didn't take a detective to see that his wife wasn't the only one that had grown attached to the battle-scarred retriever.

"She's gorgeous," Veronika said, blinking away tears.

"When are you coming back to work?" Jim asked.

The change of direction was so sudden, Veronika answered before she'd had time to deflect. "I don't know if I can."

It was the first time she'd said the words aloud and now that they were out, she realised how much pain the truth held. Outside of her family, policing was her life.

Admitting that she might not be capable of being a cop anymore was gut-wrenching.

"Okay." Jim's reaction wasn't what she was expecting. "But I still need your help." He nodded to the file on the coffee table. "I've been staring at that stuff for days, but I'm not getting anywhere."

Veronika opened her mouth to protest, but Jim held up a hand. "I'm not trying to force you back to work. I just need help," he said. "I don't have your eye for these things, and this case... This case isn't like anything I've ever worked on before."

As he recounted the details, Veronika wanted to stop him. She wanted him to leave so she could draw the curtains and shut out the world, but most of all she wanted to forget about death and violence. Instead, she found herself listening to the details of the case with growing interest.

Later, after Jim left, Veronika stared at the file, asking herself if she could plunge back into a job where death was commonplace. As she paced back and forth between the kitchen and the lounge, she wondered if by seeing what was in the manila folder she would be back to waking up in the middle of the night in a cold sweat. Would she revert to where she'd been in the weeks after her surgery?

Trying to distract herself, she clicked the TV on, only to switch it off again a few minutes later. Quite simply, she was afraid. It was a deep biting fear that kept her from returning to work. No matter how she tried to reason things out, there was no getting away from the truth.

"I can't do my job in fear." She spoke to the empty room with her eyes on the folder.

Veronika had been hurt at work a number of times over the years. She'd been hit, spat on and even had a gun pointed at her by a meth head during an early morning raid. Her first year on the job she'd been assigned to police a music festival where she was punched in the face by a man wearing a T-shirt with the word *peace* emblazoned across the chest.

While the physical side of her job had made her more cautious, there'd been no trace of the yawning cold fear she now experienced. But what made it harder to deal with was the knowledge that she wasn't afraid of getting hurt. It was the inhumanity of not caring anymore that terrified her.

Being assaulted and then dragged into that pantry – dumped like a bag of rubbish and left for dead – had done something to her and that was what really scared her. That feeling of being reduced to flesh and bone, another piece of evidence to be examined and photographed, made life seem unimportant. Could she return to a job that required so much humanity if hers had been compromised?

Not allowing herself another moment of hesitation, Veronika snatched up the file and flipped it open. Along with a coroner's report, diagrams, and Jim's typed notes, the folder contained a stack of A4 photographs.

Closing her eyes for a second, she willed her racing heart to steady; then raised her lids. The crime scene images were startling. A young woman covered with dirt, damp and grainy, her pale slender body contorted into a fabric suitcase. For a while Veronika stared at the image, feeling that old familiar pull. A pull which allowed her to connect with the victim and search out their final moments.

Hours later, Veronika's bedroom door opened. As always, she flipped over the stack of images, blocking them from view. It was an automatic reaction, not wanting her mother or son to see pictures that would horrify them, but also wanting to protect the victim's dignity. After months of uncertainty, it was that action which convinced Veronika she was capable of bringing a measure of humanity to the investigation.

"You're working?" Her mother stood in the doorway, trying to stifle a smile. "I didn't know if... I mean, I just wanted to ask if you felt like Chinese."

Veronika tipped her head to the side and narrowed her eyes. "You needn't bother, Mum. I know you and Jim were in on it together."

Mary-Lynn Pope frowned. "I don't know what you're talking about."

Veronika couldn't help smiling at her mother's poor acting skills. "Thank you," Veronika said. "And Chinese would be perfect."

Chapter Forty

It had been years since Jackie last visited Rottnest, and in many ways it felt like she was seeing the island for the first time. Certainly, it was the first time she'd arrived on a private yacht rather than by ferry with the rest of the holidaymakers. A few hundred metres ahead, the unspoilt white bay and windswept sand dunes shimmered under the flawless blue sky.

Propped on the bow of the *Long Daze* and staring into the impossibly clear water at the sandy ocean bed, it seemed unimaginable that there could be any ugliness in a world where something so perfect existed. Yet, one glance at the jagged scar on her left hand told Jackie otherwise.

Over the last four months her wound had healed without the need for surgery, but there were more unseen scars that remained. Scars she suspected would always be there. Not raw and painful as they had been in those first two months, but fibrous and tough. Places in her heart that wouldn't always ache. Old wounds that could be re-opened when the nights were long and times were tough.

"Nearly ready!" Andrew called out from the runabout.

Shaking off her musings, Jackie clamoured to her feet so she could raise a hand and smile in acknowledgement.

A smile Andrew returned in a way that made her stomach flutter with pleasure. Feeling a little flustered, she snatched a pair of worn tennis shoes out of her wicker bag and pulled them on. Not the perfect outfit when paired with a colourful kaftan, but on Rottnest the only motor vehicles permitted were the bus and emergency and service vans. She and Andrew would be catching a rickety bus into the centre and walking the rest of the way, so sensible footwear was a must.

The plan was to go ashore and meet Lisa and her boyfriend Tim at the Rottnest Lodge for lunch. Then later they'd all return to the *Long Daze* for drinks. This would be Lisa and Andrew's first meeting and a celebration ahead of the launch of Helen's book that was due for release the following week. In light of everything, and now that Jackie knew about her aunt's past, she was anxious, desperately wanting *Kiss the Wall* to be well received. She also wanted Lisa and Andrew to hit it off. What she wanted was for everything to be perfect, while telling herself that she didn't need perfection because she'd found more than she ever thought possible.

After leaving the hospital, she and Andrew had continued on as client and solicitor, but in the weeks that followed that dreadful night, their relationship became something closer to friendship. A status Jackie feared was where they'd remain. While she'd secretly hoped for something closer, having Andrew in her life was more important than pushing for more.

And then somewhere along the way things shifted a second time when Andrew asked her out to dinner and they ended the night with a chaste kiss.

As Andrew helped her when she stepped onto the small vessel, Jackie was reminded of that first flicker of passion. Once aboard he let his hands drop to her hips and for a second they stood together as the little boat rocked. With the sound of distant voices and the ocean lapping at the boat, he kissed her. A lingering kiss that was only broken when a small wave jostled the boat.

Once settled on the vessel's bench seat, Jackie raised her leg. "Be honest. Do these look weird?" she asked while pointing at her tennis shoes.

Andrew chuckled and started the engine. "As always, you look beautiful and I'm sure the quokkas won't judge you."

He had a singular knack for making her feel relaxed even when her nerves were pinging. And pinging they were. Not just because of the book and the possibility that her best friend and the man she loved might not click, but because Lena had been found fit to stand trial and soon they would be given a date for her first hearing. A hearing where Jackie would have to be in the same room as the woman who had murdered her aunt and had almost killed her.

As the runabout bounced towards the shore and the smell of salt kissed her senses, Jackie realised she had a lot of reasons to hate and fear Lena, yet those feelings were as dead as the past. Ghosts which could no longer harm her.

When they hit the beach, Andrew cut the engine and jumped into the shallow surf. "Are you ready?" he asked, holding out his hand.

"I can't wait," Jackie said, and grabbed her bag.

When she stood and tried to step off the boat, Andrew scooped her up and threw her over his shoulder. Jackie let out a surprised scream that turned into laughter as he stomped through the water with her dangling upside-down over his back.

When he set her down on the sand she was still laughing and breathless at the same time. "You're a wild man," she said around another burst of laughter.

"Yep," Andrew answered, his dark blue eyes twinkling. "Once I take off the collar and tie, anything can happen."

In that moment Jackie realised that dreams of perfection were for kids. Life was often cruel and ugly, but sometimes there were moments that eclipsed all the darkness.

The End

If you enjoyed this book, please let others know by leaving a quick review on Amazon. Also, if you spot anything untoward in the paperback, get in touch. We strive for the best quality and appreciate reader feedback.

editor@thebookfolks.com

www.thebookfolks.com

Milly assumes that her sister's invitation to go hiking in the Outback is to heal old wounds. A mutual friend joins them for the trek, and at first things seem to be going well. But a nasty surprise awaits Milly and she is thrown into a dangerous situation with a life or death choice over who and what is most important to her.

Available on Kindle and in paperback from Amazon.

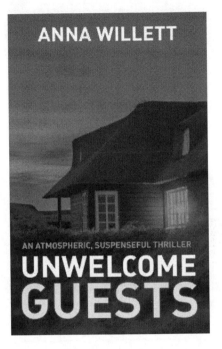

ANNA WILLETT

AN ATMOSPHERIC, SUSPENSEFUL THRILLER

UNWELCOME
GUESTS

Caitlin seeks to build bridges with her husband after the loss of their baby. Unfortunately, their holiday getaway is not what it seems when they find a man held hostage in the cellar. When the house owner turns up, armed and dangerous, Caitlin will have to quickly decide whom she should trust.

Available on Kindle and in paperback from Amazon.

Gloria's reunion with a friend triggers disturbing flashbacks of events four years ago. She is encouraged to visit the place where a woman died. Gloria goes along to make sense of the strange memories that are re-emerging. But doing so will force her to confront an awful episode in her past.

Available on Kindle and in paperback from Amazon.

ANNA WILLETT

A RIVETING PSYCHOLOGICAL SUSPENSE THRILLER

CRUELTY'S
DAUGHTER

Mina's father was a brute and a thug. She got over him.
Now another man wants to fill his shoes. Can Mina
overcome the past and protect herself? 'Cruelty's
Daughter' is about a woman who tackles her demons and
takes it upon herself to turn the tables on a violent man.

Available on Kindle and in paperback from Amazon.

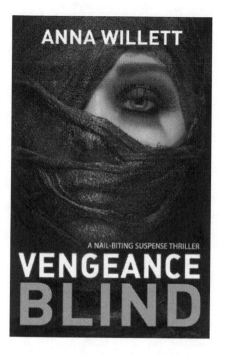

Of poor eyesight and confined to a wheelchair after a road accident, a successful author is alone in her house. She begins to hear strange noises, but is relieved when a care assistant arrives. However, her problems are only just beginning as she is left to the mercy of someone with a grudge to bear. The question for Belle is who, and why?

Available on Kindle and in paperback from Amazon.

Lucy's brother is the only close family she has. When he goes missing, she heads out to a rural backwater, Night Town, his last known location. The locals don't respond kindly. What lengths will they go to protect their secrets? And how far will she go to protect her kin?

Available on Kindle and in paperback from Amazon.

ANNA WILLETT

A KIDNAPPING, A MURDER, AND A WOMAN WHO WON'T GIVE IN

COLD VALLEY
NIGHTMARE

The Australian bush is unforgiving, so when a child goes missing an investigative journalist does all she can to find him. But she'll enter into the affairs of a small town who don't like strangers. She'll be in severe danger if she further meddles in their business.

Available on Kindle and in paperback from Amazon.

When journalist Lucy Hush's brother is accused of
murder, she goes on a desperate search for the truth. But
her inquiries are unwelcome and it's not long before she
stirs up a vipers' nest full of subterfuge and deceit. Can she
get justice for her brother, or will she become another
victim?

Available on Kindle and in paperback from Amazon.

Made in the USA
Middletown, DE
23 August 2020